I0764362

The Reconstructionists

THE RECONSTRUCTIONISTS

BIFF PRICE

Sevenhorns Publishing, A Division of SevenHorns, LLC
276 5th Avenue, Suite 704 | New York, NY 10001 | www.sevenhornspublishing.com

The Reconstructionists.

Sevenhorns Publishing
A Division of SevenHorns, LLC
276 5th Avenue, Suite 704
New York, NY 10001
www.sevenhornspublishing.com

Design: Branded Human

Library of Congress Control Number: 2017961469
ISBN-13 978-0-9838427-6-7 (hc)

ISBN-13 978-0-9976846-8-1 (e-book)

ISBN-13 978-0-9600817-5-2 (pbk.)

Visit the author's website at www.biffprice.com

Dedication

For Brian, Jennifer, Elizabeth, John and all the blessings you bring into my life. True goodness begins with family, and it is in family that we first meet love.

Table of Contents

CHAPTER 1

President Michael Stonebreaker sat behind the Resolute desk and looked out the East Door toward the Rose Garden. He was lonely. Joan, his First Lady, was away in Dallas speaking at an NEA convention. Her duties required far more of her time than he liked, but he appreciated that she took her role seriously and did her best to honor most requests for personal appearances. Two years ago, she'd worried whether the future held any possibility of meaningful work for her at all.

Vice President Eric Dryden was also away, visiting India on a mission to review a trade agreement. Michael felt Eric's absence, even as he glanced at a photo from last year's visit to the Grand Canyon.

Henry, his brother and best friend, was back home in Clear Haven, Pennsylvania, visiting their mother. Although he served Michael willingly as his chief confidant, head speech writer, and frequent counselor, Henry would have left Washington, DC behind in a heartbeat to return to his first love: fixing heavy equipment for the strip mines that surrounded their home town.

Michael sighed, already tired. His weekly six-day schedule was crammed with commitments from early morning to late evening. His regimen allowed for ninety minutes in the Workout Room three days a week. He rose at 5:3o a.m. and paced off two miles by 6:oo a.m. five days a week. They could take a man out of West Point, but it's hard to take West Point out of a man. He was one of the most disciplined men to ever serve in the office, but even with his busy schedule there were moments when the loneliness of leading the most powerful nation on earth crept in.

His first two years in office had been tumultuous. The media firestorm had not abated in intensity with the passage of time. The New York Times, Washington Post, and other media outlets were on the verge of apoplexy demanding to know what had happened to the previous administration, Congress, numerous college faculty members, Hollywood Liberals, and other Progressive elites. Their demands fell on deaf ears.

The Movement, the clandestine organization responsible for thwarting the Progressive takeover of the United States and installing Michael as president remained hidden in an off-the-grid city beneath the central Pennsylvania hills. Its members had no desire to reveal The Movement's existence to the public, in case the need to take direct action arose again.

Now, the federal government was being deconstructed brick-by-brick. Michael and the Congress were systematically dismantling the monster; it had to die in order to be reborn. Otherwise, it would have destroyed the Union in short order. The insane Progressive agenda had come to an end. Under their watch, government had grown to such a monstrous size that it would take years to reconstruct it.

No one was being thrown under the bus, however; instead huge groups of people were being retrained for a new place in commerce. Manufacturing was being stimulated in America. Thousands upon thousands of regulations were being discarded, corporate America was awakening to a world where genius and innovation were rewarded, not penalized, and the American worker was celebrating in many places again. Cities and towns that had been destroyed by over-regulation, urban ghettos, and hopelessness were seeing the promise of revitalization through private sector jobs. The days of despair and cynicism were ending.

The Department of Education was gone. A balanced budget amendment had been passed. The massive Progressive healthcare bill was no more. A restructuring of Medicare and Medicaid was in process, and when it was finished, fraud, as they knew it, would be next to impossible. Social Security was placed in a secure lock box. The money paid in by hard-working Americans would never again be placed in the general fund to be raided at will.

No one doubted that returning to fiscal sanity was going to take a long time. Nevertheless, Michael was confident that as responsibilities and revenue were returned to the states and the massive entitlements were restructured an improved economy would grow. As in times past, under those conditions American ingenuity and entrepreneurship would triumph.

The Movement's plan to revitalize the American economy was moving forward. Many government workers were being retrained for private sector jobs. With a massive Manhattan Project approach designed by The Movement over sixty years, the new leadership was overhauling every level of society simultaneously. Nothing would be allowed to stop The Movement's plan. It might require a decade or more to restore America to common sense, but the work was well underway.

Two months into the new administration, the governors of all fifty states gathered in Washington for a four-day conference. Liberals, moderates, and conservatives were confronted with the new reality, and when they understood that they would have more revenue and power in the future, as well as an exponentially increased responsibility to their citizens, they signed on to participate. There were a handful of Progressives among them, but The Movement had identified them years before. They had been confronted in a private meeting with the president, and they knew that if they wished to remain in power, they had to be helpful. Politicians are, if nothing else, well-versed in expediency.

The amazing thing about The Movement was that it had such profound thinkers among its members. They understood the cost of freedom, its fragility, its faults as well as its virtues, and what it took to maintain it. Before they had acted to remove the Progressive nightmare in America, they had watched the evil elitist plan to take over the nation grow insidiously within the halls of Congress for decade after decade. It had been like placing a frog in a pot of comfortable water on a stove, and then turning up the heat one degree each year until there was no escape.

Following Michael's occupancy of the White House, the story released to mainstream media focused on the Progressive manifesto of madman Pierce Armstrong and his plan to destroy the United States from within, including the horrific attack he'd planned for Disney World. Thanks to The Movement, the attempt was marked indelibly in the collective mind of the country as something that should never be repeated.

Michael decided to try to wind down with some reading before dinner. He made the relatively short trip from the West Wing to the White House residence. He never ceased to be fascinated by the history contained within the walls of the White House.

As had many of the others, the Treaty Room served many functions over the years, including that of cabinet meeting room, waiting room, first ladies' work room, and even as a bridge parlor under Dwight Eisenhower. The treaty ending the Spanish-American War had been signed here in 1898 under President McKinley, and the room was later named to comemorate that event by President Kennedy. For the most part the room had served as the president's private study, and Michael and Joan decided to use it that way.

Michael sat down in his easy chair and gazed for a moment at the view of the Washington Monument and the Jefferson Memorial in the distance. The weight of occupying the office of president of the United States seemed to settle on him like the years of history embodied in this house.

He picked up a copy of a novel by a new author. It was a story about a magical world where four children embarked on thrilling adventures and met fantastic characters. It was a fascinating book that reminded him slightly of C.S. Lewis's tales of Narnia, except that the images in this book were crafted as a striking metaphor for the afterlife. Normally he had little time for this kind of reading, but Joan had gone to the trouble of presenting him with an autographed copy for Christmas, so he'd decided to read it.

The soft ding of a muted bell sounded and a voice spoke into the room. "Good evening, sir. Will the president be having dinner in the study this evening?"

"Yes," Michael said, scratching his chin. "Let's make it salad, Joan's meatloaf, green beans, and cookies and ice cream for dessert."

"Very good, sir," came the reply.

When dinner arrived, Michael ate in silence. He had no desire to hear the news of the day. After dinner, he turned on the television for a half hour, but there was nothing that appealed to him.

He briefly thought about watching a movie, but he decided that an early bedtime would be a good thing. He was tired. It was probably because Joan wasn't at home. He dialed her cell number.

"Hey, First Lady, how was your day?" Michael asked.

"They adored me, but they're not too sure about you," Joan teased.

"That's to be expected," Michael said. "Did you explain to them that I adored you first?" He smiled and pressed the phone closer to his ear. He missed his wife, and just hearing her voice made him glad she'd be home tomorrow.

"Your Majesty, I'm so humbled by the attention," Joan said, and laughed.

"I miss you. I'm hitting the hay early. It's boring here without you."

"I'll be home before noon tomorrow," Joan said.

"In time for church?" Michael asked. He hoped they'd be able to go together.

"More than likely," Joan said. "I don't think there will be too much traffic on a Sunday morning heading into town."

"That's wonderful, honey." Michael sighed. "I'll be glad to have you home."

"I'll be glad to be home," Joan said. "The conference has been great, but Dallas is a long way from DC and you."

"I agree," Michael said. They spent a few moments catching up on events from the past few days before the conversation drew to a close.

"I'll see you in the morning, my love," Joan said.

"I'm looking forward to it," Michael said. He blew a kiss into the phone and they hung up.

Michael got ready for bed. He opened the novel and began reading. The children in the story climbed an old tree and were transported into an enchanted world where they met a wise old owl. It reminded him of when he and his brother Henry would go on imaginary journeys through the woods behind their house when they were kids. He grew sleepy reminiscing on those simple days.

After placing the book on the nightstand he turned out the light and settled into the big empty bed. One of the unfortunate things about being president was that he now spent more time away from his wife than he had in over twenty years of marriage.

Yet, after such an exhausting day, he fell asleep in moments. It was the best sleep he'd had in months. That was a good thing, because all hell was about to break loose.

CHAPTER 2

A soft beep-beep-beep brought Michael from deep sleep to awareness. He turned his head to the left and looked at the clock on the night table. It was 4:17 in the morning on Wednesday. The beeping continued until he brought a hand down on its top, silencing the alarm. Michael swung his legs from under the covers and sat on the edge of the bed. He pressed a button on the nightstand.

"Yes?" Michael asked, rubbing his eyes.

"Mr. President," replied an urgent voice. "I'm sorry to have to wake you—"

"What is it?" Michael said, getting to the point.

"There has been an incident, sir—"

"'Where?" Michael said.

"On the Texas-Mexican border. The team is gathering in the Situation Room."

"I'm on my way." Michael quickly hung up the phone, showered, dressed, and was heading to the meeting in less than ten minutes. He cleared the stubble of his beard with a portable electric shaver as he walked, surrounded by his Secret Service detail.

When he stepped into the room most of the team was waiting for him. He said one word: "Report."

Defense Secretary Fred Conover said, "At one minute past midnight a force of Mexican cartel members came over the border into El Paso. They were heavily armed. They proceeded from house-to-house waking people from sleep and herding them into the streets."

Michael's face was pale in the light. His stomach clenched into a tight knot as he took in the pained expressions on the faces staring at him from around the table. "Go on," he said.

"Mr. President," Conover resumed, "as many as two hundred men armed with automatic weapons fired upon the civilians they'd marshaled into the streets. Police and border patrol arrived on the scene within fifteen minutes, but it was a slaughter."

"How many?" Michael asked.

"Initial reports are that eighty-nine of our people are dead," Conover replied gravely. "Half of them are children. One hundred and seven wounded, approximately fifty in critical condition, and at least forty of them may not survive their wounds."

Michael's face was a mask of fury. His gaze was so intense that those nearest him at the table were amazed at the change in him. In two years, they had never seen the president so angry. The realization that he was capable of such concentrated fury was a revelation to them.

Michael continued, "How many of the enemy?"

"Seventeen dead, twenty-eight wounded," Conover delivered the numbers slowly. "The others fled back across the borders in SUVs, which we've determined they ditched shortly after re-entering Mexico. We have no leads on any vehicles they transferred to."

"Has the border been sealed?" Michael asked. "Maybe we can catch any stragglers trying to blend in with the local population."

"Yes, sir. We have troops on the scene."

There was a long silence at the table. No one spoke, coughed or as much as shifted in a chair.

Michael looked out into the room. All eyes were on him. His face was rigid, reflecting his controlled rage. Had his brother Henry been in the room he would have recognized the look on Michael's face. Those close to him in his family would have said Michael had gone "to the other place."

A handful of the troops he'd led in the Gulf War and a few close friends had seen that look over the years. His team members now saw it for the first time.

Michael focused his eyes on the team members one by one as he spoke. A small, chilling smile hinted at the corners of his mouth.

"This ends now," he said. "We're done with it. As of this moment we are at war. Every cartel member in Mexico is to be found and brought to justice. The border is closed until further notice."

"But, Mr. President," interjected Dean Ormsby, Secretary of State, "Mexico is a sovereign state and one of our biggest trading partners. How can we—"

Michael shot a look at Ormsby. "Dean, I don't care if they're our fifty-first state. This ends now! We're done here! We're going in with or without the permission of Mexico, rooting them out–every last one of them–and bringing them to justice! When the sun comes up, I'll call the Mexican president. His people have committed an act of war against this nation and slaughtered our citizens on our streets. He can either round up these people within the next two weeks—and I know damn well that his government knows where they are—arrest them, try them the next day, and shoot them when they are found guilty, or we'll do it for him."

"Since the border is closed, how will we proceed?" asked Ormsby.

"We'll move our troops into position," explained Michael, "where they will remain until such time as Mexico is swept clean of anyone with a mind to harm Mexican citizens or ours. All persons who attempt to cross our border illegally from this time forward will be arrested, jailed, prosecuted, tried, and, when convicted, imprisoned. If it is found that any intended to do harm to our people we will give Mexico the option to try them, convict them, and imprison them in their country, or we will do it here."

Helen Abramson, the CIA Director, spoke up. "The action is an obvious retaliation by the cartels; our work on the barrier has cut deeply into their drug traffic."

Michael turned to Helen. Her dark hair, penetrating eyes, and lovely face led those who met her for the first time to believe that she was much younger than forty-eight. She had come to her position by way of The Movement, as all the others in the room had. Michael was fully aware of her experience and credentials, which were such that everyone in the room knew that it was wise to consider her opinion or observation on any issue. Many had learned the hard way that it was never a good idea to ignore her counsel.

Michael thought about his response for a brief moment before saying, "I will tell the Mexican president to close his northern border—or we will do it for him. On our part, the legal mechanisms for people to come to this country will be enforced stringently from today forward. We will embrace those who come here in search of a better life. But they will go through the process of becoming citizens and true Americans just as millions of others have through the years."

"Mr. President, many around the world will see what we're doing as simply more American imperialism," Helen advised. "How do we handle the political fallout?"

Michael replied, "I would suggest that it's precisely because of our equivocation in the recent past that we find ourselves in this situation. Helen, I know that we are seen abroad by many as a bully because we are the only superpower left in the world, but we would have slipped to third world has-been status if the Progressives were still running things, hanging back when we have a responsibility to lead. Those days are over."

He leaned in, his voice low and steady in the silence of the room. "I occupy the office of president temporarily, and though I did not ask for it, it is my job to protect our people from without—and from within. I'm not a politician, and I'll never be one. I believe in compromise only when the best outcome cannot possibly be achieved, no matter what we do. Otherwise, compromise is not part of my vocabulary. Our people are dead and dying here, because these murderous animals came onto our soil and attacked us."

Michael returned to sitting ramrod straight in his chair. His voice resumed its commanding tone and volume. "We are about to make it clear to them, to the nation they came from, and to the rest of the world that you cannot attack Americans without paying dearly for it.

"I cannot say so enough—if Mexico cannot or will not clean its own house, we will do it for them. And right now, in this situation, I frankly don't care what the rest of the world thinks."

Helen nodded. "Understood, sir."

Michael looked at a clock on the opposite wall. "It's 5:00 a.m. I need to go to the gym. If any of you care to join me, I'd welcome your company. I have a great need to hit something at this moment. It would be best if it were a punching bag. I'll be in my office at six calling Mexico. I'm sure they already know what happened, but we'll let them stew for a while wondering how we're going to react. If anyone has anything else to add I will hear it now. Otherwise, let's get to work."

There was silence at the table.

"Good," Michael finished. "Let's get this day started. We have a lot to plan."

Michael stood and everyone else stood with him. He headed straight for the gym. After hearing such devastating news his blood was roaring through his veins. It was time to go blow off some steam.

CHAPTER 3

The Man Who Loved the Gulf ignored the tears threatening to spill from the corners of his eyes. He was a sentimental man, yet he lived secluded and nameless due to the nature of his business. Three of his four adopted sons sat silently with him in the huge living room of his estate, gazing out over his beloved body of water. They had just returned from an early morning trip to the local cemetery where the body of young Roberto Alvarez had been laid to rest.

The Man Who Loved the Gulf had left the Alvarez family with his three younger sons, the Dupree triplets. Ricardo "Rick" Rodriguez, The Man's fourth adopted son, had remained with José, his wife Consuelo, and their family as they received visitors in an upscale neighborhood a few miles away. Roberto was José and Consuelo's youngest son.

Duke, Derek, and Damien Dupree looked to their foster father with love.

"It's wrong," said The Man Who Loved the Gulf. "So wrong. He was seven years old. That's too young to die."

Duke said, "Yes, but it was an accident. He rode his bike right into the path of the truck. The driver tried to avoid hitting him. How many times did José tell him not to take his bike beyond the neighborhood? He didn't listen. He wanted ice cream and he was bound to get it."

"What the hell is wrong with this world?" said The Man Who Loved the Gulf. "He's killed because of ice cream? Where's the justice in that?"

"There's no justice that we can understand," Derek said softly, placing his hand on The Man's shoulder.

"But José's son…his only son—" Their father placed his hand over Derek's hand. "I have the four of you. What does José have?"

Damien, normally the least talkative of the triplets, said, "He has Consuelo, his daughter, his family, all of us, and you—especially you. He knows how much you love him and care about him. No one can give him back, Roberto, but we can be here for him."

The Man Who Loved the Gulf looked fondly at Damien. "It never ceases to amaze me how the three of you are so alike and yet so different from each other. If one of you were lost I would want to die. I would not want to go on living. I feel the same about Rick. You're my sons, my boys. You could not be more my sons than if you came from my body. I can only imagine what is going through José's and Consuelo's minds at this moment."

Duke Dupree, the one who usually acted as the leader of the triplets, sighed heavily. "Nothing in life prepares us for this. The death of a child is the most painful thing a family can face. Rick is alive because José led us to the farm in time to save him. José is a blood brother to him. He's also a Marine."

"It takes as much to make a Marine cry," said The Man.

No one spoke. They sat silently with their own thoughts. Grief settled like a mantle upon them.

Roberto Alvarez was dead. Nothing could change this fact. There is no pain like standing by the grave of a little child who has died too soon. The universe moved on in its impersonal way.

The afternoon wore on. The triplets got in a car and went to join the Alvarez family.

The Man Who Loved the Gulf went out onto the estate's veranda and sat staring at the waters.

His cell phone rang.

"It is beautiful at this time of year," he said, answering it.

"It is beautiful indeed," a voice said.

"Two years is a long time not to speak with you, Cousin," The Man said.

"Yes, I agree," his cousin replied, "but much has happened in that two years to keep me busy. I'm sorry for not being in touch, but I've called because our new government faces a threat. I wanted you to know about it."

The Man Who Loved the Gulf stood up and held the phone closer to his ear. "Tell me."

His cousin told him about the incursion from Mexico and the death of innocents. The Man felt his anger rising.

"What is the president doing about it?" he asked.

His cousin explained the steps that were being taken, and Stonebreaker's views on handling the situation on the border.

"Thank you for getting ahold of me," The Man said, "but why did you feel this was necessary for me to know?"

The voice on the other end of the phone was warm. "We're family. You're all I have left. Everyone else is gone."

"True. I know, and that's why I would like to see more of you—"

"My life is not my own," the voice interrupted. "The people I work for went behind the scenes the moment Stonebreaker and the others took over."

The Man Who Loved the Gulf laughed softly. "I shun the limelight, dear cousin, but the people you work for take the meaning of 'secret' to a whole new level."

"And that is as it should be," his cousin added. "However, you are a very resourceful man—"

"Ah, I knew there had to be another reason for this call," now The Man Who Loved the Gulf interrupted.

"So, I'll get to the point," his cousin replied. "You have access to a number of—shall we say, *assets*—who can blend seamlessly into Mexico. There are times when we need to go outside normal channels to achieve certain goals. I may have need of your particular talents in the near term. You'll be well paid for services rendered. I like to keep my options open."

"Are the people you work for aware of me?" The Man Who Loved the Gulf asked.

There was a slight hesitation, and then his cousin said, "They are aware of everything, dear cousin. They've been at their business longer than you and I have been alive. They know we are related, and they trust me with their deepest secrets. Your business and capability in handling such matters would be an asset."

The Man Who Loved the Gulf feared few things in life, but he understood there was no hiding from these people.

"Knowing all that you say, how then do they tolerate someone like me..." The Man asked, "a man who is a law unto himself? Why do they even allow me to exist?"

"It's a cliché, but one you'll grasp fully," said his cousin. "Simply put, the enemy of my enemy is my friend. They respect anyone who has as much power as you do, and they'll take allies wherever they find them. You can do things and run operations that are beyond even their abilities in certain areas."

"I'd like to meet them someday," said The Man.

"That will never be possible," said his cousin.

"What if my answer is no?"

"They will not harm you," his cousin answered. "If you refuse there are others we may approach."

"Perhaps," The Man said, drawing out his response, "but I'm the best."

"You are, indeed. These people and their organization intend to remain secret forever, but if the Progressives ever start to build again they are willing to work with allies on the surface to stop them."

"All right, Cousin," The Man said, mentally and verbally committing to the matter. "Call me if you need me, but I'd like to meet this Stonebreaker one day. An innocent meeting in a neutral setting—Could that be arranged?"

"I'll think about it."

"From what you've said of him, he sounds like an extraordinary man."

"You are as well, Cousin. I'll be in touch. It's beautiful at this time of year."

"It's beautiful, indeed." The cell phone went dead in his hand.

The Man stared for a long time at what he considered to be the most beautiful spot on earth. Yet, even the wondrous Gulf had shadows cast across it from both sides. He had a lot to think about.

CHAPTER 4

Michael's workout did nothing to improve his mood. When he walked into his office, he found his Chief of Staff, Harold Crosby, waiting for him. Crosby had placed a steaming cup of coffee on his desk. He could already smell the temptingly sweet scent of the French vanilla creamer. Michael looked at Harold and said, "That's not your job. Charlene brings me coffee. You run my day."

"Mr. President, Charlene is at home in bed at this hour," Harold explained. "I thought you might want it now. I know this isn't an ordinary day."

"Harry, don't be formal with me," Michael scoffed. "It's 6:00 a.m. At this hour I'm Mike to you. When the show is on and everybody's here you can use the title. Right now I need a friend—not an employee."

"Understood, Mike," Harold said, "but I don't normally break protocol. I know you've got that call to make. Do you want to talk about it first? Use me as a sounding board?"

"My God, Harry, they slaughtered our people." Michael sat down heavily in his chair. "I'm ready to invade Mexico and level the place."

"Then, I think we should talk about it," Harry insisted. "Cool heads need to prevail. I agree totally with you, but 'leveling' them could result in a worse situation. We have to go about this and be smart about it."

"You're right," Michael said. "More senseless destruction isn't going to resolve anything, but the man has to understand that we mean business." Michael rubbed his hands over his face and looked at Harry.

"I don't think there's any danger of him not understanding you," Harry said. "Just be straightforward. You always are. That's what's so great about you, President Stonebreaker. You don't beat around the bush. You're the most refreshing person that has been in this job since Truman."

"Thanks for the vote of confidence, Harry," Michael said, "but let's get this over with. We've got a lot of planning to do and a whole bunch of people to speak to. What's my day look like?"

"Busy as usual," Harry said, "but we'll keep to the schedule and make it work. The news media are already all over this. You're going to have to speak to the nation about it. I've already scheduled you across the board for 9:00 a.m. That gives us a little time to compose what needs to be said. Alex is already in his office. I called him at 4:30 so he could get in here and beat the beltway madness."

Michael knew Alex Anderson to be one of the best speech writers in the business. Alex could handle the press; he was in good hands.

"Okay," Michael said, "let's call Calderón and lay the groundwork for him."

"Yes, sir." Crosby stood up, politely nodded and left the office.

A minute went by and Michael's phone beeped.

"Mr. President, President Calderón is on the line," the White House night operator said.

"Thank you." Michael said. He took a deep breath, held it, expelled it, and then picked up the phone.

"Good morning, President Calderón. It's Michael Stonebreaker. I would prefer not to call you at such an early hour, but the circumstances of the situation require that this be handled quickly."

The voice on the other end of the line was not sleepy. The man had no doubt been awake for hours.

"Mr. President," Calderón began, his words coming in a rush, "what has happened is beyond words. On behalf of my country, I want to convey our sadness, anger, and outrage at this act. I assure you that those who committed this horrible crime are being hunted down at this very moment, and I—"

Michael cut him off. "With all due respect, President Calderón, we want every single one of them caught or killed within the next two weeks. We want every cartel member in your country behind bars within that time frame. We want you to close your northern border as tight as a drum. We will be patrolling your shores with our surveillance, aircraft, and naval vessels. We want those who have done this crime to stand trial within the month, and we want those who are found guilty executed."

There was a stunned silence on the other end of the phone. Then, Calderón said, "You can't be serious? Two weeks! That's impossible. We can't possibly—"

"But we can, President Calderón," said Michael. "If this is not accomplished within two weeks I will have no choice but to do it for you!"

On that note, Michael hung up the phone.

CHAPTER 5

The unthinkable had happened. An American president had threatened to invade Mexico. President Nicolas Calderón had hung up the phone in stunned silence. President Stonebreaker had given him two weeks to find, neutralize, and destroy the cartels. He wrung his hands. The cartels were better armed than his troops, and many were better trained. In fact, some of the cartel leaders had been schooled by the Americans. He sat alone in his office wondering what he was going to do.

It was early in the morning, but he felt he could do with a shot or two of tequila. *How to escape this nightmare?* He knew he would never be able to fulfill Stonebreaker's demands. Without a doubt, the Americans were going to come pouring over the border. He often wondered why they had never done it before. Year after year they had done nothing, allowing millions of people from Mexico and other parts of the world to cross into the United States under cover of darkness, avoiding any legal path to citizenship. Many were desperate to find work, to gain a better life and escape the crushing poverty they faced in their home countries. Most supported families by sending American money back home.

The murderous cartels made billions selling drugs to the Americans. Calderón suffered no delusions; the cartels had grown in power and strength to the extent that they had become a shadow government in Mexico. They could buy and sell almost anyone or anything. He had good intentions, but little power to enforce them. He wanted to drive the cartels out of his country, but he was outgunned, and the cartels' money made it difficult to find anyone to go against them. Their practice of beheading innocents frightened the Mexican people out of their minds. No one would talk to anyone about the cartels. The savages would do the most monstrous things to their victims, as well as their enemies. No one felt above being attacked; their silence was all they could exchange for a meager sense of safety.

Calderón paced the floor of his office, sweat beginning to bead on his forehead, despite the air conditioning. His government lived in a state of uneasy truce with the cartels. Every now and then he made a show of going after them. There would be some arrests, usually of low level cartel members, and then it would become quiet again.

Now, the world was about to change. Calderón knew little of Stonebreaker, but what he did know was unnerving. No one understood how he had come to power, or what exactly had happened to the liberal-progressive US government. To say that the government that had taken its place—headed by Stonebreaker—was conservative was to understate it.

The Mexican president sighed deeply, comforted by one thought: Stonebreaker, by all accounts, was a decent man. In fact, according to the media he was a man of faith. Such a man would not destroy Mexico; he cared too much about people to do that. However, just how far he would go to bring down the cartels remained to be seen, and dismantling them would necessarily be bloody beyond belief.

He gazed thoughtfully over tented fingers, considering what he could do in the face of the American president's determination to wipe out the cartels. Tendering his resignation was one possibility. He could let another man bear the awful chaos that was coming. The cartels had enormous power, and they were backed by foreign elements that wanted nothing less than to bring the United States to its knees, and ultimately destroy it.

The attack on El Paso had been incredibly stupid on the part of El Toro. The mastermind of the assault had yet to be officially identified, but the carnage had his signature all over it. The beast loved excess, and now he was going to be faced with something he had not bargained for: Michael Stonebreaker was angry, and he was an unknown. Nicolas Calderón was many things, but he was not stupid. One does not pick up a crocodile by its tail, nor should one ever wave a stick at a charging elephant. El Toro had vast amounts of money and power, but President Stonebreaker was the leader of the most powerful nation in the world. It would take a while, but the Americans would be coming over his border soon. Two weeks was not long enough to do very much of anything.

Resignation was sounding better by the moment. He had a place in Costa Rica, but, given the politics there, another location might be safer. Perhaps he should find protection somewhere in Europe, or perhaps even the US? He did not want to go down in history as the president of Mexico who was in power when the Americans invaded his country. The idea that this could be the greatest war on North American soil since the American Civil War curled his stomach into a knot of fear. He closed his eyes. A lot of people were going to die.

A knock at the door interrupted his musings. "Si, Margarita, adelante," Calderón said.

His secretary entered the room. "Señor Presidente, the reporters have surrounded the building. They want to know about El Paso. What are you going to do?"

Nicolas Calderón rose from his chair and smoothed his suit jacket. He squared his shoulders and looked at the woman who had served him faithfully for fifteen years in public life.

"Margarita," he said, "to be truthful, and to use an American phrase, I haven't got a clue. However, between here and the door, I'll think of something."

He strode purposefully through the door into the hallway, wearing his best suit and plastering on the smile that had gotten him elected. He was immediately surrounded by his protective detail. The strained looks on their faces confirmed it; today was not going to be a good day.

CHAPTER 6

Ernesto Ruíz's men called him "El Toro." He was a large beast of a man who loved to hurt all living things, particularly people. Knives and pistols were fun to use, but his hands were his favorite weapons. There was something incredibly satisfying to him about smashing in someone's face and breaking their bones. Oh, and the screams, the moans and groans that came from them as he beat the life out of them. His rage always lurked just beneath the surface. His followers lived in fear of his anger. The slightest thing would set him off on a destructive rampage that would not end until someone was dead.

Ruíz had planned and executed the attack at El Paso with his cartel pawns. He was brazen because the Americans were soft and weak. After all, they bought his drugs in the billions of dollars' worth, and they lived lazy lives with their many luxuries.

When he was abroad, the Americans had trained him in their ways of combat. He had always seen himself as a soldier, and Ernesto was a very eager and willing pupil. Ernesto believed that he could outmaneuver any of them in battle, and his fortress lay in what he considered an impenetrable mountain valley, far from prying eyes. Enough money could buy anything, and Ernesto had the money to hide deep inside a mountain reinforced with steel, concrete, and a level of technology that any Pentagon general would envy. Even the dreaded drones could not see him. He intended to go on living, making his billions, and enjoying his penchant for boys.

So, Ernesto had gambled, and in his mind he had won. He had no more respect for the new American president than he'd had for the previous one. At least this one had been in the military and had seen combat. That did not frighten him. Americans were not about to come over the border looking for him. It simply wasn't done by people like them. They were all bluster and show, without backup. They were losing their credibility all over the world, and Ernesto had staged his lightning strike and disappeared into the night. The ones he had left behind would not talk. They knew about cushy American prisons and did not fear them. They would get out eventually, and no one frightened them more than El Toro.

He was so sure that he would never be caught that he called for a week-long celebration when his men returned from their mission. They had brought him a present from their attack. It was a mother and her son. His men had been instructed to carefully select the most beautiful woman and her oldest male child from the people they had rounded up. The blond beauties were in a cell not far from where Ernesto was enjoying himself at the moment.

Of course, Ernesto knew nothing of substance about President Stonebreaker. He only knew what he had heard on the news. Nor had he ever heard of The Man Who Loved the Gulf. He had no inkling of what The Man was capable of doing.

Ernesto's ego was such that he was not afraid of anyone. Men hated him and women feared him. He had unlimited power, and best of all he also had a secret weapon. Buried beneath his mountain fortress was the most horrifying instrument of suffering and death anyone could ever imagine. It was the first thing new recruits saw when they were initiated into the cartel. They never forgot the lesson. He was a god with ultimate power, and he was going to keep it that way.

CHAPTER 7

Rick Rodriguez was content with spending his late morning attending to his grieving friend. José Alvarez had just lost his son. Today there was not a trace of his usual handsome, dimpled smile. Rick had always been charismatic, athletic, and had a strong sense of responsibility that was further cultivated by his foster father, the infamous Man Who Loved the Gulf. His family possessed various resources and wealth, but Rick had a sense of purpose that filled his days. Now, his purpose was to sit with and comfort José over the death of his little son.

Watching José brought tears to Rick's eyes.

José had once saved Rick's life. When the giant "Butler from Hell" had held him captive in the torture chamber of a political madman hell bent on destroying the United States from within, it had been José who had brought the news to The Man Who Loved the Gulf and the Dupree brothers.

José was a fellow Marine, and Rick loved him as a brother. They had seen each other through many hard times. Now, all he could do was sit with his arm around his friend's shoulders. Even in light of the physical and emotional agony he'd endured, the grief of the Alvarez family was almost more than Rick could bear.

The Dupree brothers had returned, and they stood quietly in the foyer beyond the large living room. The house was filled to overflowing, as friends and neighbors poured in to offer condolences and add to the already enormous array of food and sympathy cards. People spilled onto the back patio with even more expressions of grief and comfort. The murmur of voices could be heard throughout the sprawling ranch home.

Rick looked up, and seeing his brothers by the door, gently took his arm from around José's shoulders.

"I'll be right back," he whispered. He stood up and crossed the room to approach the triplets. He nodded, and the four men exited the foyer through the front door and walked out onto the large porch. It, too, overflowed with people milling about and sitting on chairs, waiting to express their support for the Alvarez family.

Rick and the Dupree brothers continued down the steps, moving through the large front yard before finally stopping by a tastefully arranged flower bed near the end of the driveway.

"Our father grieves for Roberto," Duke Dupree said. "He'll be here soon."

The men stood for a long moment looking along the usually peaceful suburban street, now busy with a solemn flow of mourners to and from the Alvarez residence.

"José is strong," Rick said. "I'm worried about Consuelo. She is very quiet. I think that she might need help—professional help, to deal with this."

"She'll have everything she needs," said Damien. "So will José. No one ever gets over the death of a child. All we can do is to be here for them when they need us, and to leave them alone when that is what they need."

Rick eyed his adopted brothers, silently thankful for their stalwart presence since rescuing him from Pierce Armstrong's chamber of death. Under the command of The Man Who Loved the Gulf, they had overcome hell and high water to get the job done.

Their regular work, though less militarized, was no less clandestine. They spent a considerable amount of time traveling to various enterprises The Man owned. The trick was that the people at the businesses they visited thought there was just one of them.

The Dupree triplets were average in appearance, dark haired, with a military bearing about them despite their longish hair. At one point they had worn their hair so that others could tell them apart. Now, they deliberately wore it in the same long style.

The Man Who Loved the Gulf had let everyone managing his affairs know that a certain vice president of his holding company would be visiting them from time-to-time to conduct evaluations of his interests. The triplets dressed alike on these visits, even carrying documents identifying them by one fictitious name. The Man Who Loved the Gulf loved the charade, and he never tired of hearing the reports they brought back from their trips. He controlled his empire with an iron fist, the fingers of which were his adopted sons. He valued his privacy above all else, and went to extensive means to protect it.

The brothers Dupree enjoyed the game as much as their adopted father, and they played it well. No one suspected that the three men visiting each company were not, in fact one man.

Rick had been given a different task. He was in charge of corporate security. The Man Who Loved the Gulf spared no expense protecting his empire. Rick oversaw the testing and implementation of each new security technology installed at all of The Man's properties. Rick also visited each of The Man's companies under a fabricated persona, in an inconspicuous disguise. No one would have ever forgotten Rick's incredibly handsome face, but the bearded, shaggy, and introverted egghead who visited routinely and oversaw security bore no resemblance whatsoever to the movie-star under the makeup. It was another elaborate, but necessary stratagem employed by The Man to protect the web of his empire. Rick enjoyed the charade as much as his brothers.

Two months before Roberto's death, Rick had recruited José as his assistant. Whether adopted son or mailroom clerk, there was no room for sluggards on The Man's payroll. Loyalty and productivity were not simply acknowledged, they were embraced, and José was a perfect fit for The Man's employ. Rick and José traveled together in disguise, visiting The Man Who Loved the Gulf's companies and communicating tersely in Spanish so as to conceal their business from all but the most senior of The Man's employees. José typically remained silent, but kept voluminous notes on a laptop he always carried.

The Man Who Loved the Gulf owned or held controlling interest in numerous companies, and it was the job of the two teams to cover them all in no more than ten days on the road each month. The three Duprees could cover the field more easily than Rick and José, but the grueling schedule was made more bearable, even enjoyable for Rick by their deepening friendship. Rick appreciated that The Man recognized the need for family time and insisted that his sons be at home with their families more often than not.

The Man Who Loved the Gulf arrived at the Alvarez residence by limousine promptly at 5:00 p.m. His sons were waiting for him when it pulled into the driveway. The Man was dressed in a dark suit with a white shirt and somber tie. The four men surrounded him as he walked to the steps that led to the large front porch.

Family members looked up in interest as the men approached, and seeing that the newcomer was José's employer they smiled warmly and called to him. Ever gracious despite his careful nature, The Man shook hands, accepted the warm greetings and responded in kind. He touched shoulders, kissed cheeks, and patted children gently on their heads. The irony that this man, who had killed more men than could be counted, was capable of such tenderness was not lost on his sons.

The Man Who Loved the Gulf entered the Alvarez home and stepped into the foyer. He slowly made his way to the living room and stepped lightly into the doorway, pausing there for an instant.

Eyes turned to him and his sons, and a pathway opened for him. He walked forward, toward the couch where José consoled his grief-stricken wife. The sound of her sobbing tore at The Man's heart.

José stood as he neared them, holding his wife's hand and gently bringing her to her feet beside him. Consuelo stood shakily, helped by her husband, and in that moment The Man reached them and embraced them in his arms. The three of them cried openly, the men's sobs joining Consuelo's, filling the crowded room with the sound.

CHAPTER 8

General Avery Thompson, who had been Michael's section chief at the Pentagon in Michael's previous life, stood in the center of the Oval Office, his face a mask of incredulity. General Thompson looked at Michael, his normally smooth brow wrinkled in consternation.

"Permission to speak freely, sir," he said.

"Certainly, Avery," Michael said. "We've been together too long for you to stand on formality now."

"Thank you," General Thompson said. The general's forehead relaxed, but his tone was no less cautionary.

"Mr. President, you can't be serious. We'll be declaring war on Mexico! We'll have rioting in the streets all over this country. The Hispanic population will go mad! Are you willing to declare martial law over this?"

"I'm not taking anything off the table at this point," replied Michael.

"Isn't that what the administration you replaced was planning to do?" General Thompson said. "The gangs in Los Angeles will attract more recruits than they can handle if you do this. Taking troops over the border will start an outright war. I can't see an upside to this no matter how we look at it. I strongly urge you to consider the alternatives."

"There may not be an upside, Avery, except that we finally take a stand for ourselves as a nation and stop turning a blind eye to the cartels encroaching on our land and slaughtering American citizens with impunity. Run down the alternatives."

"If we use Special Ops maybe we can ferret out the animals that did this in a reasonable amount of time," General Thompson suggested.

"The audacity of this attack demands a more visible response." Michael was adamant.

"If this scenario plays out the way I think it will," Thompson said, "wholesale rioting in the cities will necessitate deploying the National Guard, and there will be no way to avoid declaring martial law. We really don't know how many unauthorized immigrants, including Mexicans, live here illegally. The DHS estimates close to twelve million. We don't want to fight another civil war on our soil."

"That's for certain," Michael said, "but we were attacked from the outside."

"Plunging over the border into the sovereign nation of Mexico will become a total disaster in quick time," General Thompson continued. "The national media will eat us alive. The world media will pile on, and we'll be declared the pariah of the earth. The U.N. will condemn us and demand that we be thrown out. China, North Korea, Iran—all our enemies will declare that we are indeed the Great Satan, and use it as justification for mounting a counter-attack."

"Agreed," said Michael. "But we need to take decisive action on the world stage. Anything less will embolden not only the cartels; you can bet any number of terrorists will consider it open season on us—on our own soil."

"You know that you have my support no matter what you do, but I would not be doing my job if I did not tell you what I think."

The president of the United States looked steadily at General Thompson. When Thompson had been Michael's boss, he had been a brigadier general. He was now a two star general, permanently assigned to the White House, where he served as the president's liaison with the Pentagon. Avery Thompson was one of the most intelligent and capable men Michael had ever known, and while he had not been a member of The Movement, he had proven his mettle to Michael and his troops during the Gulf War. Michael chose his words carefully out of admiration for the man.

"Avery, you've been my boss," Michael said in an earnest tone. "Not only do I respect you, but I honor you for your love of this country and your untiring service. Our circumstances are such that now you work for me. Having worked for each other, we each know the other's strengths and weaknesses. Frankly, I think your biggest weakness is on the golf course. I don't think I'll ever be able to play as well as you do."

General Thompson smiled.

The president knew how to take the edge off of a situation, and he also knew how to reassure a man when speaking a painful truth. "I'm not going to disagree with anything you've said. On the face of it, you're right on the mark," Michael said.

"Thank you, sir. That means a great deal to me. I never like to tell a great man when I think he is wrong, but I had to say what is in my mind and on my heart," said General Thompson.

Michael held up a hand in protest. "I am not a great man, General. I came to this job on the faith of people who believe I can do it, and I don't intend to disappoint them or the American people. History will judge whether or not that faith was misplaced, but that doesn't much impact the course of action I must choose today. I have spoken to the president of Mexico and given him two weeks to solve the problem."

"Surely you know that two weeks is not nearly enough time—"

"I know it," Michael interjected, "and Calderón knew when I said that two weeks time would not be enough. Calderón is a very intelligent and capable man, but he will acknowledge his need for our help at some point. He will try with all his might to deal with the problem, but the task he faces is enormous. He does not have the money, power, troops, or weapons to eradicate the cartels. Calderón is a consummate politician. He will ask others to come to his aid. He is a survivor. We will help him survive."

Another smile spread slowly over the general's face.

"Sir, you never cease to amaze me! You expect Calderón to ask for our help—for our intervention? We will not be brazenly rolling across the border to crush the animals who slaughtered and maimed our people. Instead, we will be invited to help the Mexican government deal with the problem of the cartels?"

"You understand me perfectly, Avery," Michael said, sitting back in his chair.

"How do you know this will happen? What if Calderón balks at the threat of aggression?" The general was incredulous. "What if he refuses to ask us for help?"

"Avery, I am part of a group of people who are both long in thought and planning for the present and the future every day. On the surface we have been building fences and a no man's land to keep people out. However, there is another way to solve this problem. It is one that has not been discussed or openly debated before. A change in direction is going to be announced soon. The world is evolving, albeit, in seemingly strange ways at times."

"What are you talking about, Mr. President?" Thompson asked.

"It is too early to tell you at this point, but you'll know soon enough." Michael rose, indicating the conversation had ended.

The general stood and saluted his commander-in-chief. "Thank you, sir. I look forward to hearing your intentions."

Michael returned his salute. "You will be among the first to know, General. I will go out on a limb and suggest that you will be pleased with what is being planned. I wish I could say more, but I cannot talk about it just now. Our innocents will be avenged."

The general walked to the door. He turned and paused before opening it. "Godspeed, sir!" he said.

Michael smiled, "God is the one who gets me through times like these."

"Amen, Mr. President." The general opened the door and left the room.

CHAPTER 9

Back in 1659, Spanish explorers seeking a route through the southern Rocky Mountains discovered the Juarez mountain region. The mountains offered a rocky, dry backdrop to an area of Mexico that is often described as the "Murder Capital" of the country. Ernesto Ruíz, El Toro, liked that. When he was looking into this particular mountain region for his exploits, he had one of his researchers read to him about the mountain range. After hearing that title, a deep devilish smile crept across his face. The researcher nervously went on to explain how an ecumenical pastor and his helpers had once long ago painted a message in gigantic white letters on the side of the mountain facing Ciudad Juarez.

"'La Biblia es la verdad—¡Léala!'" the researcher read. "The Bible is the truth—read it!"

El Toro had dismissed that part of the story with a grunt. He had never read a Bible in his life. In fact, he had never even read a whole book. He had enough money to pay people, like his researchers, to do the work for him. He had more than enough money to buy anyone. After all, the mountains had helped turn him from merely Ernesto into the great *El Toro!*

The son of a prostitute who had died of a heroin overdose not long after he was born, Ernesto Ruíz had been taken in by his maternal grandmother. She was a woman who saw nothing wrong in beating a child into submission. One day, when she began to hit him over a small infraction of her "rules," he lashed out and killed her. He was twelve-years-old at the time.

Ernesto had fled for his life into the mountains, wandering until a hermit found him dehydrated and near starvation. The man took him to a cave, where he nursed him back to health and sexually abused him routinely as part of the process. When Ernesto could not stand it anymore, he killed the man with an axe and dragged his body to a place where the coyotes would find it.

From that point on Ernesto survived alone in the wilderness, teaching himself to trap and skin small animals and stay alive as best he could. One day, an outlaw named Manuel Gutierrez and his band of brigands found the boy's cave. Ernesto managed to escape, and when they gave chase he killed one of them with a thrown rock.

Amused that that a mere boy could do such a thing, the outlaw took him into his band instead of killing him. Gutierrez liked boys, and he educated Ernesto in the subtleties of sex. He also taught him to handle a pistol, rifle, and knife. Ernesto honed his skills even as he grew in size and strength. At seventeen, he was the biggest and strongest member of the group, and he challenged Gutierrez for its leadership.

Once again, the outlaw was amused by the boy, and he laughed at Ernesto. The laughter ended abruptly as the teenager hurled a knife from twenty feet, catching Gutierrez in the throat. The force of the blow exploded the knife through the flesh, shattering the vertebrae and collapsing Gutierrez's head atop his chest. He fell, gurgling and choking on his own blood.

Cowed by the act, Gutierrez's men recognized Ernesto for a hot-headed, truculent child, and refused to follow him. Instead they drove him from their camp and threatened to kill him if he ever showed up again. The incident left Ernesto alone for the third time in his young life.

Determined to survive, he left the mountains and made his way to Ciudad Juarez, where he lived on the streets. Big and strong, he was recruited by a local gang to serve as their enforcer. He enjoyed beating people up and earned a reputation for brutality. He was merciless.

The gang took to calling him El Toro. He never backed down, and like a bull, he would lower his head and charge into the biggest of opponents.

Ernesto quickly rose in its ranks as the gang became involved in distributing marijuana and cocaine for a powerful cartel. He caught the attention of the cartel's leader, Marco Vega, who saw in Ernesto a younger version of himself. After a particularly brutal fight with a rival gang, Vega summoned Ernesto to a private meeting.

"Neto," he had said, forsaking the gang's nickname and addressing Ernesto by a pet name. "You must learn to control your anger, lest it be your undoing. We must find a way to cultivate your brain."

Days later Vega again called him aside. "I have an idea."

Vega's plan was to embed Ernesto within the police force. He fabricated an identity for him and bribed and threatened whomever it took to fast track him into the police academy.

"Play by the rules, Neto," he cautioned, "and do not unleash that murderous anger of yours while you are on the force."

El Toro excelled in the seedy under culture of Mexican law enforcement, where he did double duty as an informant for Marco Vega. Ernesto kept him apprised of any information he needed to protect his illicit interests. He helped the increasingly powerful drug king avoid being accidentally cornered and captured in the cops' sham raids.

Vega continued to mentor Ernesto. When the boy turned twenty-two, the cartel leader hand-picked Ernesto to join the military.

"Neto," he said again, "I have another idea."

Ernesto was inserted to take advantage of the fact that the Americans had begun training Mexican soldiers in special ops. He was a good student, and after a single term of enlistment Vega summoned him from the military to serve full time with the cartel.

Ernesto earned the respect of the men under him. He was disciplined; he did not smoke, do drugs or drink alcohol, and years of training had taught him to control his rage. He rose in the ranks to become the number two man in the organization, and Vega put him in charge of new recruits.

Secretly, Ernesto was biding his time until the right moment came.

Drug trafficking was becoming a huge enterprise, and the money that was being made was incredible. He chose men like himself who had been trained by the Americans and brought them into Vega's cartel, but their loyalty was first to Ernesto.

On his twenty-ninth birthday, Ernesto and his men staged a coup. They slaughtered seventeen members of the organization, including Vega, and Ernesto emerged as the new leader. Marco Vega's last words before Ernesto slit his throat were, "Neto, I have groomed you too well."

In the years that followed, Ernesto gained a reputation as the most murderous man in Mexico.

El Toro hated women and made it a point to keep up with the brutal treatment of women that plagued the Juarez region. He and his men killed scores of them. He enjoyed it like a sport, especially when the victim appeared to be innocent and helpless. He reveled in his power to hurt and kill, and his rage was such that men in his organization tried not to stand in his murderous way. One man did stand up to him at one point, but El Toro made an example of him with the second use of the murderous device that had been built beneath his mountain fortress.

Everyone in the cartel was forced to watch the torture and death of the man, and no one would ever forget the horrific scene. El Toro was many things, but he was never to be confronted by anyone in his organization. Some things were worse even than death, and the device in the chamber below the mountain was the most monstrously demonic thing any man had ever seen.

El Toro had spent a lot of money to have his Death Machine created. Its design and construction had required a lot of research and development. When it was finished, he tested it on its creator. El Toro had no wish for the man to ever build such a device for someone else. The man's screams left El Toro extremely satisfied with his invention.

Ernesto was apparently insane. He enjoyed hurting others, particularly women. It was the hurting part that was the most satisfying to him. He was disappointed when death came too quickly for some of his victims. He would do anything to delay death. He loved the suffering of others. Many of his men, brutes themselves, would watch in secret revulsion as he enjoyed his games of torture.

Ernesto allowed his men to call him El Toro, but they secretly called him by another name, one they dared not use to his face. Behind his back they called him El Diablo—*The Devil.*

CHAPTER 10

The Man Who Loved the Gulf saw to it that the Alvarez family was going to be well taken care of for the rest of their lives. Money could not replace a son, but genuine concern and compassion can go a long way to help those who grieve. Consuelo was given the medical and psychological help she needed—the best that money could buy—and José, his daughter, and the rest of the family saw how much The Man cared for them in the days that followed.

The Dupree triplets had gone off on visits to various companies, and Rick was staying close to home in order to keep an eye on José.

Later that evening, The Man's cell phone rang at exactly 9:00 p.m. He answered with his usual greeting.

His cousin replied in kind.

"I don't hear from you for two years," The Man said, "and now we speak twice in two weeks. This is good. I wish I could see you. Our José's little son is in his grave, and I need the comfort of being with family."

"Would it be alright if I come to your home this Friday afternoon?" his cousin asked.

"Yes, of course!" The Man said. "That would be wonderful! I

hope you can stay a while…"

"I'll have to leave Sunday morning," replied his cousin. "I have to meet with the president on Monday. Big changes are coming."

"What are they?" The Man asked.

"Not on the phone," his cousin said a little more quietly. "I'll explain when I see you. Is Rick at home, or is he off on his rounds?"

Surprised, The Man Who Loved the Gulf exclaimed, "How would you know about his rounds? Have you been spying on me?"

"Do you forget who I work for?"

"No, but are they omniscient? How do they know about my son and what he does?" The Man Who Loved the Gulf brushed aside the curtain, peering suspiciously outside his window.

"Don't be angry, Cousin. They know about the things that matter…and we can all be thankful that they are benevolent. I want to talk to you and Rick about a project. You'll understand why when I see you. I'll be at your gate by 4:00 p.m. tomorrow."

"After what you said, perhaps I shouldn't open the gate," The Man said.

"It's not like you to be petulant," his cousin said.

"I've always thought of that as a feminine word," The Man said dismissively. "If I am anything, I am cautious, Cousin."

"Point taken. I spend too much time in Washington, and, to use the vernacular of the day, it is a metro-sexual town. They use too many words here, and many of them are as empty as the heads that dream them up."

"All right, the gate will be open," The Man Who Loved the Gulf said. "Say hello to the guards. They'll know that I'm waiting for you," The Man said. He paused and added,"It's beautiful at this time of year."

"It is beautiful, indeed," his cousin replied and hung up.

CHAPTER 11

Promptly at four the next afternoon, a limo approached the gate of the estate, and the three guards who were on duty acknowledged the visitor, but they would not allow the rented limo to enter the grounds. The visitor told the limo driver that he would call him for his return trip to the airport, and a tram driven by a fourth guard took him to the main house.

The Man Who Loved the Gulf was waiting for his cousin with Rick. After a drink and small talk in the massive living room, the three men made their way to the dining room and sat down for the evening meal.

The Man's cousin bowed his head and offered a blessing, and the other two men bowed their heads out of respect for their guest.

When they turned their faces upright, The Man Who Loved the Gulf said, "I have not been inside a church for decades. Do you attend one?"

"Yes, I go whenever I can," replied his cousin.

"Are you a believer?" asked The Man.

"Yes, of course," said his cousin.

"I guess I should ask you, why—"

"I'm not here to discuss my faith," his cousin said, brushing the question aside. "There will be time for that at some point. I'll simply say that I could not get through the day if I didn't believe that there was something greater than Washington, DC and its presence in my life. However, I have come here to explain a problem in our country. A solution will be put forward shortly to address that problem, but I need input from your perspective."

"I will offer you what I can," The Man said.

Dinner was served, and the three men made small talk about the usual subjects. Their guest did not bring up why he was there while they enjoyed a delicious grilled tuna steak accompanied by fresh vegetables.

"The meal is immpeccable, as usual," the cousin said.

"A good life demands discipline in body, mind, and spirit," The Man said. "Starting with the foods one eats. I'll deliver your compliments to the chef."

When dinner was over they made their way to a veranda tastefully furnished with sumptuous Italian milled velvet wingback chairs and antique mahogany sidetables. They took in a spectacular view of the white sand beach and dazzling blue water of the Gulf. The Man's cousin finally began his tale.

"There is no question that the atrocity that took place in El Paso was the work of a madman."

Rick had not been told about what happened in El Paso from an insider's perspective. He had, like the rest of the public, learned of the attack through the news media. Now, The Man Who Loved the Gulf and his cousin clued Rick in on the details of the attack.

"The leader of the cartel who carried out this slaughter is called El Toro," the cousin said.

"He is worth billions. No one knows where he is, or where his hideout is located—at least no one in Mexico knows."

"Are you saying that you know where he can be found?" Rick asked.

"I don't have that information, but there are people who can ferret it out."

"Are they with the new government?" The Man asked.

"No, but they do have ways of discovering where anyone on earth is at any given moment," his cousin replied.

Rick said, "How is that possible? I work with security systems every day, and I don't see how you could do such a thing."

"Please trust me when I say this, Rick," The Man's cousin said slowly. "The people I know have been around for a long time. They are the most secretive people on this planet, and if they want to find someone they can do it. They knew about Pierce Armstrong for decades before he interfered with your men."

"Then I guess that means what you say about them is true," Rick admitted.

"They normally don't concern themselves with what is going on outside the US, but they are always aware of what others are doing. Anything that can potentially harm America is of real concern to them. The latest intel from them indicates that they have a good idea where El Toro might be located. They're awaiting verification on the ground. The cartel has more than enough money to buy the best security in the world. We're going to have to do a little personal work, and that is where you come in."

"What about the CIA?" asked The Man Who Loved the Gulf. "Can't the government handle this? I'm not sure I want to put any of my men in harm's way again."

Looking at his cousin was like looking into a mirror; they so closely resembled each other that they could have been twins. The Man returned his cousin's steady gaze.

"You know me from birth," the cousin said. "We are blood of the blood. I would not ask for your help if there was not a genuine need for it. When I said that you could do things that the government cannot do, I meant it. We did our best to clean out the rat's nest when we got rid of the key Progressives, but there are still worms in the apple. El Toro is sly and his corruption has spread. He has people inside our government. While my people are the best in the world, they have not been able to identify all of the players. His name, by the way, is Ernesto Ruíz. He likes to beat people to death, especially women."

At that, Rick sat straight up in his chair. "He's a coward, then! I'd like to spend a few minutes with him and see that he never hurts another person again!"

"Anger, my friend, won't get this done," the cousin said. "No, he's not a coward…he's just so filled with hate that he is insane. He's also well trained, and that makes him even more dangerous. However, that's not the only problem. Because El Toro has so much money, he must have people in Washington who keep an eye on things for him, but there are people outside the Beltway he doesn't know about."

The cousin returned his gaze to The Man Who Loved the Gulf, recapturing his eyes. "You, for instance. He doesn't know anything about you. That's why I am here."

The Man sighed. "That's all well and good, but Rick nearly died at the hands of that maniac in Nebraska. I'm not putting him, or anyone else in my organization, at risk without a very good reason—and I haven't heard any reason yet that would make me feel differently."

The silence hung between them for a few moments.

The cousin spoke first. "Look, I don't expect you to make snap decisions, and I don't want to place anyone you care about in harm's way, but this El Toro captured a young mother and her son when his group came over the Rio Grande and slaughtered our people. He took them back to wherever he is hiding. That's bad enough, especially for their family, but there is something worse."

The Man's face paled when his cousin disclosed what that something worse was.

"My God!" The Man said.

Rick's eyes went wide. "How is that possible?"

"How do you know? Who got this information?" The Man leaned forward, his hands white-knuckled against the fabric of the chair.

"The people I work for have their ways," the cousin said with his usual air of vagueness, "but I was only told yesterday. That's the real reason I'm here. We've got to find El Toro. The president is about to go into Mexico."

"But what about what you just told us?" Rick exclaimed. "If we invade them, it will be seen as an act of war. The whole world will condemn us. That would be all the more reason for El Toro to do something really drastic. How can the federal government take such a chance?"

"I didn't say that we are going to invade Mexico. You did. President Stonebreaker says that President Calderón is going to ask for our help…that he will invite us to come and find the cartels and eliminate them."

The Man Who Loved the Gulf looked perplexed. "Why would Calderón allow the US to violate their own sovereignty?"

"Why would our president do it?" Rick asked.

"Michael Stonebreaker will do it because he doesn't make decisions that end in failure," his cousin said with a gleam in his eye. "There is about to be a major paradigm shift in the universe. It will be up to the rest of the world to watch and learn."

"How is that possible?" he finally asked.

The view from the veranda was as magnificent as ever, but it felt as though a cloud had passed overhead.

The Man Who Loved the Gulf shivered involuntarily. "What was that old saying about someone stepping on your grave?"

CHAPTER 12

The select group of people sitting in the Oval Office with the president Monday morning included Vice President Eric Dryden, General Avery Thompson, Defense Secretary Fred Conover, CIA Director Helen Abramson, and a tall, well-built, handsome man who bore a strong resemblance to a movie star from a generation ago. He had not been identified by name to the other members of the group, and none of them had asked for an introduction.

"Let's begin," the president said. "We know the name of the leader of the cartel who attacked us. They call him El Toro. His real name is Ernesto Ruíz. He is in charge of a covert cartel with tons of money and a secret weapon, according to the intelligence that has been shared with us. The death toll from the El Paso attack has risen by five, and more may die as the result of their wounds. It is my intention to rid Mexico of this threat, and I will see that this is accomplished by any means necessary.

"President Calderón is doing his best to deal with the situation, but he lacks the resources, weapons, and will to do the job in the time frame I gave him. To that end, I will introduce a guest who, for reasons I will not go into, will only be known to us here by his alias,

Mr. Smith. He will share the scope of the situation beyond what we know."

Michael turned to the man and nodded.

The cousin of The Man Who Loved the Gulf stood up as the other meeting attendees eyed him with polite interest, noting his easy command of the room. Mr. Smith was at least six feet tall, and gave the impression of someone who was always in control of himself.

When he spoke, his voice was deep and powerful. "Mr. President, thank you for your invitation to this meeting today," he said.

Helen Abramson thought she detected the slightest hint of an accent from somewhere in Europe. It could have been from Spain, but she couldn't attest to that beyond a reasonable doubt.

"All of us came here by way of the same group," the man was saying. "My existence has been unknown to all but one of you before today, and I will cease to exist for you when we part company. I speak for the organization that we do not name outside of its walls, and I convey best wishes from its members to each of you. They have been in the surveillance business longer than most entities on the earth, and they have a good idea where Ernesto and his cartel are located. I cannot tell you how they know this. Simply accept the fact that it is so."

General Thompson cast a wary glance around the room, but the guest showed no worry over his concern.

"I have contact with people outside the government," the mysterious guest continued, "who have resources, special skills and abilities that become useful from time-to-time. This is one of those times. I have already been with them, and we have discussed possible scenarios that may play out in the next few days. In the meantime we 'Trust – but verify,' as the saying goes. It is very good to know exactly where you stand, particularly when you are dealing with people who would like to kill you. El Toro has people on his payroll inside the Beltway whom we have yet to identify, but it's only a matter of time until they're exposed."

There were a few nods around the table. Michael admired the aptitude of the man. He was well-informed and there was a confidence and firmness in his voice.

"There is also the larger problem at hand," the visitor warned.

"There are a number of cartels in Mexico, not just the one led by Ernesto. You want to eliminate all of them and close Mexico's northern border."

Fred Conover nodded in agreement, shifting forward in his chair as the visitor continued.

"That is a major undertaking, one that will require time and some cooperation between the US and Mexico to accomplish," he said.

"Beyond that goal there are two additional concerns. First, we are tasked with securing the well-being of Mrs. Adrienne Williams and her son, Charles, who are being held by Ernesto."

The man introduced as Mr. Smith paused and met each member of the group's eyes before going on. "Secondly, we must identify the location of a particular weapon that is, according to our intelligence, kept within the cartel compound.

"With that, I've shared all of the information available up to the moment. Mr. President," he said, addressing Michael directly, "I know that you and your people will be dealing with the broader issues, and I feel confident in the outcome of your decisions. I'll be in touch via the usual channels."

Michael nodded. "Thank you for coming personally to deliver the intel."

The man smiled and left the room.

Michael spoke first. "I had no knowledge of this man until recently, but I can tell you, we sit in this office today because of his tireless efforts. If it were possible—and it never will be—to publicly recognize him for what he has done for this country there would be a statue of him on every corner."

Defense Secretary Conover sat back in his chair as the president continued speaking.

"You have just met a bit of living history," Michael said, "though we cannot admit that he even exists.

"As to what we face in Mexico," Michael went on, "it is time to solve the problem of not only the drug cartels, but to also resolve the problem of the border and illegal immigration. We have been completing the fence, building a no man's land, and doing our best to secure our border. That doesn't solve the problem. It needs to be fixed in a way that doesn't need to be tinkered with in the future.

"Illegal immigration has been tolerated in this country because the Progressives were buying votes. We no longer have that problem. Term limits have eliminated that possibility on the federal level. The vice president will address our options." Michael directed the group's attention to the vice president.

"Thank you, Mr. President," said VP Eric Dryden, rising from his chair. "It is our intention to deal with the problem of Mexico in such a way that future generations will not be plagued with an on-going situation that is detrimental to the US people and our economy. We have three options: First, maintain the status quo. That would be to complete the fence and no man's land. After that, through technology and additional manpower, to so tighten the border that crossing it illegally will be next to impossible."

Helen Abramson and Avery Thompson nodded in agreement.

Vice President Dryden continued,"Our second option is to close the border entirely. That is neither realistic, nor fair to either us or the Mexican people. At the moment, people in both countries need work, and many of our businesses require workers willing to do jobs that many Americans simply won't do."

He paused, visibly assessing the room before going on. "The third possibility is that we take a new direction, one that has not been publicly discussed. There is an alternative to the conundrum that faces our nation. It will require resources on a large scale, a long-term game plan that will have to be implemented over the next decade, and the willingness of both the American and Mexican people to fully participate."

He walked to the end of the room. "Before we focus on this solution, let's look at what we are facing. While some believe that there are six major drug cartels operating in Mexico, with tentacles in the US and other parts of the world, there are also splinter groups within the country. The Sinaloa Foundation in the Mexican state of Sinaloa may have as many as a hundred-thousand operatives in seventeen Mexican states. The Zetas cartel is a hard-core group of Special Forces trained men who are lethal. There is an ongoing turf war between the cartels, and it may ultimately end with the cartel that outlasts all the others.

"There is also the Juarez cartel, but El Toro and his group are not part of it. He has delusions of grandeur. He wants to rule the world.

Whether he will survive is a matter for debate, but he has control of something that poses a great threat to everybody, and he's crazy enough to use it. When President Stonebreaker announces our plan, President Calderón is expected to embrace it. When you extend a life preserver to a drowning man, he eagerly grabs it and holds on for dear life. Calderón will end up making history, a problem will be solved, our troops will be welcomed in Mexico, the cartels will be eradicated, and a new and friendlier world will be born."

"That sounds rather simple," Director Helen Abramson said with a raised eyebrow. She had her arms folded across her blazer, waiting patiently for more information.

"Simply said, well, yes," the vice president replied. "Practically applied? That is a bit more complicated. The immediate need of dealing with El Toro is being addressed. The greater plan involving those of us in this room is going to require a new level of public understanding and acceptance. It will be presented at the appropriate time by President Stonebreaker. He will be explaining it to the American people via television, the Internet, and radio simultaneously.

"Our forces will be gathered at Fort Bliss, as well as at many other points, and we will enter Mexico when President Calderón invites us to come into his country. We will conduct ourselves with perfect restraint and good behavior in our tactical plan. While the cartels may learn we are coming, they will have no idea of the firepower we will be bringing with us. If necessary, it will be to the death, and the death will be their demise.

"In addition to what our president will be presenting to both our people and the Mexican nation, we will be moving a Manhattan Project-sized relief mission into Mexico at the same time. I'm not going into detail just yet because I have not been given all the facts. However, President Calderón faces an equal need, as our president does here, of gaining public acceptance. Mr. President, will you explain at least as much as you can of what you plan to do?"

"Thank you, Eric," replied President Stonebreaker, clearing his throat. "I will be calling Calderón within the hour and asking him to meet me at the border tomorrow. I am going to outline our plan to him, and I am going to explain how it will benefit Mexico and its people. I believe he will accept the plan. When he does, we will be moving rapidly as soon as he announces the plan to his nation. We will coordinate our announcement to our own people simultaneously."

The president took sealed packets from his desk and handed one to each of the people present before continuing. "This outlines in full detail what the plan is and how it will work. When you return to your offices, I ask you to lock your doors and read through the plan. If you have questions, call me immediately. I need your intelligence and your hearts on this. Nothing has ever been proposed like this before, and it may never be again. This is the first step of what could be a monumental success, or an unmitigated failure. I believe that it will succeed. So do the people who put us here. However, I still need your input. Thanks for coming today."

Helen Abramson said, "Mr. President, may I ask you a question?"

"Yes, of course," Michael said.

"The weapon that this El Toro has—what is it?"

Michael closed his eyes for a moment in a mild grimace. His audience stared wide-eyed as he said, "Let me answer it this way. It came into his possession because Mexico's borders are not as secure as they should be. It was given to him for safekeeping by people he helped cross illegally into the United States. Those people are here now and under surveillance. We captured one of them and questioned him at great length at Gitmo. His people had big plans for the weapon, but they recruited El Toro to keep it under wraps while they figured out the best way to get it into the US."

Defense Secretary Conover said, "They can be very persuasive at Gitmo. May I assume the man you're talking about was from another part of the world?"

"It's a safe assumption, Fred," Michael said.

Director Abramson quietly posed the question again. "Mr. President, the weapon—?"

There was real pain in Michael's face when he answered. "It's nuclear, Helen. God help us all."

CHAPTER 13

Michael looked over the case file for the missing hostages. Adrienne Williams was a very beautiful thirty-five-year-old Caucasian woman. Her twelve-year-old son Charles, or Chuck, as he was called, had inherited her good looks as well as his father's. His dad, Everett Williams, was fair, tall and well-built. A captain in the Army serving at Fort Bliss, Williams was no doubt distressed over the abduction of his wife and son. Michael read in the report that William's commanding officer, Colonel Ron MacKenzie, was keeping Captain Williams busy. At least while on duty the officer could maintain his focus. Off-duty, Michael was sure all Williams could think about was getting his wife and son back, safe and sound.

Troops were being gathered at the training facility, and members of Seal Team Six had flown in to help with the planning, and the possibility of making a secret insertion into the Juarez area.

Mobilization of forces was moving forward at a rapid but orderly pace. When the American and Mexican presidents made their joint declarations to their respective nations, the deployment would already be underway. Nothing was being left to chance.

President Stonebreaker and President Calderón met together

in a building on the American side of the border. Given what had happened, it was the least Calderón could do. There was no time for bluster and saving face. The meeting was not announced to the press, and, unlike the way things used to be done inside the Beltway, no word of the meeting had been leaked.

There were a dozen people in the room, including the two heads of state, and when the president of the United States had fully explained what the intentions of the meeting were all about, the silence of those in the room was long and deep.

Calderón was a good looking man. His smile was legendary, and he was known for his political acumen. He finally broke the quiet hush in the room.

"President Stonebreaker, are you quite serious about this?"

Michael said, "President Calderón, there is no more serious moment than now. We both face the task of getting our people to accept this plan, but it will do what has always been necessary to solve three problems—eliminate the cartels and solve our mutual cross-border drug trafficking problem, fix the illegal immigration problem once and for all, and bring your people the promise of an economy that will support them in such a way that they won't have to leave home to find work. If the people on both sides of the border accept it, it will take time to do all of it. Realistically, it may require a decade, but that is nothing compared to the time we've spent trying to rectify the monstrous problems we have between us."

Calderón said nothing. He looked grave, his graying brows knitting together as he focused in on what Michael was saying.

Michael allowed a pause for his words to sink in. "This promises us hope for a great future together. Is it going to be easy? No. People are going to die in this process. The cartels will not roll over and play dead. When men have that kind of money and power over others, they will not go away quietly. However, if the fear of the common man is replaced with freedom and economic prosperity, then the hoodlum down the street is the one who will learn to fear the strength of the people.

"Your nation is filled with good people and poised at the intersection of two roads: one leads to anarchy, disaster and ruin, and the other leads to rebirth and the kind of freedom people want. This is the time for words—not empty political promises that can't be kept—but words that are true that can stir the hearts and minds of people, followed by the necessary action to make the promises real. Will you join with me to begin this task?"

President Calderón looked across the table at the American president. What was being proposed was stunning in its design, massive in scope, and beyond his wildest dreams. He had come to the table thinking that this was the end of his political career, that he would have to leave his office in disgrace, and that his nation was about to be overrun by angry Americans. Now, everything had changed, and the possibilities that loomed in front of him were like the proverbial life raft thrown to a drowning man.

Calderón found his voice. "Yes. Yes, indeed. We can—no, we need to do this together. I have been hamstrung in my ability to help my people shake off the power of the cartels. They live in fear of talking openly. This plan will destroy the organizations, reveal the leaders, and bring them down. Our border should not have to be a no-man's land of fence, wire, cameras, and guns. If my people can build prosperity for themselves, there is nothing that will keep them from rising to the task."

Michael considered interjecting, but he wanted to give Calderón the respect of finishing his full thought. Remaining on good relations while simultaneously turning the situation around so that Calderón was on his side took precedence.

Calderón's voice took on a somber tone. "However," he said, "you must understand that Mexico is not the United States. Many of my people still struggle. Yet, despite being looked down on and stereotyped as illegals, we do have pride. Americans may have their action movies, football players, and superheroes, but Mexican men are no less machismo in their vision of themselves."

Michael smiled. "What you say is true. That does not make it right, but the blight of prejudice can be healed. Dr. King wanted people to judge character, and his dream is a worthy one for all of us. Overcoming stereotypes won't be easy. People are stubborn in their beliefs. However, if we don't begin to change now we will never change, and our people will remain estranged from one another.

"Regardless of the obstacles we face, we must resolve to be better. This doesn't have to be a zero sum game. Our people can join together and become that shining city on a hill that is the promise to those who will strive to attain it."

Calderón's eyes were gleaming. He was beginning to see Michael Stonebreaker as a remarkable man. Perhaps having him as an ally would truly be for the best. He took a breath and said, "Then we will do this together. When do you wish to announce the plan?"

"I propose that we stand side-by-side at a podium on the border between our countries and tell our people what we intend to do. However, we must take care of a terrible threat to all of us—your people and ours—before announcing our intentions to the world."

"What is that?" Calderón asked.

"Ernesto Ruíz, or, El Toro as he prefers to be called, must go."

"Aah," the Mexican president said, "He has another name that his men call him, one that he hates: El Diablo."

"Yes," Michael said. "Well, the Devil will have his due."

"The problem with the Devil, Mr. President, is that he does not like to leave quietly," Calderón said.

"Well, he forgets one thing, President Calderón," Michael said.

"What is that?"

"There are forces far greater than he will ever be in this world," Michael said. "He is about to learn, again, that there is no long term future for him."

Michael knew the look on his face was one that few had seen.

President Calderón saw that look and recognized it for what it was. No one in his right mind would make an enemy of the man who sat before him. He felt a shiver creep up his spine. Stonebreaker was a man of his word, and his word would be accomplished.

CHAPTER 14

The Man Who Loved the Gulf had called for the meeting to be held aboard his beautiful yacht, the Gulf Maiden. It was anchored a half mile out from his estate. His cousin had arrived from Washington, and they took a speedboat to the ship.

The dock at The Man's home could easily accommodate the ship, but keeping it away from land afforded better protection for the vessel. The ship was protected by every system money could buy and outfitted with special equipment used only by the US military, thanks to The Man's cousin. Two helicopters near the stern were piloted by the three Dupree brothers and Rick. There were only two other men in the man's employ who were qualified to fly the choppers.

No one on earth could hack the computers aboard the ship. Its armament was state-of-the-art, including surface-to-air missiles, torpedoes, and an arsenal that SEAL Team would respect. The lovely ship was like a beautiful viper floating upon the water. It appeared to be graceful and designed only for pleasure, but it was deadly beyond what anyone would suspect.

The ship's crew were all ex-US Navy men. They knew every inch of the ship from bow to stern. The Man Who Loved the Gulf expected total loyalty from everyone in his employ, and he made sure his people were the best in the business, extremely well-compensated, and afforded the finest money could provide in their personal lives. The crew members were family men with wives, children, and lovely homes. They drove up-scale automobiles, had country club memberships, and The Man saw to it that they had nothing about which to complain.

If there was one word that described The Man Who Loved the Gulf, it was reclusive. Those who were given access to him had been vetted better than anyone in the previous federal government. That included the crew of his ship. The man was also a qualified master pilot. He could fly the choppers, as well as fixed-wing aircrafts.

One could never be too cautious. The Man Who Loved the Gulf loved the luxuries he had, but he was no fool. He was not soft, and he did not allow his skills to rust. His four sons were extraordinary in their abilities as well, and he chose employees first for their character, followed by their ability to contribute to his organization.

The Man often remarked that had the US government been run by men a tenth of their caliber The Movement would not have arisen and removed them from power. He fancied his organization and theirs consisted of men of excellent character, real intelligence, and if his cousin were any indication, a commitment to serving the American people.

"Mediocrity has no place in human affairs." This motto was on a steel plate that hung on the wall behind the desk in his office. Although he was self-educated, The Man was a lifelong learner of Mensa-level intelligence and a gifted athlete. Only Derek and Rick could sometimes best him on the tennis court, and no one defeated him in handball, golf, and a host of other sports. While he was incredibly competitive in everything he set his hand to, he was also gracious towards his opponents.

The Man believed in living a balanced life and did nothing to excess. He took pains to stay mentally sharp and had a knack for being attentive to the smallest detail of what was going on around him. He had seen others make mistakes simply because they let their guard down.

He was not a seer or prophet, but he was most certainly a man who thought far ahead of most others. He operated on the prinicple that one planned for every possible contingency in all things, and then carefully designed the route to success. As a result, he was worth billions.

The Man's cousin, who resembled him so closely, was equally intelligent and enigmatic, but he had taken a very different path to personal fulfillment in life. He had become The Movement's point man, making it possible to unearth the secrets of the previous government, and to replace it. He was a patriot in thought, word, and deed. Money and power were unimportant to him. He was also a believer. In this, he was far more like Michael Stonebreaker than he was his billionaire cousin.

His faith gave him the strength to move ahead confidently in extremely dangerous circumstances. He had seen what the evils of the world could do to those it captured in mind and body. Pragmatic in style, unruffled in his outward composure, he kept his great passion hidden from others. He sought answers that other men could not see, or, if they saw them, denied their existence. In an earlier age, he would have been called a zealot. In the present he was careful to hide the fiery passion for truth that blazed within him.

Twelve men and women from throughout The Man's organization assembled in the beautiful lounge aboard the yacht for the meeting. Duke, Derek, and Damien Dupree were also present and sat at the table with Rick, The Man, and his cousin. The remaining attendees included six former Special Forces members who had served with distinction and were as tough as men could be. Each spoke Spanish fluently.

The Man Who Loved the Gulf was not a chauvinist, and prided himself on being an equal opportunity employer. His organization employed hundreds of hispanic and latino men and women, and the women seated at the table held positions of equal authority overseeing key aspects of his enterprise.

The Man had made two critical decisions many years before. He would base his all of his companies in the Americas, and over the years he'd built his empire from Canada and across the US, down through Mexico, and into Central and South America. He was committed to the Western Hemisphere, and he saw it as fertile ground for his ever-expanding business.

The second fundamental decision he made was to employ people native to those countries in great numbers within his personal army. While he had begun his organization within the Mafia traditions, he had quickly morphed into legitimate businesses, and he exited that arena, to the relief of the other crime families. They were wise enough not to antagonize him, and bid him good riddance when he separated from them.

Several of the captains in his organization were of Mexican, Puerto Rican, and Brazilian heritage, and others were natives of Chile, Colombia, and Costa Rica. All had attended schools in the US and returned to their home countries to serve in The Man's employ.

The Man also maintained a personal army hidden amidst well-paid, customary jobs within his organization. These men understood that when The Man called them to duties beyond the scope of their "day" jobs, they would report and serve him in whatever capacity was required. This clandestine army numbered in the hundreds. It gathered at a camp deep within the jungles of Brazil each year for weeks of exhaustive training. Here, as everywhere else in The Man's organization, there were no sluggards in his employ.

The Man Who Loved the Gulf looked around his lovely yacht at the faces of those he trusted the most within his company.

"We are here today to discuss something that must be kept so secret that we speak to no one about it until we have agreed to do two things," he said. "First, we must decide if this is something we will be part of, and, second, determine if we can successfully do what needs to be done. My cousin will explain the details."

The Man Who Loved the Gulf had spoken; his people sat listening attentively. No one said anything, and all eyes were glued on The Man's cousin. It wasn't lost on anyone that his cousin bore remarkable resemblance to The Man himself.

At the press of a button a large screen appeared and came to life with the image of a city.

"Ciudad Juarez, Mexico," the cousin began, "Population 1.5 million, lies on the Rio Grande in the Mexican state of Chihuahua, opposite El Paso, Texas. It is one of the fastest growing cities in this hemisphere. There are over 300 maquiladoras—factory assembly plants—in or near the city. Its rapid growth is something of an irony, considering that it might well be called the 'Murder Capital of the

World.' It averages eight murders a day, according to statistics, with over a thousand unsolved murders of women factory workers. The city is a major drug trafficking center, run largely by the Juarez cartel. As distrubing as these things are, we are here to discuss something far more sinister about this region today."

The scene on the screen changed to show the Juarez Mountains. The cousin continued. "Hidden somewhere in these mountains is a cartel that is led by Ernesto Ruíz, also known as El Toro. His group is unaffiliated with the Juarez cartel, and he wants to become the most powerful cartel in Mexico."

An out-of-focus picture of a man on a city street appeared on the screen, and the cousin pointed to it.

"This is the only known photo we have of El Toro. Every effort has been made to clean up the picture, and this is what we have now."

The photo changed to a close-up, and they saw the face of the man more clearly.

"Some would say he is a good looking man, but his face hides a cruel nature that has forced many unfortunate victims into a web of brutality and death. His hatred of women is diabolical. He does like little boys though, and the younger the better."

There was a murmur among the people around the table, but The Man held up his hand and they became silent.

The cousin went on. "El Toro and his men, somewhere between a hundred-fifty and two-hundred of them, crossed the border nine days ago in the middle of the night. They entered a suburban area, went house-to-house, woke up the residents and herded them into the streets. They opened fire and slaughtered eighty-nine people, half of them children, and wounded another hundred-and-seven. In this past week, twenty-three more Americans have died, and, of the remaining victims, more than half will probably be invalids for the rest of their lives.

"When local law enforcement arrived on the scene they killed seventeen of El Toro's men and wounded another twenty-eight. Ten more died from their wounds last week, but Ernesto doesn't care about those who will be in our prisons for the rest of their lives if they survive their wounds. He fled back across the border. His men captured the wife and son of an American military officer and took them over the border with them. Based on what we have learned about El Toro, if they are still alive at this point, you can appreciate what will be done to them."

The cousin glanced across at The Man who Loved the Gulf, already anticipating the look on his face. The Man's deep grimace relayed the empathy that his cousin had always known was buried in his chest.

The cousin said, "We must move swiftly. The fate of the woman and boy are certain unless someone gets them out of his hands quickly. The fate of Mexico and the US, on the other hand, is just as precarious. There is another far more serious problem facing both Mexico and the United States. El Toro helped a group of Al-Qaeda members cross into the US six months ago. One of them was captured and taken to Gitmo. He was forced to talk, and he revealed that they had left behind something in the care of El Toro for safekeeping until it could be brought into the US. El Toro himself is rumored to be a force to be reckoned with. He was well-trained by our military, and he has a low opinion of our ability to find him. He thinks that no one knows where he is. He has spent millions making his fortress secure from prying eyes, including our drones. El Toro has hidden away the Al-Qaeda secret in his fortress. Perhaps this is why he is sure that he has the power to become the biggest cartel in all of Mexico. He has a nuclear weapon."

The cousin stopped talking at this point. There was silence around the table.

Finally, Duke Dupree said, "You said that this El Toro thinks no one knows where he is, but you implied that someone does. If that is the case, who knows and how can he be found?"

"The people I work for identified a general location a week ago," the cousin said. "I have given this information to President Stonebreaker and his people. Troops are amassing at Fort Bliss at this moment. Stonebreaker and the Mexican president are cooperating with each other at this time. There will be a joint announcement by the two to their nations simultaneously about what is going to happen. American troops will be entering Mexico and a full-scale massive campaign will begin to rid Mexico of all its cartels and related elements during the next few years. Coupled with this, a huge joint economic plan will be announced between Mexico and the US. The plan will help build the Mexican economy into one where people can stay in Mexico and not choose to cross the border. I cannot explain what is involved just yet because there are many things that need to be put in place.

"However, our immediate problem is to find and neutralize El Toro and the weapon. This is going to involve SEAL Team Six, from the military end, but El Toro was trained by our people, and he expects to see signs of such an incursion every day. He isn't a fool, but his hubris is enormous. He thinks we lack the will to come after him."

Rick scoffed. He couldn't believe the audacity of such a man.

The Man Who Loved the Gulf held up his hand again. "What, dear cousin, is President Stonebreaker then planning to do from this point on?"

"That is why I am here," his cousin replied, a hint of personal confidence returning to his voice. "El Toro knows that if someone does come looking for him that they will have to be someone like the SEAL Team. What he does not expect is that there are others in this world that have the same training as he does, but who have, shall I say, a different approach to the problem. I know you have contacts throughout Mexico, as well as through all of Central and South America. You have 'ears-to-the-ground' that our government lacks. I understand that you are a world-unto-yourselves, but I also know that many, if not most of you, are former members of the American military, with an apology to Duke and his brothers, but they are well-trained ex-military, as well. The Aussies and Americans are brothers when called upon. At this point, I will turn this meeting over to my cousin's direction. Whatever you decide is up to you. If the decision is that you cannot participate, I will accept that answer—and move onto the next group. However, I believe you are the best and that is why I came to you first with my request."

The Man Who Loved the Gulf sat and looked silently at the people around the table. Their lives and loyalty meant far more to him than he could put into words. Now, they were faced with making a decision that would mean that they would be in harm's way. There was a storm of emotions raging within him. Perhaps he was getting old? The right path had to be chosen. It was going to be a long meeting.

CHAPTER 15

Adriana Cristiana Santos was raised in Fort Lauderdale, Florida, in an upscale neighborhood not far from the inland waterway. She had enlisted in the US Army as soon as she graduated from high school, despite her parents' wishes to the contrary. She rose from private to sergeant, and then left the army to attend Duke University. She went on to Wharton for an MBA, and through a family connection she settled in Rio where she joined a television and movie production company owned by The Man Who Loved the Gulf. She worked hard, and she had become the second in command in that company. Her parents, though proud of their adopted American heritage, insisted she learn several languages. As a result, Adriana spoke Portuguese, Spanish, French, and a little Italian. She developed a reputation for being one of the most knowledgeable and capable in people in filmmaking.

Adriana was also one of three women aboard The Man Who Loved the Gulf's beautiful ship to discuss whether the boss's considerable resources would be brought to bear against the cartels after the attack in El Paso. She now realized those resources included the apparently wide-ranging abilities of his adopted sons.

Seeing all three Dupree brothers together, she felt annoyed that she had not realized there were three of them. She would figure out later if she was angry or amused at the prank. She had never met Rico "Rick" Rodriguez: he had yet to visit her company in disguise on behalf of his father. Derek was explaining that he and Damien had visited her production company in Rio when Rick entered the ship's lounge.

Adriana had met scores of handsome Latin men in her work, but not one of them compared to the man who had just come into the room. He was a vision, to put it mildly. His hair, coloring, and clothing gave the impression of an easy nonchalance, and his build spoke of great strength, health, vitality, and athleticism. She watched discreetly as he made the rounds, greeting each of his father's guests.

When he reached her and took her hand, Rick Rodriquez's face and smile burned into her mind. Adriana was a good actor, and she hid her feelings well, but she felt as though a god had come down from on high, stepped onto the earth, and decided to walk among mere mortals.

She brushed the thought aside, remembering that she was, after all, a good Catholic girl, and forced herself to react normally and speak appropriately. Her heart was racing, nevertheless, and she felt like a schoolgirl who had just met the biggest rock star in the world.

As the meeting progressed, a plan was shared that would consist of inserting as many of The Man Who Loved the Gulf's "soldiers" as possible in the Ciudad Juarez region immediately. This could be done without arousing suspicion or, at least, the wrong kind of scrutiny under the guise of filming a TV pilot.

"At any given time numerous people can be working on location to film a TV pilot," Adriana said. "And there is another advantage in the amount of equipment typically needed to do it."

It was decided that one-hundred-and-twenty people would make up the crew headed to Mexico. Forty of them would be there on far more serious business than filming an action TV pilot. Any required weapons and gear would also be brought in, stowed among the filmmaking equipment. They would be carrying enough firepower to wipe out an army. The Man Who Loved the Gulf agreed to the plan, and the decision was made.

While the lives of the captured woman and her son were on the line, the threat of a nuclear weapon unleashed on the world was an even more powerful motivation to deal with El Toro and his men. The whole operation was being paid for with "off the books" money funneled into the US government by The Movement.

"Ms. Santos is in charge of filming the pilot," the cousin said, "and Rick, you will be her on-site VP overseeing the operation."

The production crew would be flying into the region from Rio. A plane was waiting to take the team out in two hours.

The cousin looked at The Man. "I assumed you would agree, and all the equipment is already onboard."

When the meeting broke up and the guests had left for their respective destinations, the brothers and their father gathered again with The Man's cousin in the lounge.

"So, we go to war again," The Man Who Loved the Gulf said. "This time it's not in Nebraska. Juarez is not a place I'd choose to go lightly." He placed a hand on his son's shoulder.

"Rick, you must promise me that you will do everything you can to be safe. I agreed to this only because of the nuclear weapon. It cannot be used by Ruíz—in Mexico or here. Too many have died already."

"Father," Rick said, "I don't plan to make the mistakes we made when we went after Armstrong and his monster. We have better intelligence this time, and we know the numbers we face. This time we go all the way in and kill everything in sight, except for the woman and her son—if they're still alive. Besides, the SEALs will be there, too. When you have that kind of back-up, you don't worry so much. Which brings up the question: why us and not the guys who do this for a living? Why aren't they the ones to take El Toro down?"

"He'll be expecting them," the cousin answered. "What he won't expect is that anyone else would be coming for him. We can't give him a clue that anyone is on to him. I am sad to admit that our military trained him, which makes him even more dangerous, but we have to find a way to take him out so the SEALs can secure that weapon and remove it. When that is done we will round up the other terrorists and ship them off to Gitmo for good."

"Do you know where his hole in the ground is yet?" Duke asked.

"We are fairly sure of the region," the cousin said, "but not yet certain about its exact location. The SEALs are already in-country. Between them, the drones, and other information, we are narrowing down the location. By the time you arrive we hope to have it pinpointed."

Damien asked, "How do the SEALs feel about us going in ahead of them? I would think they would be upset."

"There is no problem there, Damien," the cousin assured him. "They are the most professional people in the world. They appreciate the help. They have been fully briefed on why the mission is being staged this way."

He turned toward Rick. "If there are no more questions, I'll be driving you to the airport."

To the others, he said, "The rest of you are welcome to tag along, or, you can say so long now and we'll be on our way."

The men stood to form a circle. The triplets embraced their brother, and The Man and his cousin joined them.

"If you don't mind, I'd like to say something," the cousin said.

The Man Who Loved the Gulf nodded. "As long as you think it will help me accept the fact that my son is going to be in harm's way—again."

"The last time was not my fault," said the cousin.

"Touché," said The Man Who Loved the Gulf. "True. That wasn't your fault, and you did get us what we needed, so…say on."

The cousin bowed his head. "God, there are big things going on here, so I make a small prayer for Rick and all who will be with him. Protect him and them, Lord. Let Rick return to his father and brothers safely. Keep him from harm. Amen."

They all shook hands.

The cousin and Rick had started for the door when his father stopped him, embraced him, and whispered something to him that the others could not hear.

They left the ship, and rode the speedboat to the dock. Once there they took the tram to the front gate, where they found the limo waiting.

They'd ridden in silence for a mile when the cousin said, "I know he's worried about you, but what did he say to you? That is, if you don't mind telling me—"

"I don't mind telling you. After all, you're family." Rick smiled at the cousin. "He said, 'Vaya con Dios.'"

They took the rest of the journey in silence.

Everything was in God's hands.

CHAPTER 16

The Movement had done what the organization did best: spend a lot of time analyzing the problem presented by Mexico and coming up with a solution. While the fence and no-man's land served a straightforward purpose of keeping people out, it did not solve the greater problem of the desires of people. Many Mexicans were desperate to find a better life for themselves and their families, and far too many Americans who bought drugs were too great a temptation to the cartels.

President Stonebreaker sat alone in his office and read through The Movement's plan once again. The brilliance of the Mexican Resolution was its simple application of truth. People desire the best for themselves. It did not matter where they lived or what language they spoke. They wanted opportunity and the freedom to pursue it.

Michael believed that the exceptions in the world were those nations run by tyrants, despots, and power hungry maniacs where people lived in fear of their rulers. Given the opportunity to understand what real freedom was like, there was no doubt that the people of North Korea, Iran, China, Cuba, and elsewhere would fight to have lives that allowed them to speak as they chose, work where they wanted to work, and come and go as they pleased. Absolute power indeed corrupts absolutely, unless constraints prohibit it. He was wise enough to realize that even those who led The Movement would be gone one day, and those who replaced them might not possess the same idealism.

Michael sat back in his chair, allowing his thoughts to wander. Was it possible that their East Asian neighbors were in cahoots with El Toro and the cartels? The Movement had to be working on these details, and Michael trusted in them. Speculation without proof would be meaningless.

He sighed and pushed himself back in his chair, wheeling it around to stare at the paintings on the walls. In his soul, he understood that he was a guest in this room so rich in history. He also understood that all those who had sat in this chamber before him had only been guests here as well. It was a privilege to serve the American people, one that should be undertaken with humility; one that should not be taken for granted. Michael wondered for a moment what life was like on the island, and who had survived. That was not his concern, of course, but he still felt awe for the remarkable way The Movement had dealt with the problem.

However, his natural curiosity had been piqued. He opened a desk drawer and drew out a piece of paper. There was a number on it. He had not used it for months. He dialed the number. A familiar voice answered. "Yes, Mr. President?"

"Madame Director," Michael said, "it's good to hear your voice. I was sitting here wondering how things were going on the island. That's why I called you."

"It is good to speak with you, too, Mr. President. The Movement keeps an eye on things there. There's nothing new to report."

Michael laughed softly. "In other words, it's on a need-to-know basis, and I am not in the need to know."

The director chuckled.

"Yes, Mr. President, but, if we need your help we will contact you immediately. Is there anything else I can help you with?"

"No, I was just curious."

"Thank you for your call. I'm here if you need me."

The director hung up. She was one of very few people who could give the president of the United States the brush off and get away with it. He was the president because of her belief in him.

Now that he'd held the office for going on two years, questions of whether he would run for election had begun to surface. Michael refused all requests to align himself with any particular political party. Republicans, Democrats, The Tea Party, and every other political group hoped he would choose them, but he said, almost daily, "If I decide to run for a second term it will be six months before the election and I will run as an Independent."

This infuriated everyone, but he was adamant.

"If I stand for re-election and win, you all will have to put up with me for another four years," he'd tease, which often led to smiles from his cabinet. It was their solemn hope that he would run and lead for another term.

Michael thought about his family. His brother Henry had remained in Clear Haven and not returned to Washington. Henry was keeping an eye on their mother whose generally good health had been shaken by a recent bout of pneumonia. She was at home and under her doctor's care, but Michael's mind was more at ease because Henry was only minutes away from her.

Michael and Joan's daughters, Angela and Louise were attending their schools, well-protected by Secret Service details and immersed in studies and college life. He was glad they were away from Washington.

Joan was off on another appearance as first lady, this time to California. He missed her terribly. When this job was over he wanted to leave this town behind and go someplace where people were real, egos were under greater control, and family was the center of attention.

He did not like the often necessary pomp and circumstance that his role required, but was glad he had chosen to serve his country, both in the Army and now in this role. Still, he wished in quiet moments that he could go and play cards with the Old Man and his father in that quiet room behind his childhood home. Perhaps he, too, was following in his father's footsteps—becoming an Old Man.

However, before that could happen, El Toro had to be dealt with. Michael knew that his country and the world would not be safe with such a man in it.

He hoped whatever solution the mysterious Mr. Smith would bring from The Movement, that the effort would succeed. If not, he could not dare to think about what might happen. A terrorist attack was awful enough, but a nuclear weapon was beyond imagining.

Thankfully, The Movement was busy in its hidden fortress detailing how to take the weapon out. This knowledge and power would prove a vital asset in the tide of this internal war. He would not want to face such a monumental undertaking alone.

Michael also thought about the woman and her son who had been kidnapped by Ernesto. He prayed silently that they would be safe.

On impulse, the president hit a button on his desk.

"Yes, Mr. President?" came the response.

"I want you to call Army Captain Everett Williams directly at Fort Bliss in El Paso, Texas for me. When you have him on the phone, please let me know. I want to speak with him personally."

"Yes, sir," replied his secretary. "I'll get him on the phone right away."

"And, if you could, I'd like another coffee," Michael added. "I have a feeling that tonight is going to be another long one."

"Of course, sir."

His coffee arrived shortly before he received the call on his phone. He set his mug on his desk, allowing the steaming liquid to cool. "Captain Williams," Michael said.

"Mr. President," Everett Williams stammered, "I never expected a call from you, sir. I don't know what to say—"

"Captain Williams, you won't ever know what your service to this nation means to me," Michael said.

"Thank you, sir!" Williams replied. "I am honored to speak to you."

"Captain, I am the one who is honored by this call. We're both career military, or, rather, I was serving just as you are now when I assumed this office. I know how concerned you are about your wife and son. I'm calling to tell you that steps are being taken to return them safely to you. I won't mince words with you. You deserve the truth. The man who has taken them is someone who should not be walking above ground. Do you understand me, Captain?"

"Yes, sir," said Williams. "I just want to march across the border and bring them home. I'm out of my mind with worry. I'm sorry, sir. Mr. President, this is so hard to deal with. I'm military, sir. I want to charge over there and find the S.O.B. and blow him away. Forgive me, sir. I don't mean to use such language with you, but I don't know what to do!"

"Captain Williams, as commander-in-chief it is my duty to care for my men and women in uniform wherever they are serving," Michael said. "I cannot predict the outcome of what is going on, but I will tell you this: there are people working to get your wife and son back at this very moment. They are deadly people, Captain. In fact, the man who took your wife and son has never encountered such people. I hope my saying so gives you some encouragement."

"It does, sir. Thank you," Williams said.

Michael thought of Williams' seven-year-old daughter. The little girl was being taken care of by the captain's mother, who had come from Omaha to stay with them until the crisis was over.

"How is your Susan doing?"

The captain nearly sobbed aloud. He quickly got control of himself.

"She's doing okay, sir. Just okay." He stifled a sigh. "In fact, she's doing better than I am."

"Let me break ranks for a moment, soldier," said Michael. "May I call you Everett?"

"Yes, sir. That's fine."

"Everett, listen to me," Michael said, his tone serious. "I believe in God, and I believe He will see you through all of this. If it were my family I would be in the same frame of mind that you are, but try to be strong."

"Thank you, sir." Williams nearly sobbed again into the phone. "Your call means a lot to me."

"You're welcome. I'm praying for you and your family!"

"I am, too, sir."

"We'll speak again, soon." A red light began blinking on his desk phone. "I have to go now. God bless you. Goodbye."

"Goodbye, sir," Williams said.

Michael hung up the phone. He bowed his head and prayed for Captain Williams and his family; especially for his wife and son.

The buzzer on his desk sounded.

"Yes?" Michael responded.

"Your next appointment is here, Mr. President."

"Thank you," Michael said. "Would you send him in please?

"Yes, sir."

Michael focused his eyes on the door and shifted his sentimental mindset toward a more logical one. He would need it for conversation ahead.

CHAPTER 17

A moment later the door opened and the mysterious Mr. Smith entered the room. It had only been two days prior since Michael had last seen the man and he was eager to converse with him again.

The door closed behind Smith and Michael got up from his desk. He walked around it and shook the man's extended hand warmly.

"It is good to see you again. Let's sit over there where it will be more comfortable."

Mr. Smith felt the power in the president's grip and smiled.

"Good to see you again Mr. President. I won't keep you long. I know you have a busy schedule."

The two sat opposite each other in comfortable chairs.

"How did it go with your friends?" Michael said, referring to The Man Who Loved the Gulf and his private force.

"They're already in Mexico," The Man replied.

The president's eyebrows went up. "They don't waste time, do they?"

"They understand that lives are at stake," Smith said. "If they can get there in time to save the woman and her son, they'll do so. As to the other problem," he continued, "they want to—to be delicate—neutralize the situation and then call the SEALs in to remove said problem. They want no parts of handling it if they don't need to touch it."

"That's a given," Michael said, sitting back. "I would not want to touch it either. That's good news." He paused, "And with our mutual friends?" he asked, alluding to The Movement.

"They send their regards, sir," Smith said. "You can contact them through the regular channel whenever you need to speak with them."

"My 'regular channel,' as you put it, is away on extended leave."

"How is Henry these days?" asked Smith.

"You know about my brother?" Michael said.

"Yes, Mr. President," Smith said with a small smile. "I hope your mother is doing well. That is a great concern for anyone who cares about his family. My prayers are with you each day."

Michael was surprised by the man's knowledge of his family, but decided to question him on the latter half of his statement.

"Then, you are a man of faith, sir?"

The man the president knew only as Mr. Smith smiled.

"Mr. President, this world is a scary place, and for decades there was no more frightening place than this city. I've been in this work for a long time. I could not get through a day if I didn't believe. I can't share my faith often, if at all. I even attend church secretly."

"How did you come to be in this—uh—line of work?" Michael asked.

"I was recruited years ago by one of the people you know as a director. Her mother was a founder," Smith said. A hint of fond memory washed over his features. He let a pause hang between them, glancing out the window before continuing.

"Human evil never goes away, Mr. President," he said. "I am still hanging around the type of people banished to the island. Not all of them are gone. Some of the lesser players still cling to their delusions of grandeur." His face took on a more stern look. "I find their arrogance and idiocy insufferable at times. They are tedious, but I am there as a watchman to monitor what they are doing."

Mr. Smith waved a hand dismissively in the air.

"There is no trust among such as these," he said. "My task is to convince them that I am as evil and twisted as they are. There are times that my words taste bitter in my mouth."

"You have my deepest sympathy, sir," Michael said. "If I had to bury my faith beneath lies I would choke on it."

Smith sighed and returned his gaze to Michael's face.

"The people I watch also watch me. I must be very careful when I move about. I am only able to come into this building because they actually believe that I am spying for them."

Michael nodded. "The debt this country owes you is beyond measure," he said. "I hope that someday you'll be able to walk anywhere without the fear of evil. Sadly, we both know that will never be possible."

It was Mr. Smith's turn to nod in agreement.

"You've read the Book as I have," Michael said. "And you know how the story turns out in the end."

"Yes, Mr. President, I do," Mr. smith said. "I take incredible comfort in that ending."

"Why is that, sir?" Michael asked.

"The good guys win," Mr. Smith said.

Michael smiled. "Do you take coffee or tea?" he asked.

"Tea would be great," Mr. Smith said.

Michael pushed a button on his desk.

"Yes, Mr. President?" came the response.

"Please send in tea service for two," Michael said.

"Yes, sir."

"Thank you," Michael said.

"Sir, your next appointment is here."

"Please entertain them for a bit," Michael said. "My guest and I have more to discuss."

CHAPTER 18

Ernesto Ruíz—El Toro—delighted in acts of torment and inflicting pain. The twenty hand-picked men who worked his protective detail in his underground fortress knew that full well. Trained by the American military, only they were allowed near him at any given time. He felt as safe as he could with them; after all, his only loyalty was to himself, and he had gained his position at the top because these men had slaughtered others on his behalf. His guardian group knew him well, and they were wise enough not to provoke him to anger.

The bulk of his army, some three hundred men, were stationed three miles away in a small town hidden away from prying eyes. The town consisted of barracks buildings, each housing one hundred men. They also held stores of food, clothing and other necessities.

El Toro did not drink, but he recognized this weakness in others so he'd allowed saloons to be built in the town. Although he hated and despised women and their devious and corrupting influence, he also ordered brothels built. It was not unusual for women who came there to be found later mutilated and dead somewhere in the Juarez area. El Toro demanded that no bodies be disposed of near his hidden fortress.

The Williams woman was beautiful and terrified. El Toro took delight in this. Her son would ultimately watch as he had her slaughtered in his Death Machine in the bowels of the compound beneath the mountain. Then, he would have his way with the boy until he grew tired of him. He would also die in the machine.

El Toro was in no hurry. The process of inflicting psychological terror was, in his opinion, an art. He could have satisfied his murderous rage swiftly when they had returned to his fortress, but where was the fun in that? Building terror in a victim was, to him a deliberate process requiring ample time.

Reducing a woman to total fear and terror especially brought him unequaled delight. Each time he did this he saw the face of the grandmother who had brutalized him, and he wanted unremitting revenge. He always got what he wanted.

Adrienne Williams had been wearing pajamas and a robe when she and her son had been taken. She had taken off her slippers and put on sneakers when El Toro's men had forced them to leave their suburban El Paso home. The boy, Chuck, was also in his pajamas and sneakers. El Toro had insisted they remain in their night clothes.

The two of them were kept in a locked room in the complex. It had a bed, a chair, a bathroom, and nothing else. The room was monitored by cameras from every angle, and their captor would sit for hours watching the pair in his communications center.

El Toro's men knew he was insane, but they owed their comfortable existence to him, and all of them desired the woman. That would be part of the fate that she would experience. Each of them would have time to do with her as they wanted. The boy would be forced to watch her degradation.

His men were eagerly looking forward to the day when he would give them leave to be with her. They smiled wickedly and eyed the direction of the cell like jackals staring down a meal. El Toro had chosen well. She was very beautiful, indeed.

CHAPTER 19

Michael Stonebreaker never took anything for granted. The Mexican Resolution was more than a game changer. It would alter life in the Americas at profound levels. No one could have possibly thought up such an incredible plan without careful consideration of the costs, operational design, possible glitches, and countless issues that could arise.

Michael had read and re-read the plan. He had been chosen as president by The Movement precisely because he thought meticulously through every decision he had to make. This decision would be no different.

Although conditions had improved in Mexico with a better GDP growth rate in recent years and the poverty level dropping to about fifty-one percent, people were still coming over the border seeking more money and greater opportunity. Drug trafficking was still outrageous. The Movement intended to solve the problems so that, in time, the people of both nations would be productive, happy, and eager to stay at home.

The revitalization plan was ingenious. Implementing it would require a profound commitment on the part of both nations. To foster that commitment, the plan would be announced to both countries at a joint news conference. The president of the United

States and the president of Mexico would deliver the news standing side-by-side.

The problem of El Toro would first have to be resolved, however. *A maniac with a nuclear weapon is enough to give everybody heartburn*, Michael thought.

That was the one detail that he couldn't grasp—from who and where did El Toro get the device? Had it come from somewhere in Asia? He was sure The Movement was already looking into the source. It was his job to see the current plan through and theirs to deal with the rest. He trusted in The Movement to find the truth.

Michael had also received a note from the mysterious Mr. Smith indicating that things were moving rapidly into place. The operation to "remove the thorn" was underway.

The reference to the old fable by Aesop was apparent. Michael smiled. This "thorn" would cease to exist altogether. The SEALs would see to it that the hideout was obliterated, with the blessing of President Calderón. Ernesto and his men would no longer threaten anyone once the Mexican "problem" was dealt with.

Obviously, things could always go wrong. As a military man, Michael was well aware of how messed up things could become in short order. The good news was that if you needed back-up, there was no one better to protect your back than the Navy SEALs.

Michael read through the final pages of the plan and then locked it away in his desk. He needed a break and a pick-me-up. He grabbed his phone and dialed a familiar number.

"Hey," Michael said in a lighter tone, "is this the first lady of the United States?"

"Why, sir, I do declare! Is this the famous man himself?" his wife asked.

"I don't know about famous," Michael said, "but I'm awfully flattered."

Joan laughed. "How's work?"

"Oh, you know," Michael said, spinning his hair to the side, "doing that midday president grind. It can be a hassle."

Michael wasn't usually one to brag, but he didn't mind being a little more focused now and again with his wife. The sweet sound of her chuckling on the other end of the line made him smile. He dearly missed her voice.

"Don't stress yourself out too much," Joan said. "I'm quite busy myself these days."

"I was thinking dinner and a movie were in order before you rush off on your next trip," Michael said. "Whattaya say, little lady?"

"Shall we make it 7:00 p.m.?" Joan asked.

"Perfect," Michael said. "I'll bring the flowers."

"Where will you ever find flowers this late in the day?" she said.

He loved that playful tone of hers.

"I have my ways. See you soon."

"Bye," Michael said and hung up the phone. He sighed happily and checked the clock on his desk. There was just enough time for a visit to the gym before he went to their private quarters.

He had missed his morning workout, but even with a madman holding his finger on the trigger of a nuclear weapon, he could not let the day end without doing his best to stay disciplined.

CHAPTER 20

Adriana Santos was used to the organized mayhem of moving a TV and movie crew to remote locations, but Rick Rodriguez felt like everything was out of control. He was secretly glad he was not in charge.

Rick and Adriana sat together on the plane flying out of Rio and spoke quietly in Spanish. As far as the crew knew, the only person on the plane who did not speak the lanquage was Ray Karwel, an American director of action films who had flown to Rio to advise Adriana using an interpreter. Karwel was more than just an American filmmaker. He had been the man in charge of directing the "disaster" movie that The Movement created and broadcast to America during the aborted terrorist attack in Disney World two years ago. On paper, he was there to advise Santos on directing the action sequences in the new Spanish language TV series. In reality he was the point man on site for The Movement. Karwel also spoke five languages, including Spanish, impeccably.

The flight from Rio de Janeiro, Brazil to Ciudad Juarez, Mexico is a long one—over 5,600 miles—but sitting next to Rick Rodriguez in first class made it far too short as far as Adriana was concerned.

She had great outward control, and she showed a cool reserve to the incredibly handsome man sitting next to her. They discussed many things as the hours passed. Anyone overhearing their conversation would have thought they were business associates.

They talked on and off through the entire flight. Rick needed the practice, and so he had asked Adriana to speak only in Spanish on the journey. Her easy conversation helped him slip comfortably into his role as a native speaker.

Though long, the flight from Rio to Abraham Gonzalez International Airport in Ciudad Juarez was uneventful. Thanks to discreet arrangements made through the office of President Calderón, when the plane landed it taxied to a hanger normally reserved for loading and unloading cargo planes. Situated on the outskirts of the airport, the hangar provided discreet cover for the fleet of trucks and vans waiting to take the passengers and their gear into the city.

Ostensibly, due to the large number of people in the cast and crew, rooms had been booked at both La Quinta Inn & Suites and Wyndham's Microtel Inn. Ray Karwell and his interpreter were booked at the Hotel Conquistador near the US Consulate. In truth, the hotels served as mission satellites, with the Conquistador as the command post. Vans whisked the crewmembers to their destinations, while the gear was placed in trucks and taken to a warehouse at the edge of the city.

The shoot would begin the following morning. The film crew was expected to spend two weeks shooting interior and exterior scenes for the new action series. Spanish-language television was growing by leaps and bounds throughout the western hemisphere, and an audience of over four-hundred million in Mexico, Central and South America was a lucrative market for as many movies and TV shows as could be made.

After checking in at La Quinta, Adriana and Rick took the elevator to their suites, and exhausted from the flight, they each went to their rooms to catch up on some sleep. They agreed to meet at a nearby restaurant for dinner at six.

Adriana was asleep moments after her head hit the pillow.

Rick was not as lucky. He kicked off his shoes and sprawled on the bed, but sleep would not come immediately.

His thoughts turned to Adriana Santos. He was used to the attention his looks earned him, but Adriana was quite different from any woman he had ever met.She did not seem attracted to him at all, and oddly enough he found it refreshing. Rick respected her for her cool demeanor and her obvious intelligence. He could not remember the last time he had such a long conversation about a multitude of subjects with anyone else outside his family and inner circle. He was fascinated by her. Her mind was sharp.

He lay in bed for a long time, thinking about many things. His mind wandered to conversations with The Man Who Loved the Gulf that had opened his mind to new desires to know far more about everything worth learning. What had happened in the torture chamber at the farm had changed him forever. When he had been brought safely from that horror and certain death, he had discovered a new appreciation for life. He saw each day as a gift.

When José's son had died in the accident, he had comforted his friend in his grief as if he were his brother. The pain José felt was his pain. He wondered at the change in himself, and he found that he often stopped to think about God, life, and the true meaning of things. He wanted to speak to his adopted father's mysterious cousin, but contact with him was not easily arranged. Rick needed to ask him about his faith, but he did not quite know how to approach the subject with The Man Who Loved the Gulf.

Rick knew it would have to wait until the present problem was solved. As a Marine, he understood that good intelligence could mean victory, and poor intelligence usually ended in failure and death. It would be dangerous to underestimate their adversary. El Toro was, from his description, one sick and twisted man. The fact that he had been trained by Americans did not help the situation.

To get to El Toro they needed to know exactly where he was, how his fortress was constructed, and the best way to approach it without sounding alarms. It was going to be difficult to take out him and his men.

He took comfort knowing that SEAL Team Six is the best in the world when stealth was the order of the day. They would be so careful that Ernesto and his people would have no idea that they were even nearby. Nothing could tip their hand, especially since El Toro was expecting some attempt might be made to find him. He was no fool. The maniac could not suspect that they were coming for him.

The nuclear weapon was another issue. They did not have intelligence that indicated that El Toro knew how to use the device, but they could not take the chance that he did have the knowledge to set it off. Rick shuddered at the thought. That would be a nightmare.

Saving the woman and her son was also important, but Rick wasn't sure if they could get there in time to find them alive and unharmed. It was maddening, but the path had to be clear before they went in to shut El Toro down for good.

A second, but no less important issue, was keeping news of Ernesto's removal from the other cartels for as long as possible. President Stonebreaker's plan to remove all the cartels from Mexico could not be jeopardized.

There was a major paradigm shift coming to North America, one that would reshape how things worked from now on. Unlike the former American regime that had telegraphed its intentions again and again to America's enemies, Stonebreaker believed in action followed by explanation, and not the other way around. The element of surprise was still viable.

Rick finally rolled over and fell asleep. He dreamed of Adriana Santos, but the the dream changed into a nightmare about being in an underground dungeon. The Butler from Hell chased him down a dimly lit passageway.

He woke up and was disoriented for a moment before he remembered where he was.

He checked his watch. There was just enough time to freshen up and change his clothes before heading to the restaurant. A quick shower washed away the memories brought on by the nightmare.

He rarely thought about what had happened to him, but he missed the men who had died fighting beside him, especially Big John.

Rick was grateful to be alive. His thoughts about Adriana were even better. He looked forward to having dinner with her. Life was good.

CHAPTER 21

The Man Who Loved the Gulf recognized the incoming number and answered his cell phone with the customary code words.

His cousin gave the appropriate response and asked, "Would it be acceptable for me to visit you this evening for dinner...unless you have other plans?"

"I had no idea you were in town," said The Man. Of course you can come for dinner. Make it 6:00 and we'll have time to talk. Can you stay the night?"

"Yes, I can stay over," his cousin said. "I'm not in town yet, but I am in the air and on my way. I want to speak at length about certain things, and that would require that dinner be served aboard that beautiful ship of yours, for security reasons. Would that be too much of an inconvenience?

The Man Who Loved the Gulf said, "No, that's fine. I'm in the ship's lounge at the moment. When you get to the gate ask the guard to have the tram take you to the dock. The speedboat will be waiting. I'll see you tonight."

When his cousin arrived, The Man welcomed him aboard and

led him to the lounge. A sideboard was set for coffee and tea. When they'd filled their cups, they sat down together.

"I know how wise you are," The Man's cousin said, "and I admire you for building your empire in the western hemisphere while others look to expand in Asia, for obvious reasons. The Asian nations are starting to come into their own, and their future looks bright, even though some of them are having economic difficulty at the moment. However, I believe you are prescient because of your desire to stay in the Americas, although I'm not sure how you've been able to deal with some of the governments and the level of corruption you must wade through in South America."

"Your description of my "empire," as you've called it, is a bit overblown," The Man Who Loved the Gulf said. "True, I've done very well, but the countries I choose to do business in need me far more than I need them."

"Your net worth is in the billions," his cousin stated. "Given the volatility of some of those governments, aren't you afraid that they will nationalize your companies and drive you out?"

"When I said that they need me more than I need them," The Man said, "please remember my past. I can be difficult when people get on my wrong side. I have found that when people understand who you are and what you can do, they are usually reasonable."

Although The Man Who Loved the Gulf said this quietly, his cousin knew that he was referring to his beginnings in the Mafia, and that The Man's personal army was not something any sane person would care to face.

"I do not forget how capable you are," the cousin said. "That is one of the reasons I am here. You believe in well-run businesses and profit, and our relationship with Mexico is going to change in profound ways in the coming years. There are going to be immense opportunities for growth and prosperity doing business in Mexico. You know the market. In fact, you understand the markets all the way to the bottom of the South American continent far better than most Americans. We have had an adversarial relationship with Mexico because of the border. Many Americans have been angry with our southern neighbor because of the illegal problem, with the exception of the farms and businesses who've been using their cheap labor for generations and looking the other way. You are extraordinary, and I am not saying this to flatter you. You saw opportunity where others saw nothing. You have deliberately chosen to seek success where others chose to ignore it. The president and his people need your insight, and my purpose in coming here is to discuss how providing that personally can be accomplished without compromising your anonymity."

"I don't see how it can be done," The Man said. "I value my privacy and freedom far more than you know. I can't go to the White House, and I cannot expect him to come to me. My identity is known to the people you work for because they have resources that I do not have, but I will not go where I will be seen and placed in some government database to be tracked, categorized and monitored. True, I did tell you that I would like to meet President Stonebreaker, but it would have to be in a protected and neutral setting. I insist on it."

"There is a way…" his cousin said, trailing off.

"It has to be foolproof," The Man said, shifting in his chair with a grim look on his face. "I don't see how you can pull it off."

"You become me," the cousin began. "We trade places. The meeting will be held at a place where the Secret Service can protect the president, and your identity can also be kept secret. We look like our fathers, and our resemblance to each other is striking. A little Hollywood magic and you become me. The president is to attend a meeting at Williamsburg, Virginia on the campus of William and Mary a month from now. I hope that will provide you with enough time to arrange your schedule. The meeting involves announcing a new policy on student loans in America. Your meeting with him will be at a nearby location. There will be two people with him in your meeting—his brother Henry, who acts as his chief confidant on many occasions, and Helen Abramson, the head of the CIA. You will appear as me. I've told the president that I have a great deal of knowledge about the region. His brother will escort you to the meeting. No one else will see you. In the meeting you may use your discretion as to what you will or will not share with them. If you are satisfied with the results, you may want to meet with them again. If not, so be it."

His cousin paused, letting his proposal sink in. Then he gently added, "I am asking you to do this not only for the country, but also in your best interests. Yes, you're worth billions, but I believe that what is going to happen in Mexico is going to result in your profits increasing exponentially. Will you attend the meeting?"

"You seem to know a great deal about my businesses and net worth, Cousin," The Man Who Loved the Gulf said. "If you know it, who else knows it? That makes me nervous. You've said the people you work for know all about me, yet you refuse to allow me to meet with them. I don't like that at all. My sons know my business inside and out. They are being prepared to take over when I am gone. I don't like anyone else knowing anything about me. I will not agree to the meeting unless you can set my mind at ease. Explain why I should not be concerned."

There was a hint of anger in The Man's tone when he responded, and his cousin noted it. He let his concern show on his face when he replied.

"You have nothing to worry about for many reasons. First, the people I work for have been in the espionage business for as long as we have been alive. They are the most secretive group on the face of this planet. They have studied and analyzed everyone at one time or another. They track every student who enters a service academy, every enemy of America, every foreign government, and everyone who does business in or with America. They know everything about you, and they hold you in such respect that they would never touch you, never interfere with you, never reveal your existence to anyone, and never harm you in any way. You don't have to accept their word on it, but you can accept mine. I have given my life to their work, and I will die serving them and our country." The Man's cousin sipped tea from his cup before going on.

"We are very different from each other. I don't care about money. I have no family, not because I dislike the idea, but because I have no time to give to relationships, and that would not be fair to a wife or children. Compared to you, I am a penniless pauper who lives like a monk. I do so of my own choosing. This country was being eaten alive by the Progressives. Their day is over, at least for now, but they're out there scheming, planning and dreaming about how to enslave the people of this great nation, but the people I serve will never allow them to come to power again if it can be avoided. I have given my life to a cause. I believe in it with all my heart. You are not in danger from my employer. You never will be. I give you my word on our parents' graves. Is that sufficient to reassure you?"

Silence filled the room. No one had dared to speak to The Man Who Loved the Gulf like this in a score of years. He was embarrassed at how he had nearly lost his temper, and he looked at his cousin with contrition.

"Please forgive me," The Man said. "It has been a long time since anyone has corrected me, and longer still since I apologized to anyone. I cannot say that I have ever felt such devotion to a cause as you do. I deeply respect your dedication. Compared to you, I am an epicurean who cares only for himself. You deserve far better from me than I have given you. I know in my heart that you care about me, but I am out of practice in dealing with family, and you are the only blood family member I have left. I want nothing more than to be able to see you more often. Your work is essential to America. Your temperament allows you to tolerate people that I could not be near. I would quickly destroy them.

"I will meet with the president. However, don't you think he will see immediately that I am not you? A disguise would have to be incredible to be effective. We do have a great resemblance to each other, but we're not twins. We sound something alike when we speak, but I don't have the vocabulary you have. I spent far more time on the streets than you did growing up. How do we pull this off?" The Man asked.

His cousin agreed that the president and Helen Abramson were clever enough to see through their ruse, but he had never met Vice President Dryden, and that could be beneficial.

"There are acceptable ways to influence tight lips," The Man's cousin said, "and even if the president and Abramson did see through the disguise, it will be of no consequence since the meeting will be held outside of the White House."

The Man Who Loved the Gulf was once again surprised by the strings that his cousin could pull.

"All right," said The Man. "I agree to do the meeting. But I will do it another way. We do it together. I want you in that room. I trust you. Other than my sons, my people and you, I trust no one. I want you next to me. Explain that I am your cousin. Tell them that I know how to do business better than most, if not all Americans, in our hemisphere, but I am to remain nameless. My identity is not to be compromised. From your description of the president, I believe that I can grow to trust him, and this Abramson woman is apparently someone who is highly thought of by both Stonebreaker and your employers. That is acceptable. Perhaps I'm getting a little reckless by agreeing to this, but I never want to have to pretend to be someone else, even someone as important as you. That's my one and only offer. If we get along well, we can meet again. If not, it will be the only meeting we will ever have, and I will return to my secluded life."

His cousin smiled. "I agree. The arrangements will be made. Thank you. There may come a day when both of us can walk openly in the light and not have to hide from others, but it may be years in the future, or it may never be possible. I deeply appreciate your help."

The Man Who Loved the Gulf sighed. "All right, let's have dinner and spend some time together. We have over a score of years to catch up on. I realize that you can't tell me everything, and I can't tell you everything, either, but it will be fun to try and see how well we do."

His cousin laughed. "In some respects, we may be the two most secretive men to ever sit down and share a meal together."

"Well, I won't keep the meal a secret," The Man said. "Fresh grilled salmon steak, wild, caught today, vegetables purchased two hours ago, homemade bread from the ship's galley, and a delightful Pinot Grigio. How does that sound to you?"

"Given the company, I'd say that this will probably be the best meal either of us has had in a long, long time," his cousin replied.

CHAPTER 22

El Toro had been certain that American operatives would have shown up asking questions, but his sources on the streets of Ciudad Juarez were silent. He was told about the people who were filming the TV pilot, and inquiries revealed that they had flown in from Rio, and they were legitimate.

He wasn't nervous, at least not outwardly. He could not let his men know that he was just a little concerned. The raid on El Paso had been outrageous, true, and he had meant it to be a warning to the American authorities who had been clamping down on the border. However, hindsight being what it is, one could not be too cautious. He knew SEAL Team's reputation, and yet he believed that he would never be found. El Toro surrounded himself with twenty hand-picked men, and another three hundred could be counted upon to come to his aid swiftly when summoned.

His stress level had been building during the day. He needed to vent his repressed nervousness, so he took the elevator from the top level of his compound down four floors to the lowest level where the woman and her son were being kept. He walked into the room, startling her.

She bit her lip to keep from screaming in fear.

His plan of terrorizing her was going well. Very soon he would turn her over to his men. He was savoring the moment in his mind. Her son was a very good looking boy, and there was defiance in his eyes. He had placed himself in front of his mother to protect her. He looked at El Toro in defiance. However, the cartel leader saw the terror in the boy's eyes, as well. He smiled evilly.

"You dare to defy me?" El Toro said. "I can swat you like a fly!"

"Leave my mother alone," the boy answered bravely, although El Toro saw that he was shaking like a dog that had just stepped out of a river.

"Who do you think is going to protect you here?" El Toro said. "I do as a please. I am master here."

"Don't hurt my son!" the woman pleaded.

"I hurt anyone I choose. There are many ways to hurt people. Some are worse than others. Both of you are very beautiful. It will be a pleasure to hurt you. Imagine what I might do to you. Think about it. Fear is good. Soon you will know how I take my satisfaction."

El Toro stepped forward, and the boy backed up against his mother. She put her arms around him and both drew back against the rock wall.

"If my husband was here you would be the one who was hurt," she said. "He would make you wish you had never hurt anyone."

El Toro reached out and stroked the boy's hair.

The boy recoiled as though he'd been bitten by a snake.

The monster drew back his hand. "Your husband will never find you here. If he did, I would kill him easily.

"As for your son, he will know my touch soon enough. You cannot imagine what I have planned. My satisfaction is all that matters. I will leave you alone to think. When the door opens the next time I promise you that our time together will be far more terrible than you imagine."

"You're a sick freak," the woman said. "And a coward! Hurting defenseless women and children makes you less than a man! You don't know what a real man is— "

Murderous rage filled Ernesto. He reached out and pulled the boy from her arms.

The woman was screaming when Ernesto slapped her across the face. The back of her head hit the rock wall. She slumped to the floor.

"You hurt my mother!" the boy yelled. "You killed her! Let me go!"

Ernesto threw the boy aside and bent down to lift the woman's head. She was breathing. She would recover. For now.

At the last second, Ernesto realized he should have been paying attention to the boy. The chair came down on his head with all the strength the boy had.

Chuck had knocked El Toro unconscious. Adrenaline had given him the power to lift the chair and swing it. He raised the chair a second time and smashed it on the monster's head again. Then, suddenly filled with the fear that someone else would come into the room, he set the chair down as quietly as he could.

He went to his mother and took her face gently in his hands.

"Mom...Mom..." he whispered. "We've got to get out of here. Please, wake up. We have to find our way out of here now, or he'll kill us!"

Adrienne Williams opened her eyes and stared into the face of her son.

"Chuck, honey, what did he do to you?"

"We have to leave here now," Chuck said. "If he wakes up he'll kill us. Please, Mom, come on! We have to get out of here!"

The boy's fear and desperation were palpable. His mother looked at Ernesto sprawled on the floor.

"What happened?" she asked. "Is he dead? Oh, please, let him be dead!"

"I don't know," the boy said. "I hit him with the chair. If he wakes up we won't be safe. If someone else comes, they'll lock us up until he can torture us and kill us. Please, we have to go!"

Adrienne got to her feet and stood unsteadily for a moment. The back of her head was on fire. She put her hand to her head. It felt sticky. She withdrew her hand and there was blood on it. Suddenly the floor seemed to rush upward and she felt like she was going to swoon. She steeled herself against blacking out.

Chuck was right. They had to get out of here. She looked down. Ernesto had a pistol in a holster. She got down on her knees and removed the gun. Ernesto moaned.

She was on the verge of panic, but she had to save her son. Then, she saw the key. It had slipped from the monster's pocket when he fell. She grabbed it and put her hand to her lips for Chuck to keep quiet, then motioned for him to follow her.

They quickly made their way to the door of the room and slipped outside. Adrienne locked the door behind them.

The tunnel ran to their left and right.

"Which way should we go?" Chuck whispered.

Oh Lord, Adrienne thought, *lead us out of here*. She led her son to the right.

She did not know that what happened in the room had been seen on camera. Even as the woman and her son fled down the corridor, three floors above them Ernesto's men were racing down the stairs.

Had she known they were coming, Adrienne might have killed her boy and then herself. It would be better to die swiftly than to suffer what the men planned to do to them.

Thankfully, she didn't know about the cameras. Adrienne and Chuck ran as fast as they could go.

CHAPTER 23

The president and the first lady were hosting a dinner in the State Dining Room at the White House. Their one hundred-and-twenty guests represented major corporations which had signed on to retrain federal employees for non-government jobs over a five year period.

Thanks to Jackie Kennedy, guests sat at round tables and enjoyed each other's company in the elegant dining space. Mrs. Kennedy had done away with the horseshoe configuration of long tables in favor of rounds to create a less formal atmosphere, which on this night suited Joan Stonebreaker just fine. Dinners for heads-of-state were normally black tie affairs, but normal suits and dresses had been permitted, setting a more relaxed and intimate mood for the gathering.

Joan Stonebreaker had welcomed their guests warmly.

"The president will be a few minutes late," she said. "He is dealing with issues that could not wait, and extends his sincere apologies."

Approximately twenty minutes after the festivities began the band announced the arrival of President Stonebreaker with the traditional ruffles and flourishes and a performance of "Hail to the Chief." The president entered the room to standing applause from the guests. His smile was warm and friendly.

He spent the next twenty minutes walking through the room, greeting people at each table, and giving fits to his Secret Service detail. He ended his tour of the room at the head table where he greeted each of the corporate heads of America's largest companies, before taking his seat between Joan and his brother, Henry.

Henry Stonebreaker was back in Washington from seeing to their mother in Clear Haven, PA.

"Mom is doing much better," he said as he and Michael spent a few moments catching up.

"It feels good knowing Mom is doing well, Henry," Michael said. "But I deeply appreciate having you by my side again."

Michael had come to think of his younger brother as another Mark Twain, with Will Rogers thrown in for good measure.

Dinner in the State Dining Room was going well. The meal was followed by dessert and candid conversation. Michael reached out to talk to as many corporate heads as possible about the re-training program, and they seemed receptive.

Henry was working the room, as well. The tall, well-built Marine was in his glory, putting people at ease with with his homespun humor. Amid the laughter he reassured everyone he spoke to that President Stonebreaker wanted to know all they were doing to absorb people out from the federal workforce into private industry.

Michael was engaged in conversation with the head of a leading textile manufacturer.

"It's a monumental task," he said, nodding. "It's taken decades for the federal bureaucracy to balloon to its enormous and unmanageable size; it's going to take at least a decade to dismantle it and redistribute the wealth back to the Americans who paid for it."

Michael did not share, but he knew that The Movement had been planning just such an operation for over a score of years. Now, with the help of corporate leaders like those here tonight, the plan would be implemented.

Henry came up to Michael as he finished his conversation with the textile magnate. He smiled and said, "Mr. President, the heads of Microsoft, Apple, Exxon-Mobile and Wal-Mart would like a few moments of your time. I assured them that they can simply pick up the phone to reach you whenever they need to discuss the program.

Everyone else in the room is also pleased to have such access. I'm assuring folks that they have your ear."

Michael grinned and said, "Spot on, First Brother! Like I said, it's great to have you back here."

"I'd rather be fixin' 'dozers," Henry replied. "But when my president calls, I answer."

"Speaking of 'dozers," Michael said, "I understand that GM, Ford, and Chrysler are considering a joint venture to build the things. Is that right?"

"Yes, Mr. President," Henry said. "They're going to be training a lot of people to build them, service them, and operate them. Now that the pipeline is online and we're beginning to revitalize the coal fields through coal-to-oil plants, tens of thousands of jobs will be created. Energy independence is going to be a reality. Natural gas, coal, oil, wind, and solar power will run our country for a long, long time without obligation to anyone else in the world."

"I think that's fantastic news," Michael said. "When this party breaks up I'd like to spend some time with you," he added. "I need to fill you in on what's about to happen."

"If it's about that thing on the border, I've already been briefed," Henry said.

"Whoops! I forgot you've been just a few miles from our friends for the last few weeks. How are things going there?"

"Things are going quite well as of my last visit," Henry said. "They're looking forward to your speech. They believe it will be well received, even though the Progressives can't take credit for the idea. There is an irony in there somewhere, but I'm sure you know it."

Michael laughed. "I'll see you when this is over. The other issue is about to be handled. I can't discuss that outside of the Situation Room. I won't keep you long, but I'd like to take a little walk and fill you in on what I know."

"Sounds like it's time for prayer, Mr. President," Henry said, his smile fading.

"I won't argue that," Michael said. "Some people are going to be very surprised by some uninvited guests. We all hope it turns out well."

The brothers separated and the after-dinner gathering continued for another hour. By 9:00 p.m. Michael and Henry were walking the

White House grounds, swapping the latest intel from The Movement and the mysterious man who had visited the White House.

"I have had word that we'll be meeting him and someone very special in Virginia in a few weeks," Michael said. "He is secretive, but the man he's bringing with him is even more so."

"How so?" Henry said.

"From what he told me the man is as close to a recluse as one can be," Michael said. "He also apparently knows a great deal about doing business in our hemisphere. My contact says that he probably knows more than any man alive about how we should go about establishing a two-continent global powerhouse, and that he can guide us in making the right choices—and avoiding mistakes."

"Do you believe him?" Henry asked.

"That remains to be seen, but there is one thing I know for certain: my contact doesn't lie, and if it hadn't been for him, you and I would not be sitting in this building at this moment."

Henry's eyebrows went up. "Who is this guy?"

"He's the insider in the Progressive world," said Michael. "The man risks his life every day as the point man for the people who put us here. The people who did not die in the happiest place on earth are alive today because of him and the information he supplied. No one can know about him except a handful of people, but what we owe him could never be calculated."

Henry said, "Holy cow!"

"Wrong expression," Michael replied. "Having spent some quality time with him, I think it would be better to say, 'Thank you, Lord!'"

"Okay, I get it," Henry said. "I'll look forward to meeting him and his friend. Are you up for a little handball?"

"Not tonight, brother, but how about 5:30 tomorrow morning?" Michael asked.

Henry groaned. "Why do you get up so early? This isn't boot camp. You need your sleep—and I do, too,"

"Are you saying no to the president?" Michael asked.

"I'll be there at 5:30, Mr. President—but I expect breakfast afterwards," Henry replied.

"Good. Get some sleep. Tomorrow is going to be interesting."

Henry smiled. "I'll bring the bagels."

Michael added, "And I'll bring the cream cheese."

CHAPTER 24

There are times when bad things work together and the outcome is good. This was such a time for Adrienne Williams and her son, Chuck. They ran headlong down the rocky corridor deep within the earth and came to three metal doors. The door on the left would take them to the compound's concealed entrance in the side of the mountain, and possible escape. The door on the right led to El Toro's ultimate torture device and the atomic weapon. Behind the middle door, a stairwell led to the upper floors. El Toro's men were coming down those stairs as fast as they could go.

Hesitating for only a moment, the boy chose the door on the left and cautiously opened it.

Adrienne looked at her son. "What about the other two?" she whispered.

In many ways Chuck Williams was just like his father. He had a mathematical mind and an instinctive affinity for numbers.

"Thirty-three percent odds, Mom!" he whispered back. "We don't have time to think! Let's go. If we're wrong we're worse than dead."

They went through the doorway and raced down the metal stairs.

The men coming down the other stairwell had reached the third level with one level to go.

Adrienne and Chuck followed El Toro's escape route down the stairs and into a hallway that led to a tunnel carved from the rock. A quarter mile in length, the tunnel opened onto a cave where his Hummer sat loaded with food, bottled water, climbing gear, weapons, and ammunition.

Adrienne opened the driver side door and quickly searched for the keys. They were nowhere to be found.

"Grab everything you can, Chuck. Take two of those canteens if they're full. Grab whatever food you can carry, and let's get out of here."

With those words she picked up an assault rifle, ammunition, a large knife in a sheath, a nine millimeter Glock, and more ammo.

She was ready to close the door when she saw blankets. She picked up two of them along with an emergency medical kit.

Chuck placed the food in a backpack and shouldered it. He carried the canteens in his hands. They turned and ran toward the light that was shining down the tunnel leading away from the Hummer.

Breathless, they emerged into daylight and a bleak, arid landscape. They ran along the middle of the dirt track away from the cave. The entrance was camouflaged by a tarp painted to look like the surrounding rock.

Hidden cameras monitored the area. Anyone seen there would have been met by El Toro's men, questioned, tortured, and done away with. But fate extended another gentle hand toward Adrienne and Chuck when they exited the cave. The man who was supposed to be watching the monitors in the control room was instead watching the men racing to El Toro's aid.

Two of El Toro's hand-picked men carried first-aid supplies. They ran to the room where their fearless leader lay unconscious. The others split into two groups. One group went through the door leading to the torture device, while the second raced downstairs toward the escape route.

Fear is a great motivator. Adrienne and her son ran for their lives.

Chuck had the natural build of a runner, and back home he ran with his father as often as he could. Tears streamed down his face as remembered his father proudly proclaiming that Chuck could run all day and not get tired to anyone who would listen. He swiped the tears away.

Adrienne went to the gym three times a week and also ran every day but Sunday. Neither she nor Chuck had ever had such cause to run as they did now.

A quarter mile from the cave entrance the dirt track veered off to the left. The pair ran into the curve and stopped short in surprise. An old shack loomed ahead. They expected someone to jump out and ambush them. Nothing moved.

They reached the shack and Adrienne saw a camera aimed out of a window. Reflexively, she smashed the stock of the assault rifle into the camera lens, destroying it.

Chuck cautiously pushed open the door, but Adrienne was making her way around the outside.

"We don't have much time, Chuck. I pray to God we can find a place to hide soon, but I don't think this is it. They're coming for us as quickly as they can, and this will probably be one of the first places they look."

She covered her face with her hands. "If that monster survives what you did to him—I don't even want to think about what he'll do to you."

She banished the thought with a shake of her head. "I see a path behind the shack," she said. "It goes up the hill. We need to find a high place. Let's go!"

Mother and son raced up the steeply climbing path. They had gone perhaps five hundred feet up the hill when they heard the Hummer's engine roaring below them.

"Down!" Adrienne whispered urgently.

With that they leaped behind some low scrub and lay there, trying to control their breathing.

From their hiding place they watched as The Hummer slid around the curve and the driver slammed on the brakes. Clouds of dust rose into the air. The driver stayed in the vehicle while four men exited the vehicle and spread out. They were armed with Glocks, and all of them were holding their weapons in the classic position. They were obviously well-trained. They did not speak. One went to the front of the shack where Adrienne and Chuck had stood moments before and looked inside.

He signaled that the shack was empty and the camera was useless.

The men spread out in a wider search pattern, obviously not afraid of being shot at. They knew weapons, food, and water had been taken from the vehicle, but what could a helpless woman and a boy do against such men? They figured she probably didn't even know how to fire a weapon, and the kid was too young to know anything.

Despite those advantages, it was hard to track them in the rocky terrain. The men moved slowly, expanding their perimeter.

After a few minutes the men re-grouped near the Hummer.

"Odds are they didn't try to make it farther up the hill," Adrienne and Chuck heard one of them saying. "They're on foot, likely trying to make it down to the main road. Let's go. It's only a matter of time before we catch up to them."

Fate was kind again.

The four men got into the Hummer and went tearing down the dirt track.

Adrienne and Chuck waited several minutes and then began racing up the hill again. They were panting like dogs when they crested the top, some nine hundred feet above the shack.

When they saw the terrain extending outward from where they stood they were nearly overcome with dismay.

"We might as well be standing on the moon," Chuck said.

Rocky hills and narrow valleys lay in every direction. Trying to determine what direction to go in was the least of their problems. The tumbled and split rock would make movement very difficult, and there were few places to hide that they could see from where they stood. The men in the Hummer would realize their mistake and come back to search higher on the hill all too soon.

Adrienne reached out and gently placed her hand on Chuck's shoulder. "If they get close to us we have a choice to make. I won't let them take me back—and I won't let them take you either—"

"I know, Mom, but we can't think about that now. Let's go down this hill and see if we can find a place to hide. If there is one cave here maybe we can find another one. We can't stand up here. They'll see us."

They started down the other side of the hill. Halfway down the slope they heard the engine of the Hummer. It was faint, but it was obviously returning to the area near the shack.

They began running down the hill as fast as they could go, trying their best not to fall and break their bones. When they got to the bottom there was a flattened area that led away to their right.

Chuck started to go in that direction when Adrienne grabbed him from behind and whispered, "No. They'll go that way first. People look for an easy way to escape. We have to think differently. We'll climb the next hill as fast as we can. We have to get high and stay above them. I would rather shoot down at them than be picked off from above like sitting ducks. Let's climb!"

Both of them were hungry and nearing exhaustion, but knowing what they would face if they were caught gave them the energy they needed to start climbing again. They got to the top of the next hill and looked back. They didn't see anyone.

"We have to go down and up the next hill," Adrienne said. "The more hills we put between us and them the better. I know you're as tired as I am, but we can't quit, Chuck. We have to go on. We have to find a defendable position. This isn't it."

"Mom," Chuck said, "I'm so tired I could sit down and not move for a week. I need a drink of water. Can we rest for a minute?"

"Take a drink," his mother said, offering the canteen. "We have to keep moving.

Chuck opened the canteen. The water was cool from being in the cave, but it tasted funny, like it had been in the bottle for a long time. He closed the canteen and they hurried down the hill.

The next hill was steeper than the previous two, and the protruding rocks made the climb more difficult. They reached a plateau that led to another upward slope. The hill appeared to crest again another five hundred feet above where they stood.

They looked at each other.

"There's no place to hide here," Adrienne said.

They stumbled on exhausted legs across the open area and started up the incline. When they reached the top could see down the steep descent to a narrow valley below. Along the crest where they stood there was a depression in the rock. It wasn't exactly a cave, but it was big enough to squeeze into and stay out of sight.

They crawled into the hollow and found a flat stone area where they could sit down. They were both panting from exertion, and it took a while to catch their breath.

They opened the backpack and checked their food supply, which consisted of military Meals Ready to Eat.

"Just MREs, but I'm so hungry they look like a Thanksgiving feast," Chuck said.

"Beggars—and fugitives—can't be choosers," Adrienne said.

Chuck offered a weak smile.

While they ate, Adrienne checked out the assault rifle and the Glock. She was glad she'd grabbed a fair amount of ammo, despite the effort required to carry it uphill.

Adrienne Williams may have looked like a supermodel, but looks can be deceptive. She was a child of ranchers who lived at the foot of the Bitterroot Mountains near the small town of Victor, Montana. She was fishing with her parents by the time she was three years old, and firing a .22 cal. Remington at the age of eight under her father's careful supervision. She could ride a horse with ease, rope a steer, brand cows, change horse shoes, hunt, install a fence, drive a tractor and a backhoe, and hold her own where a lot of men couldn't.

She wiped away tears with the back of her hand as she remembered meeting the love of her life while a student at the Colorado School of Mines. She married Everett Williams soon after graduation, and they had seen much of the world thanks to her husband's duty assignments in diverse places, courtesy of the US Army.

Adrienne may have turned heads because of her beauty, but she was deadly with a rifle. Her husband bragged about her talent, saying she was a better shot than he, even though he was no slouch. When Chuck was old enough the two of them took him to the range and taught him to shoot as well.

If a certain well-known former governor was a "Mama Grizzly," Adrienne Williams might be described as something equally dangerous. She was a lioness. Right now she and her cub were being threatened, and she was desperate to save both their lives—or die trying.

Thanks to her husband Adrienne knew how to handle some pretty impressive weapons. Everette was fond of saying the Williams family believed in gun control—they were certain that good, law-abiding people should have control of their guns at all times.

She was jerked from her memories by a noise in the sky. Chuck's eyes found hers, and she could see the terror in them.

"They've come for us!" he was near to panicking when she grabbed his arm.

"No!" she said. "If it is them, we've got to stay calm."

Chuck quieted, and Adrienne hugged her son tightly. They pressed as far as they could into the depression.

The sound of a chopper became louder and louder. Now, it was above them. There was nothing they could do. They were trapped.

CHAPTER 25

Dinner with Adriana Santos had been more than interesting. Rick and Adriana continued the hours-long conversation they had begun on their long flight to Juarez. When they had separated at the hotel to get some sleep they had been discussing doing business in South America. Now, the topic turned to making movies and TV shows, Adriana's area of expertise.

Rick was fascinated by the topic, and even more fascinated by the woman who was telling her story. He watched the way her dark eyes sparkled, and the way her cheeks dimpled when she smiled. He loved the sound of her voice and the musical flow of her words.They were speaking solely in Spanish again, having agreed to talk only about harmless things in public places, and to allow onlookers to believe they were natives.

When they had finished dinner, they decided to walk around the hotel together. Inside a gift shop Adriana pretended to be interested in the typical tourist fare that lined the shelves. There was a jewelry case at the front counter, and she was looking at the bracelets and rings.

"Perhaps your husband would like to see you in these earrings? They would look perfect on you," the clerk said.

Adriana realized that Rick was standing next to her. She felt her face flush with embarrassment for a moment as she fought for her usual self-control.

"I would love to see those on you," Rick said. "Try them on for me." He pointed at a pair of lovely gold earrings that were simple in design, but ample in their size, containing what looked like turquoise that was carved in the shape of a bird. "Let's see the matching necklace, too," Rick added.

The woman behind the counter, who appeared to be in her fifties, smiled at them and placed the glittering items on the counter.

Adriana said, "Oh, Ricardo…they are tan cara! I don't think—"

"Darling," Rick said, "nothing is too expensive for you. Go ahead. Put them on. I'll help you."

Adriana took the earrings and leaned toward a mirror to put them on.

Then, as if he'd done so a hundred times before, Rick gently fastened the necklace around her neck. As he did so the touch of his hands against her neck sent a chill up Adriana's spine. She fought for control as she said, "They are muy hermosa."

"Not as beautiful as you are, darling." Rick turned to the clerk. "I'll take them to remind us of this trip. Would you wrap them for me?"

"Certainly, señor," the clerk said, and smiled again.

Stunned Adriana was about to protest when Rick took her hand in his and squeezed it gently.

"We have to get back to our room," he said. "We have a long day tomorrow and an early call."

"Are you with the TV people?" the woman asked.

Adriana had managed to get control of her emotions, and she answered, "Yes, we have to be on location at 6:00 tomorrow morning. We start very early because it takes quite a while to set up all our equipment."

"Are you actors in the show?" the woman asked.

Adriana laughed. "No, of course not. I work for the company behind the scenes, and my husband came along on the trip. He is taking some time off from his work to spend time with me. We've only been married for two weeks. This is sort of a honeymoon for us."

Now, it was Rick's turn to blush. "Yes, I live a very dull life normally. All of this is new to me."

"What work do you do, señor?" the woman asked, making small talk while she wrapped the jewelry.

"He's a brain surgeon," Adriana said, smiling a crooked smile, and nearly breaking into laughter.

Rick almost choked, making a strangled noise. He covered his mouth, pretending to cough. "I...I spend my time in hospitals every day, señora, and my work is important, but sometimes the outcome is sad," he managed to say.

"Oh, have you had people die, señor?" the clerk asked, her eyes round.

"I do my best to avoid having that happen, señora. Not every case is successful, but I do my best. Now, we must be going. Thank you very much."

Rick paid for the jewelry, and they turned to leave the shop.

The woman stared after them. Brain surgeon? Well, she thought, he is handsome enough to play one on TV!

Adriana and Rick managed to get into the elevator and let the door close behind them before convulsing with laughter.

He finally managed to say, "You…you are outrageous! Brain surgeon? Are you kidding? Where did you come up with that idea?"

Adriana laughed even more.

When the doors opened on their floor they stepped into the hallway.

She said, "I'm in the entertainment business, remember? We were doing a little improvisational acting, that's all. When she assumed we were married, well, I thought I'd play along, but I never expected you to buy me such expensive gifts. Can you return them?"

"I wouldn't think of it, Mrs. Rodriguez," Rick said with another disarming smile. "No, the gifts are yours to keep. It was fun. I needed to laugh. You make me laugh. There has been such sadness in my life recently because of José's son…"

He had told her about the terrible accident and the boy's death on the plane trip to Juarez.

"But, I can't accept something so expensive from you. We hardly know each other. It wouldn't be right," Adriana said, her voice suddenly serious.

Rick took a deep breath, reached out and took both her hands in his. Impulsively, feeling like an awkward teenager who had just asked the prom queen to go on a date with him, he said, "Adriana, I would like to get to know you better. I like you very much. A lot of things have happened to me in the last two years…and they've changed my perspective on life. I'm not one to make speeches, but I would very much like to see you when this thing is over. I'm not being forward. We can go very slowly. It's obvious that you love your work, and you can talk about more interesting things than anyone I've ever met in my life. You made me smile today. You made my heart happy."

The heat of his hands on hers was maddening, and Adriana Santos had an epiphany in that moment. She had dated many extremely handsome men in her life. Some were actors and some were not. Her relationships had been superficial. At thirteen she had been certain that she would become a nun. She knew that she loved God, and she also knew that she must be chaste. Old-fashioned virtue was part of her personality.

Nature and good genes had made her gorgeous, but her mind and determination made her something else: selective. The man she chose to marry would be the man she would spend her life with forever. She was a rock when it came to personal morality.

She looked into Rick's eyes and she saw his soul looking back at her. There was pain there, and a vulnerability she had not expected. There was also great intelligence, a tremendous strength, true passion and a shyness that also caught her by surprise. She had thought that anyone who was so incredibly handsome had to be shallow. He was anything but that.

"Rick, I see that you're serious," Adriana said, and took a deep breath. "I must admit that I am married to my work. I love it. I also love Rio. Living there is wonderful. We would have a very long distance relationship if I said that I would date you. It would be difficult. You have your great interests as well. Being the adopted son of such a father must be overwhelming at times. You speak of what happened to you without saying what it is."

"I didn't mean to keep it from you," Rick started to say.

"No, it's okay," Adrianna said. "You can tell me when the time is right. This isn't the right time. I have a job to do and so do you. My job is to create make-believe for TV. Your job, at least as I understand it, is to help save the world. That might be something of an exaggeration, but I think it is generally true."

She hesitated and then said, "So, for now, we both need to keep our heads clear and do our jobs. Later, when the dust has settled, we can talk. I'll say goodnight now. I'll be getting up at 4:00 a.m., and with jet lag I'd better go get some sleep immediately."

Adriana gently disengaged her hands from his, turned, and started moving towards the door of her room.

Rick was standing there looking at her when she turned and walked back to him.

"There is one thing I need to give you, and I want you to take it with you when you go get the really bad guy you're after."

In the next moment she was in his arms; her kiss was sweet and long.

Then, reluctantly, she drew back and looked at him. "I've just given you my heart, Rick. I have never done that before with anyone. Hearts are breakable. I know because I work in the world of make-believe. Protect my heart. You can do that by coming back to me all in one piece."

He saw that she was trembling and he took a step toward her.

She held up a hand.

"No," she said. "I have to go. Tomorrow, we act like none of this ever happened. But I mean what I say. Always. You have my heart. Do I have yours?"

His voice was hoarse when he replied. "This is a first in my life, too. Yes, you have my heart. I will be back when this is over. Count on it."

"I will be counting the hours, Mr. Rodriguez. Goodnight."

She turned, opened the door to her room and closed it softly behind her.

Rick stood in the hallway for a long moment before opening the door to his room. Someone was sitting in a chair waiting for him. He reached for his gun and flipped on the light switch.

Ray Karwel, the American action movie director sat facing him from a chair in the suite's sitting area.

"How'd you get in here?" Rick demanded.

"It's simple when you know how," Karwel said. "It's not what you think, and I'm not who you think."

"Then, who are you?" Rick said, his hand still resting on his gun.

"Let's say that I am someone other than you believe me to be, just as there is far more to you than meets the eye," Karwel said softly.

"What the hell does that mean?" Rick asked. He had no patience for the man's riddles.

Without answering his question, Karwel said, "We know where he is. Now, we have to go and deal with him."

"Who are you talking about?" Rick asked.

"El Toro. Ernesto Ruíz. We found him. I won't say how, but the people I work for are the best in the world at finding people."

Rick leaned in from where he stood near the door. "What about the SEALs?" he asked. "Did they find him for you?"

"I'm not affiliated with them, and I don't discuss the people I represent. The important thing is that we know where he is—and there's something else."

"What?" Rick asked.

"The woman and her son have escaped from Ernesto," Karwel said, "however, the odds are against them. We need to move swiftly if we're to save them. They don't have much time, and we need to plan."

Karwel motioned toward a chair opposite the one in which he sat.

"Please sit down. I've ordered some strong coffee. We're both going to need it. That plane ride was a bear."

Rick took his hand off his gun and sat down.

Karwel spread a map on the table.

CHAPTER 26

President Stonebreaker was happy to hear that The Movement had located El Toro's mountain hideout. The mysterious visitor who had set the wheels in motion to capture and kill the madman explained that the people in Mexico would be moving swiftly. He had also learned that Adrienne Williams and her son had somehow escaped, but that they would be found very quickly by the cartel if they were not rescued as soon as possible.

Michael picked up the phone, then put it down again. He decided against calling Captain Williams. There was no sense getting the man's hopes up if things went badly.

The latest intel from the mysterious Mr. Smith described The Movement headquarters as abuzz with activity after pulling the latest feed from its satellites targeting Juarez. They suspected El Toro and his cartel were in the area, and new images showed Adrienne Williams and her son climbing the nearby hillside before disappearing into a crevice in the rock. They had indeed managed to escape and were running for their lives.

The SEAL team was on alert for the extraction. They were several miles from where the woman and her son were hidden. They were tasked with neutralizing El Toro's army in the village. No doubt, doing so would be bloody, but the real problem would be keeping

El Toro from finding out that they were moving against him until the last possible moment. The biggest unknown was the nuclear weapon. They had to be inside the mountain before Ernesto could move to detonate it.

Michael worried that rescuing Adrienne and Chuck Williams presented another problem. Saving them would surely tip off the enemy. Accoring to Mr. Smith, El Toro had a chopper in the air, and could be very close to finding the woman and her son.

The Movement's plan, code named the Mexican Resolution, lay spread out on The Resolute desk. In it, Michael read what some might describe as a hostile takeover of Mexico. It was anything but that. Before he stood before the cameras with Mexico's President Calderón to tell the world how relations between the US and Mexico were about to change for the better, American troops would enter Mexico clandestinely from all points on the compass. Drones and paratroopers would fill the air, landing on shorelines and crossing borders so swiftly the cartels would not register the massive attack until it was well underway.

The Movement had been planning the event for years. Ports of entry from the Gulf and Pacific were on out-of-the-way beaches and lonely spots where they would go unnoticed.

Initially, no one would believe that America would do such a thing. The previous administration had been too busy turning its head to allow illegal aliens to cross the border so they could buy votes. But The Stonebreaker administration was cut from different cloth.

Michael Stonebreaker wholeheartedly approved the decimation of the cartels and their drug operations by the US military. A day would soon arrive when law-abiding Mexican citizens could go to sleep at night without the fear of attack or reprisals from criminals. Members of the cartels would be rounded up, tried, convicted, and dealt with summarily. They would not spend years in prison and American taxpayer money waiting for their fates. Justice would be swift.

The Movement's three-step plan was elegantly straightfoward. Step One: Neutralize the cartels. Step Two: Normalize the American presence over a specified period of time. Step Three: Begin the reformation of the Mexican economy. The plan was simple, but by no means would executing it be easy. Implementing the last step would take the longest.

The intention was not to make Mexico a smaller version of the United States. Mexico would travel its own road to prosperity, just with a lot of help from its neighbor to the north.

Part of the goal was reaching a place where the border between the two nations would not be a barrier, but rather a line on a map denoting the connection between two great friends. On a larger scale, North America, with Canada, Mexico, and the US would become a world power to be reckoned with because the trading partners would also become the good friends that they should have been all along. They would establish a benchmark for the countries of Central and South America to follow. Ultimately, the Americas would lead the world in economic prosperity, strength, and security. Capitalism would flourish again. Just as the US workforce was being retrained, and government was being downsized and restructured, the people of Mexico were about to open their eyes to a new day—one that would bring education, good jobs, and the desire to share in the goodness of life, liberty, and, yes, the pursuit of happiness. It should not be necessary for mothers and fathers to hide in darkness to sneak into the US to find work. They ought to be able to stay at home and have opportunities to build far better lives.

Michael rubbed his forehead as he continued going over the plan.It would be difficult. The cartels had firepower. They would not give up easily, but they had no experience in dealing face-to-face with the best military force in the world. They would be eradicated from the earth. The drug culture in the US was also about to be dealt with in ways none had anticipated. Not only was a new way of life coming to Mexico—the crime, hopelessness, and despair of the drug trade in US cities and affluent suburbs was also going to be shaken on every level. A new way to solve the drug problem was being born. Michael sighed heavily. It was long past time to change.

Michael read each word, weighing it within its sentence, seeking imperfections and mistakes, making sure the language was as close to the ideal as possible. He believed to the very core of his soul that anything worth doing was worthy of the best that human beings could do. Mediocrity had no place in any government that he was part of because the people deserved the best that could be done for their tax dollars.

While it was true that there was an incredible amount of work to be done to heal the harm inflicted by politicians and their minions over many decades, Michael knew that love of country and the desire for the ideal could carry the nation forward to a place where it would achieve extraordinary things again. Yes, much had to be done, but The Movement was hard at work solving the nation's problems. A great deal of thought had gone into shrinking the government, retraining the workforce, enlisting business to aid in the process, and the myriad other problems that had to be resolved.

Michael Stonebreaker did not consider himself a cynic, but he would never be anyone's fool, either. He understood the human personality in all its twists and turns. He had been chosen to work in intelligence in the Pentagon precisely because he was anything but naïve. He brought the enthusiasm that led him to success as an athlete, West Point cadet, army officer, son, brother, husband, and father with him to the job The Movement had called on him to do. He believed in the American Dream. It was not dead.

The phone on Michael's desk sounded softly. He picked up the receiver.

"Yes?" he asked. The look on his face changed from one of quiet concentration to concern. He had not considered having to deal with the news being delivered to him from the other end of the line.

CHAPTER 27

El Toro had a headache. In fact, he had much more than that. In all the brawls and fights he had been in during his lifetime, no one had ever managed to do as much damage to him as the boy with the chair. The first blow had knocked him unconscious. The second blow had nearly fractured his skull. He had a severe concussion. He was disoriented when he regained consciousness. His men had carried him to an infirmary two floors above where his on-site physician was nervously examining him.

He swore and told the man to leave him alone. As he lay there waiting for the pain to subside, his thinking cleared and he was filled with such a rage that he lashed out and struck the doctor in the groin.

The man fell backwards, landing on the floor and moaning in pain.

One of his men snickered and was immediately sorrier than he had ever been in his life. El Toro screamed for the others to take the man to the cell near the Death Machine. Kicking, screaming, crying, and begging, the man implored him not to send him there, but Ernesto screamed even louder and told his men to do as they were told.

The sound of the man's yells receding down the corridor

momentarily diverted El Toro's attention from his headache.

He thought of the woman and the boy. Not only would he prolong their torture and deaths to an exquisite degree, he would slow down the process of the Death Machine until its horrific mutilations would be so subtle that the victims might die at the thought of the next injury it would cause. He would have his fun and then some!

No one had the courage to tell him that the woman and her boy had escaped.

When he demanded that they be brought before him, his second-in-command gathered up his courage and revealed that they had gotten away. El Toro screamed in rage, and sat up quickly from the table he had been lying on. The sudden movement nearly made him blackout again, and he nearly swooned and fell to the floor.

His lieutenant grabbed him in time to keep him from falling, but he immediately pushed the man away.

"Don't you dare touch me!" he yelled. "How the hell did you let them get away? If you don't find them, you'll die in their place!"

The men in the room began scrambling to get out the door. The men who were outside looking for the pair had yet to find their prey.

High on the hill within the rock indentation, Adrienne and Chuck pressed themselves tightly against the wall trying to avoid detection. Adrienne raised one of the assault rifles.

The chopper had been called up from the village where El Toro's army lived. The pilot and another man were searching everywhere for signs of the woman and her son. He landed the helicopter on the rocky plateau that extended out from where Adrienne and Chuck were hiding.

Chuck thought it sounded like the helicopter was nearly on top of them.

Adrienne was shaking with fear, but no one was going to take her son back to that animal. She would rather kill him and take her own life than be dragged back to that hole in the ground to face God-only-knew what awful things the fiend had planned for them. Her weapon was loaded. She was ready.

She edged forward slightly and placed herself between the opening and Chuck. The chopper touched down and the passenger opened his door and stepped to the ground. The pilot remained at the controls with the rotors spinning. The noise was deafening, and the wash from the blades filled the small space with a rush of air and a continuing roar.

Adrienne opened fire as the man rounded the front of the chopper. The impact of the bullets sent him flying backward.

The pilot was quickly trying to ascend when she turned her weapon on him and emptied the clip into the cockpit. She and Chuck watched as fire appeared from somewhere inside the chopper. It was about seventy feet in the air when it started to whip around. The craft spun around twice, three times, before it seemed to float over the plateau and into the rock wall rising above it.

The explosion was so loud that Adrienne and Chuck were stunned. They cowered back into their small cave. They were momentarily deafened by the blast. It would be some time before their hearing returned to normal.

They looked at each other in wide-eyed disbelief. Neither had expected to still be alive, but here they were. Adrienne lay the assault rifle down carefully and hugged her son. She released him and he smiled a slight smile.

"Way to go, Mom!" he said.

She couldn't hear him, but she smiled and placed her right index finger to her lips for him to be silent. Someone might be close enough to hear them.

El Toro's men were racing up the hill. The pilot had radioed that he thought he had seen something on the plateau.

"The woman knows how to shoot!" he said when the first man went near the a cleft in the rock. "I'll be damned if I'm going to die on this mission."

When they heard the rifle and then saw the chopper explode El Toro's men knew this was no longer going to be a walk-in-the-park.

There is something sobering about realizing that what you thought would be easy prey is really something deadly. It takes the wind out of your sails. These men were immune to the carnage of

El Toro because they had seen much as his hand-picked elite since the man took power. They had raped and murdered to their heart's content, but now they had a problem.

The old cliché' about being between a rock and a hard place was true. On one side was the one they secretly called El Diablo; on the other was a woman desperate to protect her child, who actually knew how to fire a weapon. The time for fun and games was over.

The American military had trained El Toro's men well. One thing they had learned was not to be stupid. The woman had ammo. She knew how to shoot, and she had the high ground. She did not have to come down to them. They had to go up to her.

"Damn!" the lead man on the hill said. "We can't get above her without being seen."

They had been spread out half way up the hill when the chopper exploded. The only thing they could do was go back down and regroup. They wore body armor. They were going to need it.

The lead man turned and signalled for the other to start down the hill when a burst of fire came from above them.

One of them did a cartwheel and fell dead.

The remaining men surveyed the damage.

"Head shot," one of them reported.

"Who the hell is this woman?" another said out loud. He readied himself to keep moving downhill. A second burst of gunfire killed him where he crouched.

Four men and a chopper were gone. The last two men started running in fear, but there was no place to hide at the bottom of the hill. No doubt they wondered, *how the hell could anybody shoot that well?*

From her perch on the plateau Adrienne could see the last two men. She took a deep breath and squeezed off another round, picking off one of them as they reached the bottom of the hill.

The last man started for the cover of some shrubs halfway up the next hill. He'd made it about a third of the distance when a burst of gunfire cut him off at the legs. He was screaming as he tumbled back down the hill. He lay there yelling in agony when Adrienne fired again. Then he was silent.

Adrienne knew that their safety would not last long. The maniac would be coming for them. Now, they had to choose to stay where they were, or to get further away.

After the chopper exploded, the driver had left the Hummer and found a place where he could watch what was happening. He had broken protocol, but there was no one around to report him. When he saw the woman easily kill his companions, he was enraged and afraid. He raced back to the vehicle and drove like a madman to the secret entrance to El Toro's mountain fortress.

High above the plateau, The Movement's satellite transmitted the images they'd been waiting to verify.

Ray Karwel's cell phone rang where he sat in his Juarez hotel room. He answered it on the first ring. Now he knew where the entrance to the hidden fortress was located.

CHAPTER 28

Getting forty men and heavy firepower to El Toro's location was not simple, but if Adrienne and Chuck Williams were to have any chance at all, Rick and his men had to get in position fast.

"Buzz about the new action TV series has been spread everywhere," Karwel said. He and Rick sat hunched over the map spread out on the coffee table in Rick's hotel room.

"A dog fight will be staged and between five bad guys in choppers and the hero of the series, who'll be flying a fighter jet."

"Sounds like the intent is to make as much noise as possible," rick said. "with a lot of expensive aircraft."

"Money is no object," Karwel had said. "Particularly when a maniac has a nuclear weapon and might use it."

The five mock gunships were armed with blanks, as was the fighter jet. Karwel would direct shots from a sixth chopper acting as a camera plane.

"We'll ostensibly be recording exterior footage to be edited into the story, coupled with special effects and interior shots done later in the studio," Karwel said. "But two of the choppers will actually be carrying you and your teams to El Toro's hideout."

"Got it," Rick said. "One team will secure the perimeter and I'll take the other into the mountain fortress. We'll deal with any unfriendlies there and make our way to Ruíz."

The distraction would begin near the edge of the city and drift over the place where El Toro thought himself hidden from the world.

"We're counting on people on the ground near the hideout to buy into the helicopters chasing the jet as part of the TV action," Karwel explained. "Most movies had one or two choppers in some sequences. Going over-the-top might involve as many as three, and big budget productions could have more. It depends on how spectacular the director wants the end result to be."

"Obviously, the goal here is on the uber spectacular side," Rick said.

"During the dogfight the hero will shoot down all of the choppers," Karwel said. "They're rigged to look like they're hit and going down. The hero's plane will also fall from the sky, but not before he escapes to fight another day."

"I imagine this will look pretty realistic," Rick said. "The last thing we need is to incite panic on the ground."

"Great point," Karwel nodded. "People have been advised that the choppers will fly low in controlled drops, appearing to be smoking and falling from the sky before disappearing out of view of the cameras. Special effects of them exploding on the ground would be added later."

"You guys do amazing stuff with CGI," Rick said.

Rick's men would be rappelling to the ground at two points far enough away from the fortress that they would not be noticed. The choppers would lower their gear, and then swiftly ascend into the sky to fly back to Juarez. The fighter and the choppers would be really mixing it up over the area where El Toro's hideout lay beneath the mountain.

"The hope is that everyone, including the cartel, will ignore the whole thing as harmless," Karwel said.

The second part of the assault on El Toro's compound involved SEAL Team Six.

"It's probably safe to assume," Karwel went on, "that when you and your men enter the fortress, whoever's guarding it will immediately signal Lago."

"No doubt," Rick agreed. "They'll want to mobilize El Toro's army of three hundred men living there for back up."

Karwel nodded. "There's an easy arrogance among the men working for this maniac. Lago is nicknamed Hell, and they're fearless to do as they please there. They have enough weapons and training to destroy local law enforcement. They strike fear in Juarez and they laugh openly about the power they hold over people."

"They haven't met anyone who's made them afraid," Rick said.

"Verdad," said Karwel. "True, many of them have been conscripted from the Juarez Cartel itself, and they've grown even more fearless with El Toro's rise to power."

The Movement had been preparing for a possible Mexican incursion long before El Toro and his men had crossed the border and slaughtered innocent civilians, and they had prepared a certain number of the SEALs. Commander Jonathan O. Chalice, whose code name was "Jock" had called Lieutenant Ralph Spengler to his office as soon as word of El Toro's attack reached his ears.

Spengler was of medium height. On the street he had the ability to blend in with a local population. He spoke fluent Spanish, French, German, and Farsi, and was an expert in explosives, weapons and tactics. He had a reputation among the SEALs for being one of the toughest S.O.B.'s to walk upright on Mother Earth—and he was still walking only because he was a SEAL and did not know the meaning of the word quit. He had been wounded three times, two of them seriously. His dress uniform boasted a host of decorations, but despite his valor in the field he was a man comfortable spending most of his time in fatigues.

"Intel says we have a gold-plated maniac on our hands this time," Chalice said. "The terrain is a nightmare, they don't know exactly where his hole is, his close detail is American special ops trained. He's got an army of several hundred men and enough firepower to smoke a major US city."

"So, what else is new?" Spengler asked. "If it was easy, anybody could do it."

"That's what I like about you, Spence," Jock Chalice said. "Your emotional level is overwhelming."

"How long have we trained for this? Seems like forever. It probably has been," Spengler said. "They call him El Toro, right? I could use another word for him, but I won't. The Bull is about to become a burger and fries. He killed a lot of our own. He shot children. Payback is going to be enervating, to say the least," Spengler said.

Chalice laughed softly, "Well, alrighty, then! It's time to plan to get our man."

"Breathing or not?" Spengler asked.

"The world will be a far better place without him," Chalice replied. "But, there is one wrinkle. We will recon his army and prepare the target. The Marines will be cleaning out the rat's nest once we know the lay of the land. Another group will be visiting the maniac. When they're finished we will take care of the big problem in the basement."

"Whoa!" Spengler said, aghast. "Sir, may I ask who this other group is, and can they do the job? In fact, nobody is better than we are! What's wrong with this picture? What about the thing in the basement?"

"It's okay, Spence," Chalice assured him. "They are private contractors unknown to anybody. From what I have been able to find out, they don't even exist...at least in any discernible records that I know about. Apparently, they are all Hispanic. Ernesto is expecting us to show up, but he won't be expecting them."

"That's fine, sir, but how do we know they can pull it off?" Spengler questioned him. "What kind of rep do they have?"

Chalice eyed Spengler for a long moment. "Normally, I could not tell you this, and what I am going to tell you is classified forever. Two years ago the change in government in this country was sparked by a real nut case in Nebraska with his own private army, named Armstrong. That wacko and the former government planned to bring this nation to its knees. Problem was, he captured and killed six men from the contractor's group we are now paired up with. In return, they obliterated him. Case closed. We do all we can to avoid mistakes. These people operate on the same principle."

"We will neutralize El Toro's army with the Marines. The contractor will take out El Toro. We'll also handle the other task. Ernesto has been sitting on a gift he has been safekeeping for Al-Qaeda. They planned to use it on our soil. We spotted one of their men not long after they entered the US on a watch list. We extracted good data from him, so we know what El Toro's hiding, and what no one else knows. It's nuclear."

Few things fazed Lieutenant Spengler, but the glint in his eyes showed his anger had risen. "Does Ernesto know how to arm the damn thing?" he asked.

"We don't know, and we can't afford to wait to find out," Chalice answered.

"When do we move, sir?" Spengler asked.

The phone rang on Chalice's desk. He motioned for Spengler to sit tight as he picked up the phone.

"Hello, Starlight Bowling Alley. Summer leagues are now forming. We have a two-for-one special on weekends. How many lanes do you need?"

Chalice listened, then answered, "Very good, sir. Can we put you down for the weekend?"

Again, Chalice paused to listen. "Good. We'll see you on Saturday. Don't forget to bring your shoes. Have a great day."

Commander Chalice hung up the phone and looked at the Lieutenant. "We go tomorrow at dusk. We've got a lot to do. Gather the team."

Lieutenant Spengler stood up and saluted. "Was that who I think it was?"

"Yes, Spence, it was POTUS, the man himself. I've discovered that he doesn't like intermediaries. He takes a personal interest in things."

"Like the woman and her son?" Spengler asked.

"You nailed it. Captain Williams is one of ours. If we can get them home safe, that would be a very good thing. POTUS wants that to happen if it's possible."

"I'd like to bring them home, but that might be more difficult than we think," Spence replied.

"It is always more difficult than anyone thinks. That's why we are who we are, Spence."

"Yes, sir," Spengler said. "I'll round up the guys."

CHAPTER 29

El Toro did not feel much better. His splitting headache had worsened, his vision was impaired, and he desperately needed to beat someone to death. He walked slowly to the communication room located on the second level of his complex. The room was filled with TV monitors, audio speakers, and control panels. A massive self-contained generator system was located on the lowest level of the complex and powered by huge propane tanks accessed through the secret entrance. They were buried near the entrance and camouflaged so that a casual hiker would have to be on top of them before he saw them.

The exterior cameras and microphones would make the fate of that same casual hiker a horror show because said hiker would end in the Death Machine if he showed up. One camera had been disabled by the woman, the one at the shack near the curve in the dirt road that led away into the hills. That was unfortunate. It would have to be repaired.

The driver returned to report the death of the other members of the team and the destruction of the chopper to El Toro. The complement of his inner circle had been significantly reduced, but his anger overrode his better judgment, as usual.

He ordered the man beaten and taken to the holding cell to await his turn in the Death Machine.

El Toro stood staring at the monitors when a sudden blast of sound from the speakers made him flinch.

"What the hell is that?" he screamed.

"It's the movie people," one of his men said. "It was on the TV. They're shooting a fight in the sky between a jet and choppers. It's nothing to worry about. It's all made up for a new TV show."

"What are they doing here?" Ernesto roared. "Do they know we are here?"

"They just flew this way for the scenery. They explained it this morning on the news. They do all this stuff in the air. They have the choppers and the jet rigged to look like they're hit. There are smoke-machines on the choppers and they pretend to be shot and then crash," the man said.

"I don't like them being above us," El Toro muttered. "What if they suspect something?"

"There's no way they could know anything," his lieutenant said. "It's nothing but a movie. There's nothing real about it."

Miguel Sanchez, El Toro's second-in-command, was even bigger and stronger than El Toro, but he was not filled with hate like his fearless leader. In those rare moments when El Toro would allow someone to speak reason to him to help calm him down, it was always Sanchez who was doing the talking. Sanchez had the ability to speak to him, where others were not allowed to question anything he said.

Ernesto knew, deep down, that he could not best Sanchez in a fight. He also knew that the loyalty of such a man was worth more than any amount of money.

Sanchez also maintained the pretense of civility when he spoke.

"Señor Ernesto," he said, "from the air, one hill looks like another. There is nothing that tells them we are here. Please. We will find the woman—"

"I want them both in front of me within the hour!" El Toro nearly screamed the order. "No more excuses. Go and get them. I want them alive. They go to the machine, but not before I have had my pleasure with them."

"The woman is armed," said Sanchez. "And she knows how to shoot. We have lost at least six men and—"

"I don't give a damn if we have lost sixty or six hundred!" roared El Toro. "Find them! Bring them alive to me!"

"We may have as few as half the men left, including the two in the holding cell," Sanchez said.

"Goddamn them," El Toro said. "They are dead to me! They will suffer and die! Send a team now and bring back the woman and her damn son! Do it now! No one makes a fool of me—no one!"

Sanchez was no fool. He knew there are times to speak and times to keep silent. "Yes, Señor Ernesto, I will lead the team," he said. "We'll get them for you."

El Toro made his way to the elevator and returned to his suite on the first level.

Everyone but the man who was watching the monitors left the room following Sanchez, who chose the best men to go with him on the mission. He left the others to guard El Toro.

Sanchez and the men with him gathered at the armory. They put on body armor, chose the most powerful assault rifles, side-arms, and knives before heading to the lowest level of the hide-out. They got into one of three Humvees parked in the cave, started the engine, and sped out onto the dusty track.

High above the earth a satellite broadcast the emergence of the vehicle clearly to monitors in a mighty fortress deep beneath the central Pennsylvania hills. The Movement relayed the information to Ray Karwel.

"It's go time," Karwel said after updating Rick.

"Got it,"Rick said. "If they are to have a chance we need to get on the ground now!"

What followed was a like a scene played out in the best action movies. The jet engaged one of the choppers and it was shot down, smoke streaming out behind it.

A second chopper shot its guns at the jet, and the hero managed to evade being hit. The jet flew straight up, and then rolled over and shot towards the chopper with its guns blazing. The second chopper began smoking and streaking towards the earth below. Both choppers disappeared behind the hills. In the movie, when the special effects were added, both choppers would be shown hitting the earth and exploding in gigantic fireballs.

In reality, Rick and his team were rappelling to the ground as swiftly as they could. They hit the ground within seconds as, according to plan, the choppers reappeared from behind the hills and flew back to the airport.

CHAPTER 30

Adrienne Williams had to make a decision: stay where they were or move. The men would return—that was certain—but the next time they would not come unprepared. She checked her cache of ammunition. It wasn't going to last very long if they got into a fire-fight.

She looked at Chuck. She loved him so much. She was so proud of him at that moment. He was a brave boy. He looked so much like his father it brought tears to her eyes. She turned her head away and stared at the rocky face of the hill rising up from the plateau where the chopper had exploded. The twisted wreck was still burning. *Where could they go?*

"Chuck," she said. "We can't stay here. They'll be coming back—"

"I know, Mom," Chuck said. "Where should we go?"

"Higher," she said. "I think we have to go higher. Your dad says to take the high ground. We have to go up that hill to the top. We need to find another cave or hiding place. There is no safety here. If they can send choppers after us there is no telling what they'll do next time. We took them by surprise, but we won't get that chance again. Let's go."

They left their sanctuary and hurried across the plateau. They passed the chopper where it lay burning on the ground.

Chuck turned his head away. He had seen a blackened human form within the wreckage.

Adrienne did not turn her head. She looked at it to steel her resolve to fight on. These people were animals. They had no mercy in them. She knew it. She knew what they would do to them if they were caught.

They began ascending the hill as fast as they could go. They saw a jet and choppers high above them in the sky. A roar of sound washed over them. She nearly bolted in sudden panic. For a moment she was tempted to grab Chuck and race back to the cleft where they had hidden, but something told her not to do that.

They kept on climbing up the hill, their breath coming in ragged gasps as they reached the top. The view revealed more of the same: rocky hills and steep, narrow clefts between them.

Chuck said, "Look, Mom, over there!"

Adrienne saw a shadowy opening in the face of a rocky surface. It might be a cave. She led the way and they ran as fast as they could go. They reached the shadowy spot and discovered it was another opening in the rock face. It was deeper than the one they had left.

Adrienne carefully entered it and discovered the opening went back into the hillside about thirty feet, more like a real cave in the hillside. Her first thought was that they could hide here. Her next thought was that they might die here as well.

Chuck had come into the cave behind her.

In that moment a voice shouted from outside the cave. "¡Alto! Stay where you are!"

With superhuman speed born of sudden fear, Adrienne whipped around, ready to fire her weapon. Chuck flattened himself instinctively against the rocky wall to get out of her way.

CHAPTER 31

President Stonebreaker was in the midst of a policy discussion with Chief of Staff, Harold Crosby when the phone on his desk rang. The two men had been sitting in easy chairs while they were talking.

"Excuse me, Harry," Michael said, rising from one of the pair of easy chairs the two sat in while they talked. "Hopefully this call won't take long and we can get back to the issue quickly."

"Mr. President," Crosby said, "you have a meeting with the vice president in five minutes. Why don't we take this up again this afternoon? I have some things I have to attend to, so I'll return after 5:00, if that is all right, sir?"

"That's fine," Michael said, "I'll see you at 5:30."

Harold Crosby stood up and left the room.

Michael crossed the room and picked up the phone.

"Hello, how are things going with the situation?" Michael asked.

Michael listened to the voice on the other end and replied, "If you can wait a minute I'd like the vice president to hear this. Please hang on for a moment."

Michael punched a button and instructed his secretary, Charlene to have the vice president to join him.

When Vice President Dryden entered the room and closed the

door behind him, Michael motioned for him to take a seat by his desk. He punched a button. "I'm putting you on speaker phone. Please speak freely."

"Thank you and hello, Mr. Vice President. Good to speak with you again." It was the voice of The Movement's inside man, the man known to them only by his code name, Mr. Smith.

"Likewise," Eric said, "I hope you are well."

"Yes, I am fine, sir, and I have some news."

"Is it good news?" Michael asked.

"That remains to be seen," the caller said. "The assets are in place. The hard part is about to begin. It will be more difficult in reality than it is on paper."

"It always is," Eric added.

"We anticipate that we will be successful," Smith said, "but I have learned to temper my judgment with prudence. I know that both of you have learned that lesson as well. Combat can go sideways in seconds, but our operatives are well-trained. A plausible distraction has been orchestrated to draw attention from the mission. We can only hope that our orchestrated feint will work. I am where you would expect me to be, so I'll let you know how we progress."

"Thank you, Mr. Smith. We'll look forward to hearing good news. God speed!"

"Thank you, Mr. President and Mr. Vice President. You'll be hearing from me soon."

Michael hung up the phone. "Smith is in The Movement's fortress deep beneath the Pennsylvanian hills—where we would expect him to be." He stared at the phone for a moment, and then he shifted his gaze to Eric. "Are you ever going to forgive me for getting you into this, Eric?"

"I'm sure some men have found the vice presidency less exciting than life on the front lines, Mr. President," Eric said with a grin, "but my term has been quite busy to date."

"Well, the Post did describe you as the most active vice president in many decades in that article in the Sunday edition," Michael said.

Eric laughed.

"I can't be in two places at the same time," Michael went on. "I would if I could, but this job is easier because you're here. In a very real sense, we are co-presidents. You've dealt with some pretty hefty things since we came here. My thanks to you can't be measured. I owe you too much to adequately repay you."

"Does that mean you'll spot me ten strokes in our next golf game?" Eric asked, laughing hard.

"We haven't played golf in—how long has it been—eight or nine months?" Michael said.

"Ten months, but who's counting?" Eric said. "Time flies because we are both workaholics, and because this country was in the *terlet* when we walked in here. Archie Bunker was ready to hit the flush lever. We've come a long way in two years."

"We've got a long, long way to go, but we have an outstanding group of people on the case," Michael replied. "The amazing thing to me is just how bad our predecessors had let things go before we got here."

"What do you expect when you let evil people railroad morals, faith, and core values out of the government, schools, and every other public institution?" Eric asked. "Progressives have been around as long as mankind has been on the planet. I love our system of government, but a representative republic only works well when the people are paying attention and actively engaged. I blame all of us for what happened. Before The Movement came into our lives we were as bad as everyone else."

"Touché," Michael said. "That's true. But we got the wake-up call, and if we have anything to do with it, the American people are getting that call, too."

Michael ran a hand through his hair and brought it down on his desk. "Back to the present crisis: The assets are in place. We can only pray that the maniac doesn't know how to push the button. If he does, I don't even want to think about what that might mean."

"That depends on how big it is and how deep it's buried," Eric added. "If it's dirty and big, things could get really nasty. I'm going to think positively. I'm going to believe that the good guys will win. The level of insanity in this world is hard to believe at times. It's only a matter of time before some wacko gets his hands on a bomb and blows up a lot of innocent people. The best we can hope for is that we can keep it from happening on our soil."

"It would be good if we can keep it from happening anywhere on Earth," Michael said. "It's also hard to believe that there is so much hatred in the world. However, on a promising note, The Mexican Resolution is, in my opinion, a masterpiece of work. The thinkers at The Movement have outdone themselves. I'm sure you've already read through it several times. I gave it my review."

Eric chuckled. "Mr. President, I know what one of your reviews is like. I would rather jump into a sea of sharks with just a knife than go through a Stonebreaker review."

In spite of the gravity of the discussion, Michael laughed. "All right, I am overly cautious, I admit. However, I have marked things that need to be changed. There's nothing major, but I would like you to read through the changes and let me know what you think. Feel free to change anything that you think needs to be altered as well.

"Will do, sir," Eric said, "It will be my honor."

"When we're done I'll send it along to The Movement for final review. Now, I have a free Saturday coming up in two weeks. Can we get in eighteen holes? If so, I'll give you three strokes. The last time we played you beat me pretty badly. In the Middle Ages, when someone beat the monarch in any contest, they assigned him to a new job."

"What job was that?" Eric asked, laughing.

"Food taster—and it wasn't usually a long-term job back then," Michael said, laughing hard enough to bring tears to his eyes.

That set Eric off. The spectacle of the two most powerful men on the planet laughing out of control was not something often seen, but it was a welcome release. Michael Stonebreaker and Eric Dryden may have been heads of state, but they were also something equally important: best friends.

CHAPTER 32

The Man Who Loved the Gulf had insisted that his cousin keep him informed of the status of Rick and his men. His cousin had called him and told him that things were coming together quickly. The teams were on the ground. If someone had been able to overhear their conversation they would not have understood what the two men said to each other to be anything but an ordinary conversation between family members.

The Man marveled that with all the advances in technology, they had been speaking in code, of course. The security aboard ship was the best in the world, but of the many very bright people all around the earth, not all of them were good and right-minded. To think otherwise was to be both naïve and stupid. Evil would not be reasoned with; and so they spoke in code.

The Man left the lounge and walked to the stern of his lovely ship. He took a deep breath and stared out at the Gulf. A huge manta ray swam off the stern, perhaps thirty feet down, gliding leisurely through the water. He estimated it to be about twenty feet across its body, the biggest of its kind that he had ever seen. He was thankful to be there to see it.

The silent world of the sea appealed to The Man Who Loved the Gulf in a way that he did not understand. The beauty of the world under the surface of the waters was incredible. For him, the sea reflected nature in all its aspects. It was truly a place where human psychosis had less impact than on the land, but the effects of pollution and human greed were becoming more evident if one sought them out. It was a sad testament to progress.

He found himself thinking about predators and their prey locked in an endless ballet in the oceans of the world. The hunger of a shark isn't personal, he reasoned. It is simply an instinctive appetite on steroids. Such animals don't hate as men do. A shark will eat anything or anyone if hungry enough and given the chance.

The Man found thinking about such things edifying. He had come to believe certainly that men are more dangerous than sharks, not only because they can create fantastic weapons and ingenious means of killing their fellow humans, but because they are often truly evil. For all the terror a great white brings to a beach when it is spotted, the animal is nothing more than what nature made it: a killing and eating machine without a soul—despite what the movie Jaws made people believe. He smiled at the thought.

Getting mad at a shark, or a tiger, for that matter, is silly, he mused. To swim among them is to risk being eaten as merely food. To certain men, however, other men are to be slaughtered, or controlled, to take their property. Some men want to cut the heads off other men because their religion tells them to do so. Still others subject their fellows to abject servitude because they believe themselves to be superior.

He sighed, allowing his thoughts to play out further. The truly diabolical among men are happy to beat, rape, torture, and kill in the worst of ways because they are the most evil of all. Some find a perverted release in hurting others.

He, himself understood this better than most men. He'd lost count of the number of men he had killed in his lifetime. Some might find it strange that he was not evil. He had avoided killing others out of anger or greed. He had killed men in self-defense, or when they had done such evil to innocents as to deserve it. Unlike a shark, he understood the need for mercy, and he balanced it against judgment.

Thinking back over his life, he admitted making some errors in judgment early on in his career with La Cosa Nostra. He quickly saw the fallacy on which the Mafia was built. Crime paid well for some, but the human costs were too high. He resolved to go legit.

When he told the families that he was leaving to follow on his own road, the battle lines had been drawn. They wanted him dead. That had been a costly mistake on their part, and the ensuing war cost them a lot of soldiers. In the end, the dons relented, acknowledging that they could not break him. So a truce was made—he would stay out of their businesses, and they would stay out of his.

Free from his early entanglements, he sat down and thought for a long time about where the United States of America appeared to be heading at the time. Some would call him prescient. He saw a future coming that would belong to those who reached out and took it. Others looked to Asia, but he had his eye on the Americas. The lack of competition in the western hemisphere beckoned to him. He would build his empire from the north in Canada to the southernmost part of Argentina.

While others sought to control the manufacture of electronics and semiconductors from Japan, Taiwan, South Korea, Hong Kong, China, and Singapore, he steadily gained control of the world's food supplies. People love gadgets, but they loved food more. Everyone has to eat, he concluded. He capitalized on the timing of the world's growing seasons and made his first fortunes on the idea that it's nice to have fresh fruit in New England in the dead of winter.

After his success in the food industry he branched into shipping, logistics, airlines, and related systems. Then, he bought manufacturing operations in other domestic areas. He dealt with the ordinary and the notorious, yet he himself was known to be a man of his word. When people tried to pressure him in Mexico, Central, and South America they quickly discovered that he was not someone they should cross.

By the time he adopted his sons, he had spent years building an empire that was fully flourishing.

As a young man he had been diagnosed with a genetic abnormality that mitigated against naturally fathering children. Adoption was to be his only means for building a family. Becoming a father was a dream he had longed to fulfill.

When the Dupree brothers entered his life, he recognized in them a strength of character that he had rarely seen. Immediately, he wanted them to be his sons. They had no real father. He would be their father.

When Rick came along The Man felt the same fatherly tug on his heart, and he soon adopted him as his fourth son.

His wealth and empire encompassed more than any of them would ever need, and he loved each of them generously. As a result they were not jealous of each other, but instead loved each other and were loyal to their adopted father.

The Man took pride in knowing that his empire would go on when he was gone. His sons would see to it. He had chosen wisely.

Now, he wanted Rick and his men to come home safe. He had no illusions of invulnerability. Rick and his people could be hurt, or killed. It was a terrible thought, and he did not like to worry. Worry was counter-productive. But, he was human. Perhaps it was his age? He would not sleep until Rick was home again.

He spotted the manta ray again. He gave instructions to the men on the bridge to keep a sonar eye on the creature. Two of his crew members had been expert divers in the US Navy. He often went scuba diving with them. He summoned the men and they headed off to don scuba gear.

Back on deck, he readied his camera before he and the former Navy divers dove into the water.

The manta ray was even bigger than he thought. He couldn't wait to show Rick and his brothers the shots he took. The animal was a magnificent creature. His cousin would have said that the sea creature was God's handiwork. He liked the idea of that. It was a nice thought.

He wondered if his cousin was starting to wear off on him. Perhaps he was getting soft?

A school of fish was approaching. He swung his camera and caught sight of a ten foot shark closing in on them from his right.

His dive buddies had their spear guns at the ready—just in case. The shark kept following the school of fish.

The Man smiled, watching as the manta ray appeared to ignore the whole thing. Indifference has its place when you're the biggest kid in the schoolyard, he thought.

CHAPTER 33

El Toro had never wanted something so badly in his life. He must have the woman and her son. His rage was beyond anything he'd ever felt toward anyone. When they were in his hands again, he would torture them as long as he possibly could. They would not be allowed to die for as long as he could keep them alive. He wanted them to suffer more than anyone had ever suffered at his hands.

His head hurt. His neck hurt and back hurt. His vision was impaired. Pain killers had knocked down his pain somewhat, but his anger was building, sending his blood pressure too high. His reckless habits made him a candidate for a heart attack or a stroke. He didn't care. His personal doctor lived in quiet desperation, wondering if each day would be the man's last. He often advised him to relax, but the maniac would have none of it.

El Toro had descended to the place where he kept his Death Machine. He stood admiring it. To his mind it was a thing of beauty.

The inventor—now long dead in the machinations of his horrible creation—had tried to incorporate all of the painful things that were applied to victims of torture in the Middle Ages. He then added even more terrifying adaptations gleaned from the Nazis and others. The entire machine was run by a control box in an observation podium set above it.

El Toro became El Diablo when he had a victim in the device. The horrors he could bring to afflict a helpless victim were many, numbering nearly a hundred in count. There were cutting devices, piercing devices, twisting devices, pinching devices, pressure devices, and variations on the theme. He could implement one, some, or all of them—depending on his mood—and he added his laughter to the screams of his victims. The degree of severity of the applications ranged from the uncomfortable to the excruciating.

The Death Machine had systems for removing the residues and fluids left over from his horrific play. It could be positioned in any way necessary to induce maximum suffering. From its neutral flat position on a raised platform it could be elevated, inverted, and rotated at various speeds. Had a demon from hell been assigned to build the thing, it would have won an award from Satan himself.

El Toro's gaze zeroed in on a steel door on the other side of the chamber. He had been given a huge sum to safeguard the thing behind that door. The men who left it did so with the promise of a great deal more money for him when they returned. They had also provided him with something he prized even more than the cash before they crossed the border into the US. He had insisted that he be told how to activate the bomb.

It was a dirty bomb, indeed. The locked chamber that held it nearly one hundred feet below the surface of the mountain was actually an elevator. With the press of a button it could be raised to the surface. He, Ernesto Ruíz, *El Toro*, *El Diablo*, possessed the key to the kingdom of death and destruction. If he was provoked or attacked without the ability to escape, he would take as many of his attackers with him as possible. He would raise the bomb to the surface, set it off, and wipe out everything from Juarez to El Paso. The land would be uninhabitable, and his name would live in infamy for generations to come.

He was certain, however, that no one was going to attack him. The Americans were all talk and no action.

His thoughts returned again to the pleasure he would soon have when Miguel Sanchez and his team came back with his prey.

In his mind's eye, El Toro considered himself a great predator. He was cunning and crafty. Had he not been injured by the damn boy, he would be leading the hunt right now. He would have liked to be there to see the terror in their eyes when they were recaptured. That would be a true high that the purest and most powerful drugs could not match. Like a lion or an eagle, he was spurred to bloodlust by the panic of the prey. Fear, bordering on madness on a human face was a sweet and heady elixir to El Toro.

Sanchez understood the directive he had been given. The woman and child must not be harmed. Their horrible end must come at the hands of El Toro himself.

He would not approach her last known location directly with his men. Her skill with the assault rifle was sobering. She obviously knew that going high, maintaining cover, and carefully picking her shots gave her an advantage. They would need to get above her and flank her.

Miguel and his men knew the terrain far better than the woman did. They would circle the hill where the chopper crashed to get above her. Then, they would draw her fire until she exhausted her ammo and move in to recapture them.

The woman had already shown how well she could shoot. Sanchez' men weren't fools; when she returned fire they would stay well out of her way. But the Glock sidearm could be a problem. Knowing how to use an assault rifle, she would not use the pistol until they were well within range. Wherever she had come from, however she had learned to shoot, someone had taught her well. No doubt she would keep the pistol for close work.

Miguel, knowing what awaited the pair, shuddered involuntarily. Had he been in her shoes, he would have saved two bullets for her son and herself. She might do just that. If she did, he would have to figure out how to placate an enraged El Diablo, robbed of his fun. The monster would probably put their bodies in the machine just to see them destroyed. After that, there were two men waiting in the holding cell. It was going to be a bloody, nasty day.

Sanchez wished he could take off, get away from the maniac. His relationship with Ernesto Ruíz had reached a nadir. He no longer wanted to play the game. Spain sounded nice. He hadn't yet been there. The money in his Swiss account would last him a lifetime.

CHAPTER 34

Adrienne Williams tried her best to peek out of the cave without being seen. She was anxious at the chance of a possible rescue, but suspicious of foul play. The voice from outside the cave spoke again, this time in English.

"Mrs. Williams," it said. "Stay in the cave. Don't let yourselves be seen. We are here to take you home. I know you don't believe me, but I have to try to win your trust—and do it quickly. I don't blame you for being frightened. You've been through a horrible experience. Events are speeding along now. A couple of things have to happen. One of them is for you to trust me. I spoke with your husband and I asked him to tell me something only you would know, to verify that we are genuine. In a moment, I am going to step in front of the entrance to the cave. I will not have any weapons. You can train your weapon on me and blow me away if you choose to, but obviously I hope you won't. When I am in front of you, I will ask the question Captain Williams said that only you could answer. If you are satisfied, I will ask you to step back into the cave and not come out. We don't want you seen by anyone at this point. I will then come into the cave entrance and we will talk. If you are ready, I am going to step in front of the cave now."

"Wait, dammit, just wait a minute!" Adrienne said. "There is no way I can allow it. You could kill us easily. This is a standoff. You can't be trusted, even if you say that you are here to take us home. Home could be back to the maniac."

"Captain Williams said that you might react this way," the voice said. It was a male voice that remained calm. "I admire your intuition, and your courage. Okay, let's try it a different way. I'll ask the question first before I step into the entrance. Your husband said, 'Where did you place Maria—beneath the big oak, or by the rock wall?' He said that it was a hard decision."

Adrienne placed her hand over her mouth and stifled a sob. Before Chuck had been born, she had lost a little girl in a miscarriage. They had named her Maria, and they buried her under the big oak in the cemetery. She answered, "Under the oak. All right, step in front of the entrance. My rifle will be on you. Any sudden movement and you're dead. No one is going to take us back to that monster! Not now! Not ever! I'll kill you and anyone else who follows you. Then, I'll do what I have to do!"

She heard a boot on gravel and a vision filled the opening. The man was tall, dressed in the same type of clothing worn by El Toro's men, and he was incredibly handsome. Her husband, Captain Everett Williams, was equally as tall, but very blonde. She had hoped that it would have been her husband who would rescue them, but she was still grateful nonetheless. This man had the flashing dark looks of a film star. His smile was warm and his eyes gleamed in the sunlight. He appeared to be of Latino ancestry.

"Are you military?" Adrienne demanded.

"No, the man replied. "I'm a contractor working for the government."

"Which government?" she snapped.

"The US government," the man replied.

"Why a contractor?" she asked. Adrienne was close to yelling. "Why not the military? Answer quick or I'll start shooting!"

"Be calm, Mrs. Williams," said the Latino man. "My name isn't important. The military isn't far away. The man who was holding you prisoner has a small army a few miles from here. The military is addressing that problem. My men and I were chosen because we can blend in among the locals. We are dressed the same as Ernesto's men to fool him into thinking that we belong to his group. As of this moment, Ernesto has sent another team of men to search for you and your son. As we speak they are being monitored by satellite. They're in a Humvee and on their way to this location. They don't know that you left your last location. It appears that they believe that they can get above where you were located and flush you out of your hiding place. We don't have much time." Adrienne was beginning to believe the man, but kept the rifle on him. "Go on."

"Listen, I am going to ask you to do something very brave," he said, "but there is no other way to pull this off. We look like El Toro's men for a reason. We have to take possession of that Humvee and gain entrance to the compound. They have to think we are part of their army. My men and I are going to pretend that you are our prisoners. We'll surround you, and I want both of you to kneel on the ground in front of this cave. Place your hands behind you so that it appears you are tied up. If they are convinced that you are secured by their own people, they should approach us. When they do, keep your heads down and your eyes on the ground. Things are going to happen very fast. My men will take over the Humvee and deal with El Toro's men. Get ready. We don't take prisoners. When they have been dealt with, we will drive to the entrance of the compound and do our best to take out Ernesto and his remaining men. Can you tell me anything about the compound? How it's laid out?"

"What happens to us when you take over the Humvee?" Adrienne asked. "I'm still not sure about any of this. If we're supposed to pretend to be prisoners, how do I know that you are real? You won't give me your name! Our lives are on the line here. That maniac was going to do unspeakable things to us. We were brought to the compound in blindfolds, and kept in one room. The only time we left was when we escaped. There were three doors leading to God knows where. Chuck guessed we should take the one on the left. We did. It led us to a hallway, into a cavern, and to here. Neither of us knows about anything else in that place. How can I trust you?"

"My name is Rick," the man said. "Your husband's name is Everett. This young man is Charles, or Chuck as he prefers. My employer was approached by the government through a third party because we work without fanfare and notoriety. We speak the language and look the part." "I believe him, Mom," Chuck piped up.

"He's for real. Let's get out of here. I want to go home so bad!"

Adrienne looked at her son. Though he was young, he had good sense of judgement thanks to the way she and her husband had raised him. She nodded and turned to Rick. "If he says you're okay, then I accept this, but how do we get home when this is over?"

"There is a chopper behind the next hill," Rick said. "When we're done with them, one of my team will bring you back to this cave and exchange clothing with you. We'll get in the Humvee and head for the compound. The two of you will be airborne and on your way home immediately. Are you ready?"

"As ready as we'll ever be," Adrienne said. "Chuck, say a prayer. Let's go home."

The three of them left the cave. They were surrounded by about twenty men, dressed like the ones who had held them captive.

Adrienne and Chuck got on their knees and put their hands behind themselves, pretending to be tied. The sound of a motor was heard a few moments later as a Humvee lumbered over the hill and came to a stop.

One of the men in the back of the Humvee said, "The Boss must have called Lago for more men. They've got them. Let's take them back and let him have his fun."'

"Turn this thing around," Sanchez said. "Something's not right."

Another man said, "Miguel, chill. We have the woman and her brat! Let's get them back to El Toro. This is enough for one day."

"Turn it around," Sanchez said. "Be ready to drive. I don't like it. This is too damn easy."

They were about to turn the Humvee around when about twenty more men appeared over the ridgeline behind their vehicle.

"What the hell do we do now?" another man in the back seat exclaimed.

"Full automatic," Sanchez said. "We get out together, we move together, and if they're legit, we make this transaction and get the hell out of here. Move now!"

They wanted to stay in the truck, but with forty men surrounding it they knew they had no chance if someone began shooting.

Sanchez and his men moved toward the group holding the captives. They stopped about fifty feet away. He could see that the prisoners were indeed the woman and her kid.

He said in Spanish, "Thanks for catching them for us. We'll take them off your hands. Go back to the village. The drinks are on El Toro tonight."

A cheer went up from the others, and two men lifted Adrienne and Chuck from their kneeling positions.

Sanchez thought they would be bringing the pair to them, but they were walking in the other direction instead. At that moment his men were hit by silenced fire, and they fell dead on the ground.

Miguel Sanchez brought up his assault rifle in a fluid motion, but before he could fire a man stepped out into the open and shot him through the throat. The bullet knocked Miguel backwards and he sprawled on the ground.

As he lay dying he looked up into the face of an angel wearing fatigues and holding an assault rifle. It was no one he knew. He tried to ask, "Who are you?" but no sound came out except a gurgle.

He would not be going to Spain.

CHAPTER 35

Ernesto Ruíz hated most American things, with a few exceptions. One of these exceptions was American movies, and, in particular, Clint Eastwood movies.

Ernesto's unknown father had been an American soldier who had gotten very drunk, made Ernesto's mother pregnant, had all his money stolen, and awoke in a ditch near the Rio Grande at 5:00 a.m. He made his way back across the border to his base and passed out of his son's life forever.

Ernesto had a private theater room built just off his bedroom for watching his favorite Eastwood films from the 1960's. *A Fistful of Dollars*, *For a Few Dollars More*, and *The Good, the Bad and the Ugly* featured Eastwood as a nameless gunslinger and Ernesto loved the unexpected twists and turns in the stories and the violence. He imagined himself like Eastwood, a menacing loner who could overcome all odds.

Depsite his penchant for Eastwood movies, Ernesto's favorite film of all time actually starred Charles Bronson, Henry Fonda, Jason Robards, Claudia Cardinale, and Jack Elam. Directed by Sergio Leone, who was also the director of some of his favorite Eastwood films, Ernesto considered *Once Upon a Time in the West* the greatest movie ever made.

In the film, Charles Bronson plays another nameless man who plays the harmonica, plaintive, sometimes ominous sound is heard as Bronson sets the stage to kill all of the men who murdered his brother when he was a boy.

Ernesto Ruíz had a harmonica, which he played very badly. Fortunately, he rarely played outside of his bedroom suite. Had he done so someone might have laughed and ended up in the Death Machine.

El Toro sat back, wondering if the idiot woman and her son would wander into Lago, the town that was built for his army. He put signs up at the edge of town with Lago painted in white letters on them. Then, he had the name crossed out and Hell was painted in red over it. He thought that was funny.

The people who lived in Hell didn't care. The town was shaped like an X in a small valley that lay at the center of four gaps between high hills. Ernesto had spent a lot of money building Hell to his liking. He recreated storefronts on streets that resembled a typical Eastwood movie set. Six saloons, four brothels, a large general store, a doctor's office and clinic, a storage building that looked like a hotel, a movie theater, and a few smaller buildings were all identified by signs out front. Lago looked like a pleasant American small town, but it was swarming with the ruthless mercenaries in Ernesto's employ. There would be nowhere for the woman and her son to hide.

Near each of three of the four legs of the X there was a military barracks-styled building that housed his men. Humvees, a motor pool, and other transport equipment was garaged at the fourth leg next to an armory.

Ernesto Ruíz may have been crazy, but he was not stupid. There were four ways in and out of Lago in case big trouble arrived. With enough money to buy almost anything, Ernesto put the finishing touch on the town he called Hell by camouflaging it to avoid detection from the air. The town was hidden beneath a huge camo screen at an enormous cost, but El Toro thought it was worth the investment.

Beneath the camoflage the atmosphere in the town was always dark and murky. There was a perpetual dim twilight. The sun was never seen in its full glory. To Ernesto, the lack of light in Hell seemed appropriate for the men who lived there.

El Toro's army was conscripted from other cartels and gang members from the streets of Juarez. They were required to wear military uniforms. In fact, they had to pay for their own upkeep, booze, cigarettes, food, clothing, and shelter under a "company store" arrangement. He built the town, complete with employee housing and other provisions for their needs. In exchange for work, the employees were allowed to buy everything from the company on credit, and the costs were deducted from their pay. The arrangement worked quite well, allowing Ernesto to recoup much of the expense of maintaining his army from the men themselves.

Ernesto paid better than the average wage in Juarez, but a good portion of that money came back to him through the compay store town. None of it had been his idea, though. Instead, his lieutenant, Miguel Sanchez, had suggested it when they started planning to raise an army and have a place to house them. Lacking a proper education, Ernesto had given Sanchez carte blanche to run Lago. He didn't know it, but Sanchez had been skimming huge amounts of money off the top and sending it to an account in Switzerland for years.

El Toro's army, such as it was, was not terribly well organized. Most of the men had no military training. Sanchez did. He saw that they were trained up to a certain level and then stopped. He did not want to run the risk of a coup and his own skin. He had placed his own informants among the men, and they kept an eye on things for him.

Sanchez knew from experience that criminals love all of the vices. He made it a point to supply their needs. Girls were routinely brought to the brothels from Juarez to augment the losses resulting from abusive men. The most innocent and beautiful girls found were brought to El Toro, and of course this meant certain death.
it hadn't taken long for Sanchez to figure out El Toro's hatred for women as outsiders., and that his rule regarding them was simple. If an outsider came into El Toro's domain, that outsider did not leave to return home.

The brothels and cantinas fit the scene, but the movie theater was a modern anomaly on the western styled street. But, just as the Romans had built the coliseum for the Roman masses to enjoy free bread and circuses, Sanchez understood the need to amuse and entertain the hired thugs. The movies were another perk to try to keep them happy, along with satellite TV service, but internet service was not allowed in Hell. Communication with the world outside was punishable by death.

Once a cell phone was found in the possession of one soldier. He was hung on the gallows in the center of town after being beaten nearly to death by El Toro. Everyone had been ordered to watch. It was a lesson that no one would forget.

Ernesto was certain that his town would never be discovered. He had not reckoned on The Movement and its extraordinary ability to search out and find hidden things. He knew nothing of their existence. At the moment, he wondered what was taking Sanchez so long to return with the woman and the boy.

Unbeknownst to him, real hell was about to come calling on Ernesto Ruíz, and the Navy SEALs would be expediting the delivery.

CHAPTER 36

President Michael Stonebreaker and Vice President Eric Dryden and their wives were enjoying a rare a double-date for dinner and a movie. For security reasons, their night out would take place within the White House residence. Dinner was served on the Truman Balcony with it's breathtaking view of the Washington Monument under the moonlight.

The meal was excellent, and the couples enjoyed each other's company. It was rare that they could get together, given the demands of their offices and responsibilities. In the years before they came to 1600 Pennsylvania Avenue, they vacationed together as families, and their love and regard for each other was strong.

"Eric, I broke my 5-iron," Michael said. "It was wild. I hit the ball off the fairway and the head snapped off and must have flown a hundred feet. I've got to get a new one."

"Mr. President, you're still using the clubs you got when you were at West Point. They're ancient. I'm surprised that they've lasted this long!"

"Michael—" Michael said. "It's Michael after hours!"

Eric smiled. "That's easy for you to say. You're the president!"

"Okay, I'm ordering you to call me Mike!" Michael said with a laugh.

"Yes, Mr. President," Eric said.

Everybody joined in laughing. After the meal, family talk about their children, colleges, and day-to-day things took a little of the edge off of where they lived and what they were doing.

"What say we take a drive this Saturday and get me a new 5-iron?" Michael said.

"Why not get a whole new set of clubs?" Eric asked. "It's time you bought a new set anyway. We need to play a round, too. I'm so rusty that I probably couldn't hit straight. We both need to go to a driving range."

Joan Stonebreaker looked at Yvette Dryden and said, "Well, if they can shop for golf clubs and hit the driving range, why don't the two of us visit the new mall and do a little shopping of our own?"

Yvette laughed and said, "Can you imagine the insanity it would cause the Secret Service if we tried to do that? We can't walk outside without letting half a dozen people know what we are planning to do. If this life steals anything from you, it takes away the ability to be spontaneous."

"They are an extraordinary group of people dedicated to our protection," Michael said. "I respect their desire to protect us. If we have to give up a certain amount of personal freedom in order to stay alive that is a small price to pay. However, I meant what I said. Why don't the four of us plan an outing? We'll arrange it with our details, coordinate everything with them, and head out this Saturday."

He patted Yvette Dryden's hand. "Honest, Yvette, you and Joan go where you want to, and Eric and I will get those clubs and go hit a few balls. We'll be discreet about it."

"That's a great idea, honey!" Eric said. "I need tees, golf balls, and a new glove, too."

"I'm in if you are, Joan," Yvette said.

"Then it's a date! How about heading to NoMa early to check out the shops in Hecht's Warehouse?" Joan said.

Yvette nodded with delight. "That sounds awesome! We can sneak over to Masseria for Italian afterward."

"Then it's settled," Michael said. "So where shall we go, Eric, since the girls are off and running?"

"There's a super golf shop in a mall not far from the Virginia line," Eric said. "We'll go there. There's also a range about two miles down the road. We can go hit a bucket of balls and then meet the girls for lunch. Sound good?"

"Perfect," Michael said. "Now, all I have to do is explain to Frank Anderson why we want to do this, and he'll tell me why it's a very bad idea; I'll explain that it is for our mental health, he'll counter by saying that we could all be slaughtered in the streets. I'll add that we'll be in and out before anyone even knows we're there, he'll say we're driving him crazy, I'll finish with, 'Please!' and he'll go off to make the arrangements."

Michael said all of this in one breath with a straight face, and the others laughed insanely. Nothing relieves tension like humor, he thought.

They got up from the table and started for the Treaty Room to watch the movie. The phone rang. Eric looked at Michael.

Michael returned his stare before clearing his throat to say, "I'll take it across the hall. Go on and get the movie ready. I'll be there as soon as I take this call."

Joan looked at her husband. "What if it's something major—like the end of the world?"

"Then you'll just have to watch it without me," Michael said.

Everyone laughed again and continued to the living room. Michael closed the door of the den behind him, picked up the phone.

"Hello."

The voice at the other end of the phone said, "It's the Starlight Lanes calling again about the Saturday league. I'm afraid the last two slots have been filled. Sorry. You could consider another day. Thanks for your inquiry."

Michael placed the phone on the receiver. He went to the living room where everyone was seated, and the movie was ready to go.

"Good news?" Eric asked.

"Mrs. Williams and her son are safe," Michael said.

"Who is she?" Yvette asked.

Eric said, "A very brave and lucky woman who doesn't have a Secret Service detail. Let's get that movie started. Otherwise, I'll be falling asleep after all that food."

"You wouldn't dare fall asleep after the president invited us to dinner!" Yvette chided her husband playfully.

"That's all right, Yvette," Joan said, "Michael may fall asleep even before Eric does. All these two do is work!"

Michael smiled. Adrienne and Chuck Williams were safe! He wished he knew who had pulled it off. He wanted to give that man his genuine thanks.

CHAPTER 37

Getting sixteen Navy SEALs in place is one thing; delivering six hundred Marines is another. They were all going to Hell. SEAL Team would come down in groups of four to do recon and special prep. They were not to openly attack, and they were most certainly not to be discovered. Secrecy was the rule.

"Okay, gentlement, we're in and out, do some dirty work, and bring home the intel," Lieutenant Ralph "Spence" Spengler addressed his team. He and his men dropped into Hell from over the top and quickly blended into the terrain beneath the massive camo coverings draped between the hills on high towers to hide the town from the air. It was a surreal scene.

The gloom provided cover. They placed explosives under the three barracks buildings, counted heads, took measurements, and established coordinates. Four SEALs headed for the motor pool to set explosives at key points before moving on to set massive charges at the armory.

"When this goes boom, it's going to be spectacular!" one of the explosives specialists whispered as he set the last charge.

Spence signaled to the leaders of three of the squads to return to their hiding places on the hills above the town in its tight valley. He then led his men to the downtown area, such as it was.

Like ghosts, the SEALs reconnoitered the town and took more coordinates. They had began to slip away when one of Spence's men met a drunk in an alleyway between a brothel and a saloon. The man was not armed, except with his mouth, and when he opened it to yell, the SEAL sent him on to the next world quietly and efficiently.

Spence appeared as his man silently lowered the dead man to the ground.

"What do you want to do with the body?"

"We don't want to carry it back up the hill," Spence said.

"There's that dumpster near the side door to the saloon," his man said, motioning with his head toward the back end of the alley.

"We'll have to chance it," Spence said. "Time is slipping away. These guys fight all the time. If the body is found, they'll likely attribute it to a brawl between men in the town, and that someone simply hid the evidence. Case closed."

The two men picked up the body and went deeper into the alley toward the dumpster. It was not the best idea, but it was the only visible solution.

They put the body in dumpster and got out of Hell.

The Marines had finally arrived. It had been no small feat to get them into place with the utmost secrecy. A good time to come calling is at 3:00 a.m. when most humans are fast asleep. In Hell, sleep could be quite deep thanks to alcohol. The wake-up call would be loud, bright, and hot. The good guys had no intention of letting El Toro's men get to the armory. The building was about to be turned into matchsticks.

Six hundred Marines in groups of one-fifty each were in position to enter the four legs of the X-shaped town of Lago. The bombs at the barracks were designed to blow the buildings apart, and at exactly 3:00 a.m. local time they went off. The camo coverings above the town caught fire, resulting in a spectacular inferno.

Lago appeared to be ablaze with the fires of hell itself, and devils danced in the streets in the forms of men on fire running and screaming until they could run no more.

A quantity of ammunition was kept in the large general store. SEAL Team had not expected it, and it began to ignite in the heat of the inferno. Live rounds were shooting into the night, and El Toro's men were cowering in the dirt.

SEAL Team remained hidden on the hills above. At first, Spence thought that someone might be shooting at them, but he quickly realized what had happened. The Marines hadn't moved yet. The fire raged on. No Marine or SEAL had engaged an enemy. The inferno did its work.

Two hours passed. The sun was glowing behind the hills to the east. Because of the way the town had been designed and built, it had ignited like a tinderbox. By 6:00 a.m., everything was smoldering. As the cries and whimpers of those who managed to survive began reaching their ears, the Marines moved in. The SEALs came down from above.

They met with a hellish scene. Of the five hundred people in town, seventy-two remained alive. Forty of them were so badly burned that they would probably not live. Twenty prostitutes had done their best to survive by jumping into a swimming pool built below one of the brothels.

Twelve men in fairly good shape surrendered immediately at the sight of the Marines. One of them asked, "Why did it take you so long to get there after what we did to the Americans in El Paso?"

Spence translated the man's statement for the Marine Colonel in charge of the operation. They ignored the man and surveyed the damage. Hell had been burned to the ground, and not a shot had been fired.

The Colonel looked at Spence. "This is the strangest battle I've ever been in. What the hell did you guys do? This place went up like a Roman candle!" he said.

Lieutenant Spengler said, with a slight smile on his face, "Sir, sometimes we don't understand the whole picture, but you can bet that the rest of what we have to do in this country isn't going to be so easy."

"I wouldn't bet against that, Lieutenant," said the Colonel. "We got lucky today. There's nothing I want more than to bring the men home at the end of the day."

Both of them noticed the sign by the road at the same time. Somehow, it had not been burned, but the red paint that had spelled the word "Hell" had liquefied and run down the face of the sign.

"They called this place Hell," the Colonel said. "That seems appropriate under the circumstances."

"I'd say amen to that, sir," Spence said.

CHAPTER 38

Adrienne Williams and her son were surrounded by soldiers. A solider stepped forward and Adrienne saw that the person was not a man, but a woman.

"I'm Maria," the woman said, motioning for Adrienne and Chuck to follow her.

Maria Angelos was the assistant manager of a food importing company owned by The Man Who Loved the Gulf. She also had black belts in two martial arts, was deadly with rifles, handguns, and knives, and held her own within the ranks of the personal army of The Man.

Adrienne quickly noted that the woman was fair skinned and taller than herself, and her raven black hair was a stark contrast to Adrienne's blond. Her piercing dark eyes lent her an air of authority, which Adrienne gratefully accepted. She followed as Maria led her and Chuck back into the cave.

"I will change clothes with you," Maria said to Adrienne as she produced a blond wig from a knapsack.

Adrienne was grateful since they had escaped into the hills in nothing but pajamas. She and Maria quickly changed clothing, and Maria donned the blond wig.

Adrienne and Chuck were led away to the helicopter that waited for them two hills away, while two of Rick's men checked the bodies of the cartel members.

"Delgado, Guerrera, Vargas and Morales, you're with me," Rick said.

The four men got into the Humvee along with Rick and Maria for the journey to El Toro's fortress. Rick and the men would use their slight resemblence to the dead bandits to buy time to enter El Toro's compound with Maria disguised as Adrienne. There was no one on the team small enough to pretend to be a twelve-year-old, blond American boy. They sat in the Humvee in such a way that Maria would be visible to surveillance cameras. Rick had covered his face with dirt and sat in the back of the vehicle with his face hidden.

The maniac and one of his men were in the surveillance room when they saw the vehicle approaching the hidden cavern. The men in El Toro's compound had heard the explosions in Lago during the night, but no one had the courage to wake up their fearless leader to tell him that something bad had apparently happened in the town. They knew what would happen to anyone who dared deliver bad news to the boss.

"I don't want to die in that damn machine," one of them had remarked. They all agreed.

"It looks like Sanchez is returning safely," the man said to Ernesto in the surveillance room.

"Do they have them?" El Toro demanded.

The surveillance expert looked closely at the monitors. He could see the woman's blond hair. "Si, Señor Ernesto. They are in the vehicle. I see the woman!"

"What about the boy?" Ernesto asked. "Do you see him?"

"No, but if they have her they must have him, too," the man assured him.

"Good!" El Toro said. "I'm going to the machine room. Tell Sanchez to bring them there!"

He turned and went through the door into the hallway. He took the stairs down to the level where the door led to his torture chamber. Anticipation took his mind from the pains in his head and neck. He would kill the woman as slowly as possible, and make her son watch every moment of it. Then, it would be the boy's turn.

The Humvee arrived at the entrance to the cave and slowly drove through the camo-covered the opening. Rick noted two men in the cave waiting for them. They were both armed.

"Delgado, Guerrera, get out of the jeep slowly, showing your guns," Rick said softly. "Maria, once they're out, get out of the vehicle on the passenger side and keep your face averted. Don't let them see you clearly."

To Vargas and Morales he said, "Get close enough to them to take them out before they can sound an alarm. When they see we don't have the boy it's going to get dicey. They'll be looking for the leader of the group, so I'll stay in the vehicle to give us a few seconds before they get suspicious. If that happens, this could get very bad."

Carlos and Sebastian got out on the driver's side, while Ramiero and Fortuno exited the passenger side with their guns trained on Maria. She kept her head turned as she stepped down from the Humvee, using its height to prevent El Toro's men from getting a good look at her.

"Where's the boy?" one of the men asked. One of Rick's men on the passenger side of the car mumbled a reply in Spanish.

"What did you say?" the guard said, getting nervous. Something wasn't right about what he was seeing. "Answer me," he said. "Where's the boy? Where's Sanchez?"

There have to be cameras in the cavern, Rick thought. *Someone must be watching this.* He exited the passenger side of the truck with his cap lowered over his forehead. He was about the height of Sanchez, who was taller than the other men in El Toro's protective group. He kept his head turned away so they could not see his face. He said in Spanish, "Está muerto. He got hit in the firefight."

It wasn't Sanchez's voice. Too late, the guard raised his rifle and took a bullet between the eyes from Delgado's silenced weapon. Before the second man could react, he was shot through the head by Vargas.

"Dammit!" Rick exclaimed. "If they lock us out of the compound we have no way to get in. Run!"

They raced up the tunnel as Maria shed Adrienne's pajamas to access her weapons. She was dressed in boots, shorts, and a T-shirt. She ran after them.

The door at the end of the tunnel was unlocked. Rick pushed

down the handle and opened it very slowly. He didn't know if they had been seen, and if so what waited for them. He entered the corridor followed by Maria and his men. There were two doors to their left and the passageway that led deeper into the mountain on their right. They had no idea how many men remained in the compound.

Rick spotted a camera trained on them on the ceiling. "They have to know that we're here!" he said. "The bomb could be higher up, or somewhere down here. We've got to find it! No prisoners. There's no time to play guessing games. Maria, you're with me. We'll take the next door. Delgado and Guerrera, you take the next door. Vargas and Morales, you take the corridor. Kill everyone. Maintain radio silence until we find the bomb. Hand signals only. I want all of us back here in twenty minutes. The objective is that bomb. If you find it, secure the location and radio me. I'll call our friends to come and deal with it. Let's move!"

They separated and Vargas and Morales headed down the corridor with their weapons at the ready. Delgado and Guerrera opened one of the doors on the left and headed for a stairwell leading upward. Maria and Rick opened the other door to a hallway about thirty feet long with a steel door at the end.

"There's no telling what lies beyond that," Maria whispered.

Rick nodded. "We'll know soon enough."

CHAPTER 39

President Nicolas Calderón read through the document that had been couriered to him from the president of the United States.

He felt something on his face and reached up. He was surprised to find tears on his cheeks. He brushed them away and continued reading. The pages in the plan detailed a dream. It was hard for him to contain his emotion. Calderón loved his nation and its people. He had always desired to be a good president. His frustration came not only from the power and threat of the cartels, but also because of the poverty of so many people. He understood Mexico to be a nation of haves and have-nots. The haves live lavishly; the have-nots suffer greatly.

If implementing the Mexican Resolution was possible, his country would undergo a paradigm shift in the next decade that would alter the life of every citizen. The document outlined the overhaul of government, infrastructure, manufacturing, resource development and conservation, energy resources, agrarian reform, the military, healthcare, and education for all of Mexico's people, including the establishment of universities and entrepreneurial institutes. It detailed how each area would be treated, strategies for setting and meeting goals and providing the guidance and nurturing necessary to achieve the dream.

Calderón was mesmerized by the planning and detail that had gone into the document. It was fantastic in vision, enormous in scope, and pragmatic in its design. The people who had created it were frightening in their ability to envision such things and outlay them with perfect sense. Most importantly, their plan was doable! This could be done. It was going to be done!

The ideas contained in the work were uniquely Mexican in design. The plan took into account how Mexicans lived, worked, and thought in every part of Mexico. This was not some American idea to be imprinted onto the Mexican people. Rather, it allowed for cultural differences, modes of thought, tastes, styles, and structures. The cultural sensitivity with which the document was written sent more tears streaming down Calderóns face. Again, he wiped them away subconscoiusly and said a silent prayer to God.

Finally, someone who was intelligent, caring and deliberately careful, had taken a look at Mexico and seen its reality, pain, suffering, desires, and hopes, and translated them into a plan that could be followed to a better life for his people.

When he finished reading, he sat for a long time looking out the window of his office. He had given orders to his secretary that he was not to be disturbed until he called her. A half hour turned into an hour.

He glanced at the clock on his desk and realized he should get back to the duties of the day. But first, he had to make a call. He buzzed his secretary, Margarita and asked her to place a call to President Stonebreaker. When the connection was made he picked up the phone.

"Mr. President," he began.

"Please, call me Michael, President Calderón," Michael said.

"Then you must call me Nicolas," Calderón said.

"Yes, of course. We are new friends who are about to set out on a great journey together."

"I have been sitting here reading what you sent to me," Calderón began.

"Thank you for going through it," Michael said. "It is pretty long. There's a lot in it and a lot to be done."

"Do you know who wrote it?" Calderón asked.

"I do, but their identity must remain secret," Michael replied. "The one thing I will say is that there are no better minds on the planet. It is a beautiful thing, isn't it?"

There was silence on the other end of the phone for a long moment. Michael thought that the connection had been broken when Calderón said, "I must say that I have been moved beyond words. The people who created this know my people well. They know how we live, how we think, what we find to be important, our hopes, dreams and aspirations…and our souls. If someone had spent the last twenty years walking the length and breadth of Mexico and talking to our people, he might have an understanding of my nation, but the insights in this are far beyond anything I ever expected to read."

Calderón's voice broke.

Now it was Michael's turn to be silent.

After a moment he said, "Nicolas, things are progressing according to plan. El Toro's army is no more. The woman and her son are free and returning to their home. Our people have entered the hideout and when I have something more to report I will call you immediately. Thank you for smoothing the way for our people to get into position. It helped far more than you know."

Calderón cleared his throat. He was a bit embarrassed at his show of emotion before the president of the United States.

"You're most welcome," he said. "You said that his army is gone. What does that mean?"

Michael related the story he had received from his SEAL contact. When he came to the part about the name of the village, Calderón exclaimed, "My God…They named it Hell and it burned to the ground? What a horrible thing."

"The things they did to earn that name have apparently led most who lived there to the real Hell," Michael said. "Only God knows someone's heart, and He determines where we will end up. However, there is a long fight ahead. We will not be so fortunate when the cartels are confronted all over Mexico. It will be bloody, but your people will soon be free."

"I am most concerned about those who are innocent," said Calderón. "I can't see how you can protect them. The cartels are filled with bloodthirsty animals that don't care who they hurt. They won't go quietly. It will be an open war in many areas. They have a lot of firepower."

"I know," Michael said. "And I would not hurt any innocent person if it can be avoided, but El Toro didn't care when he came over our border and slaughtered our people. You've read the plan. You know what we want to do. I think you agree that it will be a wonderful thing for your nation if we work together to make it come true. There will be pain and loss of life, but it will be done with your guidance. You know your people better than we do. I have contacts with others who know your people well, and they live in my country. When this begins we will be committed to each other to succeed or fail. We can't afford to fail.

"Nicolas, there is nothing more I want than to see a day when your people and our people are equal on every level: economically, governmentally, and educationally. I dream of a day when your citizens will be able to stay at home and not cross the border in the dark of night, but only when they desire to see a relative or friend, or they simply want to come here and be a tourist. We've had a one-sided relationship for far too long.

"You have a wonderful country. If everything is organized the way it is visualized in that document on your desk, Mexico will become a place that draws people from everywhere who will want to come and learn why your nation is so prosperous! It is my hope that Mexico will be a template for all the other nations in the west who will want to use your example as a design for their own success. The Americas united together as a community of nations would be a formidable force for good in this world."

"Michael, I am overwhelmed by what is being proposed," Calderón said. "But our people have been promised before, and then left in the cold by empty rhetoric. I mean no disrespect because I have never known a man like you. There is a fire and determination in you that I have not seen before."

"That's because this isn't about me," Michael said softly. "I am not a politician. I am a military man, but not one who subscribes to the idea that mere might makes right. Right is born in the heart when a man realizes that there is something vastly more important in this universe than him. I believe in my nation and people. I trust their collective desire to live a decent, moral life, and to train their children in the ideas of faith, patriotism, and dedication to things that truly matter. Our nation was on the brink of being utterly destroyed when the change was made two years ago. There was a great evil here, and it was excised from our country. You are dealing with great evil in the cartels and the inequities of opportunity that plague your people. We have begun our healing process. Your healing is about to begin."

President Nicolas Calderón gave a heavy sigh. "I must admit, Michael, that I am not the man of faith that you are. I am a lapsed Catholic, and not very good at that either. I would have to spend a month in the confessional with a priest to list my sins to the Almighty. I sometimes think that I am beyond redemption. However, you give me hope. I am glad that we have come together at this time. I am so terribly sorry that it had to be because of such a horrible thing that these animals did to your people."

Michael said, "So, let's begin a new thing. We'll be friends because our nations need us to be just that. True friends. If you have someone close to you that you trust, you might want to have that person read the plan, too. I am fortunate in that the people who put me in the position also placed the others throughout this administration and government. There is strength in numbers. Having someone evaluate the plan with you will help you to see its truth, and to also see any flaws. In my government I have the final say on the things that should require my attention as president and commander in chief. That ought to be true of you, as well. Is there someone you trust that much?"

"Sadly, Michael, the person I trust is just outside my door," said Calderón. "My secretary has been with me from the beginning. You probably know that my wife died three years ago. We didn't have children. Margarita is loyal to me because she thinks of me as a son. I was able to help save her husband's career years ago when he was falsely accused of bribery in a contract dispute. I am like an uncle to her son and two daughters. I can tell her anything."

"Ask her to read it," Michael insisted. "It is about the people of Mexico and the future of everyone. When she has finished it, please call me. I want to discuss it with both of you. As to trusting someone else, I am sure that there must be someone you can trust in addition to her. We need feedback. You have a say in this, too. If there are parts of the plan that need to be corrected or adjusted in some way, we need to know it. We have no desire to impose something that is doomed to fail. I hate government bureaucracy. Assuming that government knows best in anything is exactly why we got into the horrible situation we were in. Bureaucrats are too often people who have no practical experience and got their job through manipulation, seniority, or, worst of all, nepotism or payback. This plan must be instituted carefully from the bottom up, not the top down. In other words, the people who will be most affected by it are ordinary citizens of Mexico, and they must have a say in its structure and application. There are people on my side of the border who don't understand your people at all, but they like to think that they do. Stereotyping has no place in this plan. You've read it and you know that the authors have gone to great lengths to be sure that the plan is Mexican in its design. However, that doesn't make it perfect."

"Margarita's son, Rinaldo, went to school at Johns Hopkins," said Calderón. "And he returned home to start a medical practice near Juarez. I can ask him to read it. Since he went to school in your country he knows a lot more about the American perspective than I do. I've talked to him often in the last year. He's very bright, and he cares about people. He would read it with an open mind. He came back home even though he could have started a better life in your country because he really wants to help our people."

"He sounds perfect," Michael said. "Please ask Margarita and Rinaldo to read over it carefully. If they are willing, have them make notes about things they don't think are right or that might need even slight changes. In the meantime, if there is someone else you trust to read it, please have them do so, but this must remain secret until we bring in our troops and make our joint announcement. Please call me in a couple of days. As soon as I hear something about Ernesto and his hideout I'll call you immediately. Have a good afternoon. Be well, my friend."

President Calderón gently replaced the phone on its receiver. He turned again to his windows and looked out at the view. He did not feel the tears on his face. Hope had been born in his heart. He had never wanted anything so badly in his life.

CHAPTER 40

The chopper settled gently on the tarmac and the doors opened. Adrienne and Chuck Williams were helped from it and stood on the ground.

Captain Everett Williams approached the chopper, holding his daughter Susan by one hand. Colonel Ron MacKenzie held her other hand. Officers and enlisted personnel made up the balance of the party.

Within a moment, Captain Williams was holding his wife, son, and daughter in his arms. There wasn't a dry eye within a hundred feet of the scene.

A cell phone in the Captain Williams' pocket rang and he took it out and answered it. He talked for a moment, and then he handed the phone to Adrienne.

"It's for you," he said.

Adrienne looked at him in wonder and took the phone and put it to her ear. She was startled by the voice on the other end of the phone and her eyes grew big.

She said, "Yes, that would be wonderful. We'll look forward to it. Thank you so much. It's incredible to be free and home again."

She handed the phone back to her husband.

Captain Williams put the phone to his ear.

"Thank you, sir. I can't tell you how happy I am..." His voice broke. He mumbled a goodbye and put the phone in his pocket.

He looked at Adrienne. There were tears on his cheeks. "What did he say to you?"

"We have a dinner invitation," Adrienne said. "Colonel MacKenzie and his family are invited, too. We're to bring the children, as well."

"Where are we going, Adrienne?" Colonel MacKenzie asked.

"If I remember the street number from civics class, it's 1600 Pennsylvania Avenue, I believe," Adrienne said as she smiled at the Colonel. "Now, Chuck and I are very hungry, we both need long, hot baths, and we will both fall asleep standing here if we don't sit down soon."

The party moved away from the chopper and boarded a Humvee waiting to take them to Walter Reed National Military Medical Center.

Adriana Santos watched as they went, and then returned to the work at hand. As far as her show was concerned, the dogfight between the choppers and the jet had gone well. She was reviewing digital images when Ray Karwel to the production trailer.

"This is great stuff," she said. "When the SFX guys get their hands on it we should have a super sequence for the series. What do you think?"

"I think," Karwel said, "you're right. It will make a great sequence for the show. The hero has outdone himself. It's James Bond all over again."

"Speaking of Mr. Bond, how is that other issue coming along?" Adriana asked. She spoke vaguely in front of the editing technician who was operating the equipment.

"So far, so good," Karwel said. "The action continues and the story is unfolding. The players have to get it right because there will be no chance for a re-write on this one. I'm heading back to my hotel. Do you need a ride?"

Adriana gave Karwel a questioning look. "No, I am going to stay here for a while longer. Why do you say that a re-write isn't possible?"

Karwel returned her stare and said, "I meant that the action sequence has to play out and the script is set. When it's wrapped there can't be a do-over. It's one and done. We can't re-shoot it."

The two gave each other a long look.

Adriana said, "Well, let's hope it goes well. It's very important to the series."

"That's putting it mildly," Karwel said.

Fortunately, the video tech was so engrossed in his work that he had missed the byplay between Santos and Karwel.

The action director turned and left the trailer, and Adriana took a deep breath and looked again at the screen where the imaginary dogfight continued. Her thoughts were on the man who had taken her heart with him. She said a silent prayer.

Adriana wasn't the only one thinking of Rick. The Man Who Loved the Gulf had also received the news that the woman and boy were free, that Lago had burned, and that his son Rick and his men had entered the fortress. He thanked his cousin, left the house, and took the launch to his beautiful ship.

Once there, he called his dive buddies, they put on their gear and went into the sea.

There was no manta ray swimming nearby today. They saw two sharks, some schools of fish, and a large grouper. The Man swam deeper and his men went with him, one on his right and the other on his left. He was a believer that physical activity, especially one that's enjoyed, is an excellent way to relieve stress.

His mind was on Rick and his men. He thought about what Rick had been through at the hands of the giant in Nebraska. He had adopted Rick, not only because of his ordeal and dedication to him, but because he needed to keep him close and protect him. Rick's strength, intellect, and character were amazing. He saw himself in Rick. The Duprees and Rick were the sons he had always dreamed of having.

Now, he could not help but worry. Rick was in harm's way, and he could not protect him. He felt helpless. He was the kind of man who never felt such weakness.

His thoughts shifted to his cousin. He was extraordinary in so many ways, and his obvious faith was one of them. He hadn't realized how deep he'd gone until one of his men approached him in the water. The man quickly signed to him that they should go higher. He was going too deep.

The Man abandoned his contemplation and followed the diver's lead. They ascended slowly.

He was one of the most disciplined of men, yet, as they made their way to the surface, his thoughts were raging within him. He found himself thinking, indeed, hoping that his cousin was right. Perhaps there was a God?

"If You're there," he nearly spoke the thought, "please protect my son and the others."

At that moment he surfaced into the light.

CHAPTER 41

For the immoral men at El Toro's base, it was time for Plan B.

Unlike their leader, The Man Who Loved the Gulf had no criminals in his employ. He hired fiercely loyal men and women only after strenuous vetting, first on the basis of their character, and then on their experience, skills, and talents. They worked as one and they were utterly devoted to the principles embodied by The Man's companies, even when they were unaware who the real owner of the empire was. .

The Man's army refused to take prisoners. Prisoners complicated things. They were by no means without compassion. On the contrary, the innocent women who had been set free at Pierce Armstrong's farm two years before were only one small example of their commitment to sparing innocent lives whenever possible. Strict adherence to a code of right and wrong were part of The Man's personality, and he saw to it that those who followed him understood his principles.

El Toro's surveillance man had seen what had happened in the cavern on his monitors. He knew that the world, as he had known it, was about to end. The time of the mighty El Toro was over. To heighten the probability of saving his own skin, he did not say a word to anyone. He abandoned his post, took an escape passageway through a door hidden behind a storage shelf and ran in fear for his life.

He ran to the end of the tunnel, which exited to the outside world near the edge of a cliff above the secret underground hideaway. He burst from a camouflaged door into the glaring sunlight. With an assault rifle in his hands and a pistol on his belt, he was ready for anything.

He had gone just three steps before a bullet passed through his skull sending him somersaulting over the cliff.

Rick's perimeter team entered the hideout and began moving through the secret tunnel into the complex.

Without the men in the cavern, the dead surveillance expert, and the two men in the holding area near the Death Machine, El Toro's security forces in the compound were dwindling fast. Even in such small number his men were very good, but Rick's men were far better.

Carlos Delgado was a manager with a food importing company in Mexico City. He was tall, athletic, married with two children, and had an MBA from Wharton at the University of Penn. He was also gifted in hand-to-hand combat, martial arts, weapons, and explosives.

Sebastian Guerrera served as senior vice president with a logistics company in Costa Rica. He appeared to be a man who loved life, laughter and the ladies, and he was known as a bit of a playboy because his family had money. In reality, he was deadly serious about his combat skills, spoke three languages, and was a former SEAL team member. When The Man Who Loved the Gulf showed up at the training camp each year, Guerrera was the man in charge.

At 5'7" and 160 lbs., Ramiero Vargas was the smallest man in the outfit. He spent his days running a banana plantation owned by The Man Who Loved the Gulf. His physical strength and skills were legendary in The Man's army. He held all the records set at the camp for physical training. Despite being well-liked by everyone and gracious in manner, he was also one of the deadliest men in The Man's employ.

Fortuno Morales, a tall man who had the grace and dexterity of a cat rounded out Rick's inside team. He was lean and muscular with a permanently amused look on his face. He was second-in-command at a massive farming operation in Argentina. When winter came to the northern hemisphere a lot of fresh produce was shipped north from the huge farm. Morales loved hand-to-hand combat, and he was one of the younger men in the group at age twenty-five.

All of the people in The Man's army were exceptional in one way or another. What they had in common, aside from their military training, was that they were loyal to their employer far beyond his ability to pay them. Their kind of loyalty could not be bought with money.

Fortuno and Ramiero made their way into the top floor of the compound and were happy to discover that no one was waiting to ambush them. Level Four, with the three doors that accessed the escape route to the cave, the door to the stairway, and the door to the bomb and torture chamber, was where Adrienne and Chuck had been held. This was also where the armory was located. The highest of the levels of El Toro's hidden complex housed common areas, including the kitchen and dining spaces, a theater room outfitted with comfortable seats and a large flat screen TV equipped with surround sound. Here, El Diablo's favorite movies were shown over and over again to the dismay and consternation of his men.

Fortuno and Ramiero searched every room, closet, and cabinet as they made their way through a recreation room with ping pong and air hockey tables, a fully equipped gym, and a meeting room large enough for twenty-plus people.

They were amazed when they got to the armory. The number of weapons, amount of ammunition, calibers, and configurations were enough to equip a lot of people to do an incredible amount of damage. El Toro evidently kept as many weapons in his mountain fortress as he did in Lago.

"This guy's prepared for anything," Fortuno said.

"Except his present situation," Ramiero said.

The two men moved on past a surveillance room equipped with latest state-of-the-art-gear, and stopped outside what appeared to be El Toro's private suite.

"Cover me," Fortuno said, working quickly to short the access panel outside the door while Ramiero stood guard with his rifle raised.

"We're good," Fortuno said.

The two men stood at either side of the unopened door.

"We go on three," Fortuno said.

Ramiero nodded.

As Fortuno reached a count of three he triggered the door access and the two of them burst into El Toro's bedroom. They immediately swept the lavishly appointed room, closing the distance from one end to the other within seconds.

"It's clear," Ramiero said.

"Time to head downstairs," Fortuno said.

They exited the bedroom and made their way to the third level of the compound.

Level three was devoted to a massive vault where Ernesto Ruíz kept part of his vast fortune.

"There must be nearly five hundred million dollars in here," Ramiero said, surveying the cash, precious gems, gold coins and bullion El Toro stashed in his private vault.

"Word is he keeps half his fortune in banks around the world," Fortuno said. "Now we know where he keeps the other half."

They cleared a room full of servers that appeared to be devoted solely to accounting systems for tracking El Toro's wealth and possessions, but there was no sign of the madman or his army.

Carlos and Sebastian weren't so lucky. When they opened the door off the steel stairway that led to Level Two they were greeted with gunfire.

They returned fire, killing one of El Toro's men and wounding another.

"You hit?" Carlos asked.

"Grazed," Sebastian answered. He had a slight wound on his upper left arm. "I'll survive."

The men's sleeping quarters, bathing, and toilet facilities were located on this second level. There were also three rooms where the men took the women they kidnapped before turning them over to

El Diablo for his machine. These rooms were decorated like something out of a palace complete with luxurious beds and furnishings. The women were led to believe that they would be safe there, which added to their terror when they were forcibly removed from the rooms and dragged to the horror that lay on the lowest level.

Carlos spotted poorly hidden wiring leading to a hidden camera high in the corner of one of the rooms.

"El Toro likes to watch," he said, motioning for Sebastian to move on, out of the camera's sight line.

They cornered and killed two of El Toro's protective squad in a storage room full of paper goods and other supplies.

The men continued making their way through the compound, hunting for El Toro and cutting down any of his men that remained.

CHAPTER 42

El Toro had lost count of how many women he had tortured and killed with his bare hands, knives, guns, and in his beloved Death Machine. Until the contraption from Hell had been designed and created, he had settled on less dramatic methods for destroying helpless victims. The names of the ones he'd slaughtered before the machine existed would never be known, but the names of those who had died in the machine had all been carefully recorded in the book that lay next to the controls on the podium above the machine. His Glock lay there as well.

He was standing roughly a dozen feet from the door to the tunnel when it burst open and a man dressed in fatigues that resembled those worn by the men in his army along with a woman in what looked like low cut combat boots, military green shorts, and a white tee-shirt without markings entered on the far side of the chamber.

El Toro had very little time to take the two in and assess the situation. The man had a pistol in his right hand and a rifle in his left. The woman carried a pistol, and there was a military-style combat knife in a sheath on her hip.

He did not recognize the man, whose face was covered with the black camo used to disguise soldiers in the field. El Toro judged the man to be as big as himself, and he looked fit.

The woman's dark hair was cut short, and her eyes were set wide and green in color.

Fear flashed up his spine. He knew instinctively that everything was wrong, and that nothing would ever be right again. He instantly forgot the pain in his head, neck and shoulders, and he reacted instinctively, charging both of them, trying to grab the woman to throw her in front of the man.

It didn't work. Ernesto had smashed, beaten, gouged, and ripped so many women that he expected nothing but weakness and whimpering from them. When he tried to grasp the woman's arm, she moved with dazzling speed.

He found himself flying through the air, his head and neck smacking into the side of the Death Machine as he landed. Stunned, he jumped up immediately, his rage building like a volcano within him.

The man had stepped aside to give the woman room, and El Toro charged at her like the bull he was.

With a move that he had never seen in any training before, the woman sent him headlong into the rock wall of the chamber. The blow knocked him nearly unconscious.

"A mere woman will not do this to the great El Toro!" he shouted, staggering to his feet as he gathered his wits. Roaring expletives, he charged her again.

He nearly reached her, but the man stepped between them and smacked Ernesto in the face with an open palm. The blow whipped his head to the left, and he missed his target and slammed into the floor, sprawling awkwardly before them.

He rose again. A lesser man would have stayed on the floor, but El Toro had another idea in mind. He stood wavering on his feet, swinging his head back and forth like a bull, and then feinted, pretending to charge again. Instead of heading for them, he went in the opposite direction this time, lunging back toward the Death Machine. He reached the console and hit two switches.

The machine whirred to life with a deadly metallic sound, but the other switch activated a nearby elevator beyond a set of closed lattice like doors at the other side of the room.

The distraction worked. Rick and Maria looked in the direction of the noise and saw something huge and heavy on the floor of what was obviously a massive cargo elevator.

El Toro grabbed his Glock and squeezed off two rounds. One round grazed Rick's right temple, while the second burrowed into the wall above him.

Maria returned fire instantly. Her shot hit El Toro in the right shoulder and spun him around. He yelled in pain, his trigger hand hung useless at his side.

Maria looked to Rick. His wound was bleeding but superficial.

He wiped blood to keep it from going in his eyes. "Take him," he said. "I'll try to stop the elevator. He sent that damn thing to the surface."

Maria was moving before Rick finished his sentence.

The control console was set on a mechanical arm that raised and lowered it. It was at its lowest point now, and when Maria rounded the wide console El Toro lunged at her again.

She sidestepped his clumsy attack and squared up to take him on.

"No woman on earth can stand against me and live!" El Toro snorted. His shoulder was bleeding profusely, and the pain was intense, but he did not care.

"You will die here by my hand, along with the many others that have done so before you," Ernesto said.

"I fully intend to kill you first," Maria said.

"When I activated the elevator, the bomb clock was automatically turned on. When the bomb reaches the surface it will go off in five minutes. The blast will vaporize everything. There will be nothing left of this place but a deep crater. Everything from Lago to Juarez will be destroyed as well."

"Your hellish town has already burned," Maria spat.

At this, Ernesto's hatred overflowed it's scant bounds. He screamed as he reached for her, but Maria easily avoided him and kicked him from behind as he passed her. He went sprawling on his face again, breaking his nose on the unforgiving stone floor.

The new pain was excruciating. He lay there in agony, and then his rage pushed its way to the surface again. He rolled onto his back. Blood was streaming from his nose and his eyes were filled with the sting of tears. He looked up at her standing above him. If hatred alone could have raised him upright, he would have gotten to his feet, but he lay there and smiled up at her, his lips curled in a sneer.

"Pronto, serás nada más que polvo!" he snarled. "You will soon be nothing but dust. Your skin will burn, every part of you will be burned with atomic fire, and you will not even have time to scream!"

"¡Callaté!, o te mataré ahorita," Maria answered him, her tone no less biting than his. "Shut up or I'll kill you right now."

She held her Glock steady in the classic two-handed grip, the barrel fixed on his forehead.

"Go to hell!" Ernesto shouted. I will speak if I— "

He didn't get to finish his sentence. Maria landed a well-placed kick between his legs. His tirade ended in a howl of pain.

Fortuno and Ramiero reached Level One seconds after Carlos and Sebastian. The four men entered the chamber amidst Ernesto's screams.

"Radio the SEALS," Rick said. "The bomb is above ground. I don't think we have much time— "

"Got it, Boss," Sebastian said. He spoke into his handheld briefly, then turned to Rick and the others.

"They're already on it.," he said. "When it hit ground level up top two of them were at it in seconds. Sounds like they know what they're dealing with."

"Well, if they can't stop it from going off, none of us will be going home," Fortuno said.

"I'm betting on the SEALs," Rick said. "Prayer might be wise, too!"

"Who's this guy?" asked Fortuno.

"Yeah," said Carlos, "is this the great El Diablo himself?"

Ernesto screamed in rage, but his broken nose made it sound like a burbled bleat.

"No one calls me that name. I am El Toro— "

"Yeah, maybe so," Sebastian said, laughing. "But it looks like Maria made hamburger out of you, muchacho!"

"Rick, look at this," Maria said. "This is unbelievable."

She had picked up the journal and was thumbing through it. She handed it to Rick as one of his men was bandaging his head.

Rick took the book and opened it. He read page one and the

date. He scanned the first column of names and the dates. He turned to the next page. There were more names and dates. Notes were scribbled here and there detailing what El Toro had done to his victims. Ages were also written in the book. The list went on and on.

When he saw that some victims were only children, his rage grew.

CHAPTER 43

On the hill above the hidden fortress two members of SEAL Team were working feverishly to stop the bomb. CPO Dick Zabela had the task of disarming the bomb. His talent was based on years in the field. To say that he practiced all the time was to put it mildly. Before Zabela had joined the navy he had spent a year studying to be a priest. His code name was Father Z. He believed strongly in the power of prayer, and his buddies respected him for it. No one was better at his job, and they all knew that when Zabela was called in on a mission that life could get very interesting.

Lieutenant "Spence" Spengler was the second man on the task. Other SEAL Team members stood by watching them work.

"There's no need to take cover," Spence said. "If the damn thing blows up there won't be anything left to clean up."

"This isn't anything I've encountered before," said Zabela, "and I'm good enough at what I do to know that sooner or later the odds are not in one's favor."

SEALs are the most pragmatic of men. They stood calmly, bravely by as CPO Zabela studied the bomb.

"Time?" Zabela asked.

"We've got three minutes and fifteen seconds left, Dick," Spence said. "What can I do to help?"

"Hand me the cutters and pray," the CPO mumbled.

Zabela was known for nerves of steel. The man had a well-deserved reputation for being unflappable.

"Two minutes, thirty seconds," Spence said.

"I said pray, not complain," said Zabela, trying to concentrate. "Come on! Where's the damn wire?"

"Which one?" asked Spence.

"The red one," Zabela mumbled. "There's no red one—"

"Maybe the tech was colorblind," Spence managed to joke. "One minute, forty-five seconds," he said.

"That's it!" Zabela said. The CPO reached out with wire cutters and snipped a grey wire. "Dammit!" he said, livid.

"One minute," Spence said. "Should I make confession, too?"

"Wait, there!" Zabela cried and snipped a green wire.

This time, the timer froze. Zabela sat back, satisfied.

"Fifty seconds," Spence said. "That's cutting it close."

Zabela grinned at Spengler. "Are you getting anal on me, Lieutenant? We're alive!"

We have to get this thing to El Paso. This is a big bomb. It would make a very big hole, and all of us would now be standing muster in front of the real commander-in-chief, trying to explain why we do what we do."

"Well, before we send the call to him," Spence said, "We should let the team below know they are safe."

"Right you are," Zabela said. He radioed the news back to the main team.

Rick was still engrossed in the journal when Maria said, "The bomb has been disabled, Rick!"

Rick, however, was not listening. He put the journal down and smiled at El Toro with no warmth.

"Get up," he said. "Stand on your feet!"

Ernesto rose to his feet. Glaring at Rick, he said, "I am your prisoner and you will treat me correctly. Your code demands it!"

"We don't take prisoners," Rick replied.

"But you're American military," El Toro sputtered. He put his hands behind his back, expecting to be cuffed.

Rick looked at the control console. He reached out and hit the button that would stop the machine. The whine of its motor slowed and stopped.

"Maria, take a look at that thing," Rick said. "See how it opens."

Maria stepped to the machine.

Sebastian and Carlos stood nearby with weapons trained on El Toro. They were ready to shoot if he moved.

Sweat broke out on the madman's forehead as Maria examined the capsule.

"There are four locks positioned on the top of it," she said. She released them and that the whole upper lid lifted up, much like a coffin.

"How sadly fitting," she said, "given the fact that so many have died in this...thing."

El Toro was shaking now. "I am your prisoner," he pleaded. "You must take me to your superiors. What the hell do you think you're doing?"

"No, in that you are wrong, El Diablo," Rick said, pacing in front of him. "We're not American military. We're private contractors. We answer to no one. Get in the machine."

Fear spread wide over El Toro's face. "Please, no! Don't do this to me! Please!"

"How many?" Rick began. "How many of your victims begged you not to hurt them? How many screamed inside that thing to be released? How many children and women? Surely, more than every bone in your body. You will now feel their pain. Now, get in the machine!"

The rage in Rick's face made Ernesto take a cautionary step back, only to be caught in the unbreakable grip of Fortuno and Rameiro.

"Please, I have millions," the babbling large man said. "Take the money and let me go!"

Rick finally broke. "We have your money!" he roared and the sniveling man. "It is no longer of use to you. Get into the damn machine! Now!"

With a mighty thrust, El Toro broke the hold the two men had on him and rushed at Rick. He was like a freight train smashing into an immovable wall.

Rick released his anger, hitting the rushing man in the face with all his power, pivoting and stepping out of the way in a fluid motion. The maniac crashed into the wall behind him and lay moaning on the floor.

"Seal him inside!" Rick roared again.

His companions had never seen Rick in this state. Fortuno and Rameiro joined Carlos and Sebastian. They quickly picked El Toro up and carried him to the machine.

El Toro fought them all the way. He was a big and heavy man, and his strength was multiplied by his fear. He thrashed and screamed in vain as they placed him in the machine.

He lashed out at them, but Carlos subdued him with a punch to the face.

Sebastian and Fortuno quickly put the restraints on Ernesto and stepped away.

"Maria, close the lid and lock him in," Rick said, regaining some composure.

Maria smiled sweetly at El Toro, even as he screamed a torrent of curses at her.

"I've read the names of the women and children you put into this machine," she said. "Now, the last thing you are ever going to see is a woman's face."

She closed the lid and locked it.

Ernesto's screams and curses and pleading echoed through the chamber.

Rick stepped behind the control console and studied the levers, knobs, and dials. It was clear that the machine was unlike anything that any sane person could have imagined. There were many, many things the machine could do to a victim. Rows of toggle switches activated various functions. Levers and knobs enhanced other functions. There were minimum and maximum settings clearly marked.

Everything was labeled in Spanish. A set of levers said "Elevation." A second set said, "Rotation." A third set said, "Speed."

Maria joined Rick. She pointed and said, "Looks like he had hours of fun in this hell hole. I can't believe someone would do this to anyone."

Rick shuddered recalling what had been done to him in another chamber beneath the ground by an equally insane man. He studied the console, and then turned and looked at Maria. "I have no stomach for this. I'd just as soon shoot him and be done with it."

Maria said, "You've read their names. Their families need to know what happened to them. This journal is going to solve a lot of crimes. How do you want to proceed?"

"I don't want to prolong this," Rick said. He seemed like his normal, sentimental self again. "He loved to hurt people. My father has always said that the punishment should fit the crime. There's a maximum setting for everything. There is a master power switch that starts everything at the same time."

Maria reached out and snapped all the switches one-by-one to maximum. She punched the master power switch and the machine roared to life at full power. El Toro's screams were incredible, but they lasted only a few moments. The capsule rose up on its complex support system and whirled at a sickening rate of speed.

"What are you doing, Maria?" Rick asked, his face pale in the light.

"Making sushi," she replied, the same light reflecting in her eyes.

After seeing Ernesto off, Rick and his team made their way back to the surface. The SEALS were waiting, and a huge chopper of the type that carried very heavy loads to construction sites appeared overhead. Engine roaring, blades whirling, it sent a huge cloud of dust flying everywhere. The pilot lowered a huge steel skid, and the SEALs attached massive cables to the bomb. The chopper lifted the bomb and lowered it very gently onto the skid, where it was then secured with chains and heavy tie-downs. A system of links had been attached to the chains, and the chopper pilot positioned the lift line. SEALS secured the bomb to the line, and it was gently lifted until it and the chopper disappeared into the sky.

"We found this guy in a cell on Level One," Rick said.

Fortuno led a handcuffed man along behind him.

"Says he's seen a lot of people die in the machine," Rick said. "He's willing to talk."

In fact, the man was talking so much Sebastian told him to shut up.

Rick spoke to Lieutenant Spengler, "This place is all yours. It's unbelievable. There is an armory of weapons, and the vault has millions of dollars in it. The S.O.B. had a machine to torture and kill people. You're not going to believe it when you see it. It's the most horrible thing I've ever seen. Whoever designed the thing must have been one twisted freak."

Rick ran a hand through his dark hair. "Ernesto kept a journal," he continued. "It should be turned over to the right people in Mexico. It's going to solve a lot of murder cases." He handed the journal to Spengler.

"We'll secure the place," Spengler said. "The commander-in-chief says the money is going to be used to help the families of the victims, both here and in El Paso. I understand that the records in the vault show a lot of other money and property the S.O.B. owned. Apparently, they are going to track it all down and include it in the money to help the families and any who survived in the US."

CPO Zabela approached the two men.

"Meet Chief Petty Officer Father Z," Spengler said, introducing Zabela to Rick. "He's the bomb expert who neutralized that sucker with less than a minute to go."

"And you are—?" Spengler said as he and Zabela extended their hands.

Rick shook both men's hands. "We don't have names," he said, "and we were never here."

The SEALS laughed.

"You guys sound like us," Zabela said. "It's nice to know there are others who do this kind of thing."

"Maybe," Rick said. "But you guys do this for a living. We don't, and frankly we don't want your job. This was a special case we were called in on because we speak the language and look the part. If there ever is a next time, and I sure hope there won't be, I would rather we back you up than the other way around."

"Point taken," Spengler replied. "So, what happens now?

"We say goodbye," Rick said with a smile.

Two choppers descended as the SEALS and Rick's team shook hands all around.

One SEAL approached Maria, handing her a slip of paper while bashfully inviting her to dinner. She took it and looked at him.

"I don't fraternize with warriors," she said. Smiling, she slipped the paper in a pocket, turned, and walked toward one of the waiting choppers.

Rick, who was standing nearby, looked the SEAL in the eye. The man was handsome and well-built. His blue eyes stared back at Rick.

"What's her name?" the SEAL asked.

"Can't tell you," Rick said, "but she's the one who took out Ernesto. I would not mess with her if I were you."

The SEAL smiled, "No kidding? Well, if she is that good I might want to marry her. It would make for an interesting life."

"If you survived it," Rick said with a laugh. "She'll call you if she wants to."

The SEAL saluted him. "Thank you for your service."

Rick returned the salute. "You have a good day, soldier. Gotta go now. Maybe we'll meet again, maybe not, but stay well, my friend."

Rick turned and walked to the chopper. He climbed aboard and strapped himself into the empty seat next to Maria.

"What did he say to you?" she asked.

"He wanted to know your sign," Rick said, grinning.

Maria jabbed him in the side. "What did you say?"

"I told him to be careful," Rick said. "Then again, SEALS are wild and crazy guys."

"Just like me," Maria said, grinning.

"I won't argue with you about that," Rick said.

"See that you don't," she said with a pointed finger.

"Yes, ma'am," Rick said. He smiled and closed his eyes. He drifted off to the whir of the propellers.

CHAPTER 44

President Michael Stonebreaker and Vice President Eric Dryden sat in the Oval Office with the mysterious man from The Movement, known to them only as Mr. Smith. They discussed details of the successful operation in Mexico and reviewed the latest intelligence report.

When the update had been shared, Michael said, "The bomb was big. We can thank God the SEALs were able to keep it from detonating. The experts believe it was shipped up through the Gulf of California to Sonora, then off-loaded onto a truck and taken to Ernesto's compound."

"Whose ship?" the mysterious man asked.

The vice president said, "We believe it was Iranian."

"Isn't that a bit brazen on their part?" Mr. Smith asked.

"You could say that," Michael said. "Eric and I have been discussing what to do about it. Those folks have put their noses in places where they don't belong for decades. They suffer from delusions of grandeur. We've had quite enough of this nonsense. Once the issue south of the border is on its way to being corrected we intend to deal with them. The world needs to become safer for everyone."

Eric added, "Strength through intimidation is one thing, but the kind of power we have is beyond their ability to grasp. They simply don't understand who they're messing with, or the consequences that will come from their actions. "

"Did they build the thing?" Mr. Smith asked.

"No, but they delivered it," Eric said. "They want to be a super power and rule the world with an iron fist, and they would kill us all if they could, but the device was built by other actors."

"Then who built it?" Mr. Smith asked.

"The chubby little fellow in the East," Michael said. "Or rather, his people put it together. He sold it to the wackos who planned to bring it into our country. His hands are very dirty."

Michael's gaze was steady, and his eyes were cold. "Provocation has been part of terrorist-backed plans for years. Start a fire here, a riot there, and engineer a coup somewhere else. Mix it up, and do your best to deceive the West on all fronts. Those who lead Europe are afraid to act because their nations are filled with those who dream of throwing them down. Our southern border might as well have been a sieve for thirty-plus years. They have come here, as well, riding in trucks, walking through the night, and being picked up and hidden in our cities. We have rounded up scores of them since we came to the White House. In the past two years my policy has been to act and not discuss it with the media. If they were aware of it they would be screaming bloody murder on the nightly news.

"These people have come here for one purpose: to slaughter our people and take over this country. That isn't going to happen. As we sit here today, Special Agent Goss and the FBI are breaking down doors all over this country. The director of the FBI is one of ours; Goss handpicked him to be in charge of this effort. I sleep better because I know the kind of man he is. Within the month we will have rounded up as many of these people as we can. We don't know where all of them are just yet, but this isn't going to stop until we've found every last one of them. I will not allow another 911 in our nation if we can avoid it. I want our people to be safe."

"I agree that you must find all of them," Mr. Smith said, "but what about our home-grown variety who are radicalized by way of social media brainwashing?"

"We are ridding ourselves of the sleepers who have been planning to emerge in public places and kill innocents," Michael said. "They're to be sent to Gitmo. I won't permit them on our soil any longer. Goss is our point man in this operation. He has been given the authority to clean house. There will always be nuts who think they can get away with doing horrible things to people for the sake of impressing their peers or the leader of some radical cause," Michael said. "We will deal with them."

Eric said, "As to the bomb the operatives planned to bring here, well, we have a plan that is shaping up now. We are seeking the right moment, and it will be soon. I worked in Black Ops before I took this job. I maintain all of my contacts here and around the world. The unexpected is a powerful way to make a statement. Our enemies do such things all the time. Now, it's our turn."

"So, what exactly are you going to do with the bomb?" Mr. Smith asked.

"We are going to return it," Michael said.

Mr. Smith started to ask a question. "You don't mean—"

"I said that we've had enough nonsense," Michael said. "We're going to make a clearly understood statement."

The men in the room were silent following Michael's remark.

Michael continued. "The date has been selected for the invasion of Mexico, and ships and troops are gathering at nearly every point of the compass. It would take place before President Calderón and I make our joint announcement to the United States and Mexico. The invasion will be swift and sure. There will be no pre-announcement of intentions in the American mainstream media as there have been from the previous administration again and again."

"Sounds like it's time to get President Calderón on the line," Vice President Eric Dryden said.

"Agreed," said Michael.

Next, he spoke directly to Mr. Smith. "Only Mexican President Calderón has been forewarned," Michael said, "and I want to be sure to acquaint my new friend and ally with the details as thoroughly and gently as I can.

"I've spoken to the directors of The Movement, and now with you. With this phone call, I intend to deliver a detailed explanation to the Mexican president."

Michael picked up the phone and instructed his secretary to place a call to President Calderón, and then waited to be connected.

The two men briefly exchanged greetings, and then Michael got to the point of the call.

"The US military mission is three-fold," he explained. "We will work seamlessly with Mexican authorities, maintain the peace, and eradicate the cartels. The problems we face are complicated by Mexican federal, state, and local authorities corrupted by the cartels, and by Mexican citizens who themselves serve the cartels in one way or another."

"Finding out who's who will take enormous resources of time," President Calderón said.

"Yes, and for that reason I am requiring that the mission be open-ended, at least publicly," Michael said. "Unlike with the previous US administration, there is no timeline that will be proclaimed to anyone. It will take as long as it takes."

"The problems between Mexico and the United States are not going to go away in a day, a week, or even a decade," President Calderón said, "but we have to make a beginning."

"President Calderón," Michael said toward the end of their conversation, "I give you my word that I am as near as the telephone day or night. We can do this, but only if we have, as Henry would say, our brother's back. I have yours and you have mine. Let's do this together."

"You have the promise of my utmost cooperation, Mr. President," President Calderón said.

"Good," Michael said. "I'm confident that together, our two nations can achieve the success in eradicating the cartels and normalizing our shared borders that has eluded us for too long."

Michael hung up the phone and looked solemnly into the faces of the mysterious Mr. Smith and Vice President Eric Dryden.

"This is going to be a war," he said. "If the people on one side can be described as hardened criminals with no problems killing others, what they are about to face is the best military force in the world, trained to make every possible kind of warfare."

To Michael, the endgame was simple: to rid Mexico of such people forever. "It will be a new experience for these thugs; and one they will not survive."

"The cartels will not go gently into the night," Mr. Smith said. "It will be a hard and bloody war."

"And potentially a prolonged one," Eric Dryden added.

"I know," Michael said. "We're prepared."

Mr. Smith paused for a moment before asking, "Will you pray with me?"

The men bowed their heads. Michael felt surely that if prayer rather than politics had guided more decisions made in the Oval Office by past administrations, America would have been a very different place.

CHAPTER 45

For North Koreans, October 10th marks the anniversary of the founding of the North Korea Bureau of the Communist Party of Korea in 1945, one of the predecessors of the Worker's Party of today. The event is celebrated with military parades, speeches and tributes to past leaders. People turn out in the millions for the annual celebration and receive rations of food for their participation.

At around two in the morning, several people in Pyongyang thought they heard a strange sound near the Arch of Triumph. The sight that greeted them at dawn was a massive object on a huge wooden skid next to the arch. People who approached it heard it ticking ominously. They ran in fear and contacted local authorities.

The authorities, who chose to examine the object initially through field glasses rather than approach it, became even more terrified, and contacted their superiors.

The superiors decided to examine the ticking box with a helicopter from the air, fearing it might indeed be a bomb. The chopper crew flew high above the object, and what they saw convinced them that the supreme authorities should be called.

Someone woke up the chubby little fellow to tell him the bad news. That made him angry because he had been having a wonderful dream about being tall enough to star in the NBA. When they explained the problem to him, he turned pale.

General Bahk, one of several vice-marshals present, was the first to speak.

"Supreme Leader, the device appears to be a nuclear bomb—and a very big one, at that," he said.

Their leader listened as the heads of his defence force began to panic.

"How can we evacuate a city of millions of people? Where would they go?" Vice Marshal Choe asked.

"How long do we have?" General Rhee asked. "The thing is ticking, after all."

"No one has any guess as to when it might explode," Vice Marshal Bahk said.

"Shall we call out the army, air force, and navy?" asked General Ghim, Chief Strategy Officer.

"You are advocating we go to war?" asked Choe. "Send off missiles? What?"

Finally, General Rhee suggested that they begin the evacuation immediately.

"We send a team," he explained further, "—that could be sacrificed of course—dressed in radiation-proof gear to examine the bomb and see if it can be defused."

Vice Marshal Bahk looked for a reaction from the supreme leader. Rhee was the same general who had authorized the sale of a strikingly similar looking device to a contact a year before.

General Rhee felt a trickle of sweat run down the back of his neck. The supreme leader was strangely silent, offering no immediate response to his suggestion. He wondered why the thing ticking in the square so closely resembled the bomb he had sold a year ago, but he said nothing about this to anyone. No sense adding insult to injury. He also had no desire to be fed alive to hungry dogs.

Finally, the waiting group was given an aswer from their supreme leader. The evacuation of the city would begin.

Within the hour the team was organized and dispatched to Triumph Return Square in Pyongyang. Dressed in their protective suits, they approached the ominous bomb. The ticking had grown louder and more threatening.

General Rhee had suggested where they should look on the body of the device for a panel that would allow them access to its inner workings, but there was no such potential access visible.

The ticking grew louder. Massive speakers somewhere inside the device amplified the horrible ticking. They could clearly see now that the device was indeed a bomb. The team stood around, watching helplessly as the ticking grew louder. Within moments the sound had grown so loud that the men fought their natural inclination to run.

Suddenly, the ticking stopped.

A gong began ringing. It sounded like Big Ben in England, and it struck twelve times. Then, when they expected to become part of a nuclear cloud, an amazing thing happened. An opening they had not noticed before appeared on the top of the bomb and a rectangular sign roughly two meters wide and two meters high rose into the air and, with a click, locked in place.

A message, written in Korean, was clearly visible to all of them.

It read:

Attention Leaders of the DPRK,

We have returned your 'gift' to us. Children should not play with matches or they will be burned. The grown-ups will come and punish them. Unless you behave yourselves from now on, we will come at a time of our choosing when you least expect it. You will never know when we are coming and the 'gifts' we bring to you will function properly.

Happy 'Founder's Day!' Enjoy your gift!

While the bomb-defusing team felt incredible relief, back at KPA headquarters the anger and embarrassment among the leadership was huge.

"How could anyone bring such a thing as this hoax into the capital" Vice Marshal Bahk sputtered.

"How could it be placed so delicately in such a public spot without anyone knowing it?" General Ghim demanded of no one in particular.

"What else are our enemies capable of?" General Rhee added.

Beginning with the supreme leader, one by one everyone seated at the long conference table turned his attention to General Rhee.

"I can explain—" the general began.

Ultimately General Rhee admitted to orchestrating the sale of a bomb very much like the thing parked by the Arch of Triumph. The bomb had been placed aboard a ship, and off it went, with the hoped for result of a massive explosion on American soil.

"Something must have gone wrong," General Rhee continued, now wringing his hands and in visble distress.

"If it had exploded in the States, no one would have known for sure that we were responsible." He leaned dangerously close to the supreme leader, his voice almost pleading.

"Your botched plan isn't even undergirded by a desire to gain status as a nuclear superpower!" the supreme leader shouted, slamming a chubby fist onto the table. "Those frenzied zealots in some forsaken place in the Middle East would have claimed immediate credit!"

General Rhee was not fed to the dogs. Because of his rank, instead he was stripped, covered with shark bait and ordered to swim the Pacific toward the United States.

The odds were not in his favor.

Iran's status as one of the top twenty oil producing countries in the world was just one of the reasons it was kept on The Movement's radar. Not long before the attack on El Paso, satellite data showed an Iranian cargo ship traveling into the Gulf of California and exiting the area two days later. Heavy fog over the water had obscured the vessel for twenty-four hours, but The Movement had proof that the ship had been carrying the bomb that ended up in El Toro's hideout.

Every February 11th since 1979 Iranians have celebrated National Day to commemorate the triumph of the Islamic Revolution, the overthrow of Shah Pahlavian, and the birth of the Islamic Republic under the direction of a supreme leader. The leaders of The Movement chose this day to deliver a special message to Arshad Turani, Supreme Leader of Iran and his Guardian Council.

In the early morning of the February 11th following the destruction of El Toro and his mountain hideaway, citizens in the Iranian capital city of Tehran awoke to a strange sight in Azadi Square. Not far from the astonishingly beautiful Freedom Monument, which itself is a magnificent structure more than 160 feet tall and constructed of 8,000 perfectly cut blocks of white marble, the people's eyes were fixed upon a large wooden crate sitting atop a wooden skid. Written on the side of the crate in Persian was a message: "Open with Care."

No one rushed to examine the crate. Supreme Leader Turani immediately dispatched members of the Revolutionary Guard to ascertain the nature of the threat and put down any attempt at a coup. And, given the unrest in the world, Turani suspected that the crate might contain a bomb.

As daylight grew stronger, revealing more of the crate to people near Freedom Tower, Turani and his counselors grew less sure about what exactly to do. President Arman Ahura stood helplessly by, grimacing as Turani glared and shook his fist at the images being broadcast from Azadi Square, neither of which would make the odd box go away.

"Shooting at the crate may not be a bad idea," the president suggested.

"What if it blows up, destroying our beautiful monument?" the supreme leader said, dismissing the idea. "Even worse, what if it is a very BIG bomb?"

"Another major concern is how to determine what is inside the crate without setting off an explosion," Counselor Hirbod Mohsen said.

Stroking his beard, he added, "This is a conundrum wrapped in an enigma and encased in a paradox."

Commander Dali Shir-Del of the Guard entered the conference room. The country's armed forces had been placed on alert.

"On your order, Supreme Leader, I am ready with an explosives team and a contingent of local troops to investigate the mysterious box," Shir-Del said, bowing before Supreme Leader Ahura.

"Excellent," Ahura said. "Get there immediately and remove this insult!"

"As you command, sir," Shir-Del said and left the room.

By noon Commander Shir-Del and a team of Iranian explosives experts had cordoned off a perimeter around the crate and Freedom Tower in Azadi Square. Long-planned festivities for the day had been put on hold, instead the square buzzed with the frantic activity of soldiers and scientists trying to figure out if the object in their midst was indeed a bomb.

Suddenly the leader of the bomb team, Ramin Hashemi, shot a hand up in the air causing all activity around the crate to halt. Beads of sweat formed on Hashemi's brow as he leaned in close to the side of the crate. He thought he heard the sound of ticking coming from inside. The sound grew louder.

"What's going on?" Commander Shir-Del demanded. Near the box the ticking was so loud he nearly shouted to be heard by Hashemi, who was standing less than two feet away.

"The ticking seems to be amplified by some sort of device," Hashemi said. "I can't guarantee that the louder it gets, it's not getting closer to doing—something." His eyebrows lifted, and he wiped sweat from his brow with the sleeve of his white lab coat.

Shir-Del spun on his heels and walked quickly to the men guarding the area around the monument and the crate. Crowds of onlookers had gathered, curious about the box and possibly thinking it was part of National Day festivities.

"Evacuate the perimeter," Shir-Del ordered.

The soldiers immediately moved out in an ever-widening circle, pushing curious by-standers farther from its center and away from the bomb.

As Commander Shir-Del turned to go back to Hashemi and the box, an ominous thing happened. The sides and ends of the crate collapsed outward as if by magic. Hashemi and the other scientists fell to the ground, fully believing they would be blown to bits.

Shir-Del remained standing, though bent low with his arm up to shield his face from the anticipated blow. When it didn't come after a second he dropped his arm and looked to the center of the circle. The box remained, surrounded by the figures of the scientists trying to take cover on the ground around the crate. A smaller version of the crate stood on the spot where the larger box had been seconds before. The ticking was now so loud that he was sure it could be heard a kilometer away.

Hashemi and the other scientists realized they were still alive. They stood and cautiously approached the pallet as the ticking grew louder, still. Before they reached the crate to try to disarm it the ticking suddenly stopped, and the sides of the new crate fell flat. All the scientists except Hashemi turned and ran for their lives. The orb of a huge bomb stood in the center of the pallet. Instantly the ticking began anew.

Shir-Del saw Hashemi standing alone near the box. To his credit, Hashemi looked afraid, but it did not appear that he was going to run. If they survived—and he was not certain at all that they would, Shir-Del vowed to commend the man to Supreme Leader Ahura.

Ramin Hashemi stared at the huge bomb sitting before him on the planks of a wooden pallet surrounded by the crates in which it had arrived. If the thing blew up now there was nothing he could do. Anything this big would vaporize him in seconds. He swallowed, closed his eyes, and stood still, praying silently.

He wasn't sure how long he'd been standing there when the ticking stopped and a great gong thundered throughout the square. He had been to London once many years before as a university student, and the sound reminded him of the chiming of Big Ben at The Palace of Westminster.

Out of the corner of his eye, Hashemi glimpsed Commander Shir-Del standing midway between the circle of dutiful soldiers and where he himself stood next to the bomb. Their eyes met, and a kind of silent resignation passed between the two men, carried on the breeze blowing across the square.

Hashemi turned back to look at the bomb before once again closing his eyes to pray. When the gong struck for the twelfth time, he fully expected to become one with the universe. He had steeled himself against eternity rushing to meet him when he heard a whirring and then a whizzing sound.

"Hashemi—" Commander Shir-Del was calling his name. He opened his eyes.

The front of the bomb was open, and he spotted a briefcase sitting inside. A minute passed...then two. He screwed up his courage and stepped forward, expecting something terrible to happen, but nothing did.

Hashemi moved closer to the "bomb" and looked carefully into the compartment. In a second Shir-Del was at his side.

"It could be a fake. All I see is this briefcase," Hashemi said. He looked over at Shir-Del. "Should I try to pick it up?"

Shir-Del shook his head slowly, and stepping between Hashemi and the bomb, gingerly inserted his own hand into the compartment.

Hashemi jumped back in terror. A green flag popped from the side of the bomb into the air. A yellow happy face smiled at them from a green background. As the flag fluttered in the breeze, he saw something written in Persian beneath the happy face.

"What does it say, Commander?" he asked.

Commander Shir-Del's face twisted in a mask of anger. "Gotcha!" he said.

They stood looking at one another in silence for a long moment.

"What madness is this?" Hashemi asked. "What should we do now?

Shir-Del was out of patience. He stepped closer to the infuriating object, grabbed the handle of the briefcase, and pulled. A deafening siren went off inside the bomb, so loud that he released the handle, and half-pushed, half dragged Hashemi toward the ring of soldiers and away from the sound.

They had covered a half the distance to the soldiers before Shir-Del realized the siren had stopped. He and Hashemi had tripped and fallen while running. He got to his knees a few feet from where the other man lay, apparently unconscious. He moved over to check the Hashemi's injuries and waved for soldiers to come tend to the scientist.

Shir-Del glared at the object. His heart was pounding and he was out of breath.

"This is insane!" he yelled, so frustrated he cursed the thing at the top of his lungs, even as he started walking toward it again.

Thousands of miles away in a city hidden far beneath the mountains of central Pennsylvania, laughter rose as the scene in Azadi Square played out on giant flat-screens in a secret communication center. On the screen, the Iranian soldier stopped at a spot about fifty feet from the pallet where the mock bomb stood. His audience could not see the anger on the man's face but his body language made it clear, he was furious.

"He's got to be close to breaking," the comptroller said from his seat at the satellite control panel. "We built the mock bombs and delivered them to North Korea and Iran. As you can see, the Iranian model has many more bells and whistles," he said to more laughter from around the room.

The Iranian began moving again. He approached the bomb, but did not reach for the briefcase. He had learned the hard way that doing that was a bad idea.

Shir-Del contemplated his next move. While he stood thinking he heard a metallic noise. He watched as a port opened at the top of the bomb-like object and something that looked to him like an audio speaker rose about a meter into the air. It stopped with a click.

Suddenly The Beatles roared, "*Can't buy me love—*" overwhelming Azadi Square with sound.

The man was so startled that he backed up, tripped over his own feet, and fell on his rear in what could pass for a slapstick routine in a silent movie. In fact, laughter filled the underground cavern. The leaders of The Movement were nearly brought to tears, as though they were watching Charlie Chaplin do a pratfall.

Shir-Del sprang to his feet in the next instant, hurrying toward the soldiers as Led Zeppelin's *Stairway to Heaven* rang out at deafening volume.

The commander was shouting to be heard over the 'Stones singing, "*I can't get no satisfaction…*" when suddenly the music stopped, replaced by the smooth voice of a silver-tongued radio DJ in perfect Persian:

> *"Hey there Guards and Guard-ettes, it's the hits that make the difference on I-Ran Radio. Yes, I ran because I'm afraid to walk! It's yours truly—here to tell you that the classic hits are coming your way—bing, bang, BOOM!"*

The word reverberated like an explosion. Soldiers on the ground dropped their weapons and covered their ears, while the few spectators remaining on the square scattered.

The disc jockey's voice continued:

> *"Yes, guys and gals, your gift to Sam-I-Am was intercepted by those who see all, know all, and know just what to do! Your ship tried to deliver, but the delivery was pre-empted, and here is the result: The Good Guys—WIN!"*

The sound of a nuclear explosion erupted from the speaker, cranked loud enough to shake the ground throughout Azadi Square.

> *"We advise you to never, ever try what you tried before because, as you can see, we know where you are, we know what you're doing, and we know how to bring you gifts when you least expect it!*
>
> *"Yes, dear friends, this is the big boss with the hot sauce, playing the hits and telling you that the next time you do the dirty deed, what comes your way will be real—and it really will go BOOM!"*

Another massive explosion of sound rocked the square, followed by a 1,000-cycle tone and the voice of an official-sounding announcer, saying, "If this had been an actual emergency, you would have been instructed to place your head between your knees and kiss the world goodbye!"

Woody Woodpecker's famous farewell blasted into the air.

Then there was nothing.

In the silence, Commander Shir-Del heard a distinct "ping." He and the soldiers watched as a large sign rose from the surface of the fake bomb.

> **You may touch the briefcase now.**
> **Give it to the "Supremes"—They'll want to read what's inside.**
> **¡Adiós, amigos!**

The speaker burst to life again as Diana Ross and The Supremes belted out, "Stop! In the name of love..."

Deep beneath the hills of Pennsylvania the laughter went on for a long time. The leaders of The Movement would long recall the incident as one of the most satisfying—and meaningful—practical jokes that had ever been played.

CHAPTER 46

When Adriana opened the door to her hotel room and saw Rick standing there with his head bandaged, she was in his arms in an instant. Their kiss was long and passionate.

When she released him, she exclaimed, "Are you alright? Of course you're not alright! What am I saying? What happened? Is it over? Did you take care of the problem? Please, tell me."

Her words came tumbling out in a rush.

Rick grinned at her. "May I come in, Ms. Santos?"

She pulled him into the room and closed the door behind him.

"Of course you can come in!" She took him by the hand and led him to a sofa in a small sitting area.

When they sat down, Rick said, "It's over, the problem has been taken care of, and I am fine. It was a shot that missed."

"Not entirely, Rick. You could have been killed!" Adriana said.

"But I wasn't, and now I am here." Rick's voice was suddenly soft. "Before I left, you said that you had given your heart to me. Did you mean it?"

Adriana blushed. "Yes. Yes, I meant it, Rick," she said in Portuguese.

Rick could see she was flustered. He smiled and said, "Sorry, I don't know the language. Could you tell me again?"

"Oh," she said in English, "Yes, you have my heart."

Suddenly shy, she looked away from him toward the window. "I've never said that to a man."

Rick reached out, and taking Adriana in his arms, he kissed her long and deeply. He stopped kissing her and looked into her eyes.

"And I have never said this to a woman.Will you marry me, Adriana?" he said.

Her eyes were wide. "Oh, Rick! I, I mean, I do feel very passionately towards you, but we just met and everything is moving so fast! And even if we were to, we must wait…until…until you know..."

Rick shook his head, placing a reassuring hand on hers.

"I understand," he said. "Because you are a woman of faith I honor you, my love. You believe in the old ways, and I respect you. I know this has moved fast as well, but this last mission in Mexico made me realize what I want in life. Calling you my beloved wife is one of the things I want most. My line of work has been dangerous, and I don't want to miss any other opportunities to be with you. Do you think your parents will find me a suitable husband?"

Adriana smiled. "My parents wanted me to marry young, and they had chosen my husband. When that didn't work out they were patient enough to allow me to seek my own life. I think they will adore you, Rick. I know I do."

Rick felt his face glowing. "I adore you, too. I am concerned though, that we live so far away from each other. I don't know if we can make this work. I can't give up who I am. I have a responsibility to my father and brothers, and I would never insist on you giving up the work you love. I want you to be happy about your choices. I'm trying not to be selfish."

Adriana reached out and gently placed her palm against his cheek. "God opens doors and provides a way when two people are meant for each other," she said.

"God and I have never had much to do with each other," Rick said softly.

"Perhaps that's because you have never been formally introduced to him," Adriana smiled. "I was raised as a believer."

"Isn't that a little strange for the daughter of a university professor with a mother who works in the world of fashion?" Rick asked.

"Perhaps," Adrianna said, "but there is nothing obvious about my parents. My grandfather was a Franciscan priest who loved God with a passion so great that he could hardly speak of it until he met my grandmother. She was incredibly beautiful, but it was hidden beneath her habit. They became friends long before they became a couple. They fell in love. It was inevitable. They had to leave the religious life behind, but they loved God so much that they made sure their children loved Him as well. They are both still alive, and quite old. They live on Manasota Key on the Gulf coast of Florida. I love to visit when I can. They are full of wonderful stories about their lives and my father as a child."

Rick watched and listened as her face softened with fond memories.

"My mother's family wasn't Roman Catholic," she continued, "but they were people who went to church regularly. She was also taught the old ways. My parents met in college, fell in love, and life began for them. They took me to church as a child and taught me that there was something far greater than man in this universe. I was twelve years old when I met God personally, but that is a story for another time."

Rick felt her pride in her faith, and somehow that made him feel proud for her.

Of his own experience, he said, "Well, my introduction to faith wasn't as grand. As I told you on the plane, I grew up in the Marine Corps. I signed up the day after I graduated from high school with my friend José Alvarez."

Rick paused, knowing he was getting close to the topic he least wanted to talk about. He knew that if he wanted to marry this woman, now was the time to be honest.

"Listen, Adriana," he said, "two years ago I almost died at the hands of a maniac. I can't go into detail, not because I don't trust you, but because of what was involved, I don't want to subject you to that. I had been sent on a mission like the one we just finished. We didn't know what to expect. Four of our men were killed, and I ended up being held and tortured. Fortunately, José got away, and my father and brothers arrived just in time to save me."

He took a deep breath before going on.

"Adriana, it got me to thinking about God and what this all

means. After José's son died, I began to question again. There is such unfairness in the world."

"I understand," Adrianna said, keeping his hand in hers. "There truly is, and you've been through so much. But it's important to have some faith, and faith in each other."

Rick smiled again, feeling her warmth. "We have a lot to talk about," he said. "Hopefully we'll have a lifetime to discuss everything. I love you, Adrianna. I've never felt this way about anyone until now."

"And I you," Adrianna said, leaning in for another kiss. She had full faith that this would be one of many.

CHAPTER 47

President Stonebreaker and President Calderón huddled over a table in a secure room in the Arena Mexico. Plans were moving swiftly into place. It was going to be a logistical challenge. American and Mexican troops would be working together. The cartels were spread widely throughout Mexico, and the intent was to move into position at lightning speed. SEAL Team would be involved, along with every branch of the military. Because of the corruption in Mexico, rapid placement into position was essential to success. The big problem would be explaining why thousands of American troops had placed their boots on the ground in sovereign Mexico overnight.

Calderón knew where the cartels were headquartered. Others in the government did as well. Police knew where they were, and so did the Mexican military. The problem had always been to move on them and take them down. They had so much money and power that the people feared them more than anyone else. The cartels continued to exist because no one wanted to be shot, stabbed, beheaded, boiled alive, burned alive, beaten to death, or killed in some other horrible fashion. People kept their mouths shut, turned their heads, and looked the other way.

Under the guise of a national conference on crime and violence, the heads of Mexican police forces gathered in Mexico City along with all of the senior military leaders. The meeting was closed to the public, press, and others who would be curious. Everyone was required to surrender all firearms and submit to security scans, and anyone suspicious was taken away for extensive questioning.

The Arena México stadium routinely holds more than 16,000 pro wrestling and boxing fans, and was chosen as the perfect place to hold the meeting.

After introductions by top officials and an explanation of the purpose of the conference, the attendees were surprised to see the president of México take the platform at the arena's center.

Surrounded by his armed protective detail, he lifted his hands like a winning prizefighter as thousands of voices cheered him.

Calderón was a man admired by the people who did their best to serve their nation. He was despised and secretly ridiculed by those who served the cartels, but no one openly mocked him.

The Mexican president stepped to the microphone. He waited for the crowd to quiet and take their seats.

"I realize that my presence here today must come as a surprise to some of you. I am here for a very special reason. As you are well aware, cartel members recently crossed our border into the United States and murdered innocent people. Our relationship with the US has never been good because millions of our people have fled across their border seeking jobs and the opportunity that they cannot find here in our country."

There was the sound of grumbling in the crowd. Several in the audience wondered where el presidente was going with this speech.

"In the recent past," Calderón continued, "we had no worries about reprisal; the previous American administration lacked the desire for confrontation. Clearly they would rather talk than act."

The grumbling increased among the crowd.

Calderón stopped speaking for a moment, his famous smile transformed into a look of anger. He slammed his fist on the podium and yelled, "Silence! Hear me! The last administration in Washington, DC is not the administration that is in power now."

Several people had risen from their seats and began moving in the aisles towards the exits, rudely turning their backs on the president of Mexico.

What happened next was totally unexpected.

Calderón then said, "Arrest them and hold them for questioning!"

The police appeared and began handcuffing those trying to leave.

The crowd became noisy. They watched as police grabbed those in the aisles. Others in the crowd who had intended to join those who had been trying to leave thought better of it and remained in their seats.

President Calderón waited patiently until the police had led the rebel-rousers out of the arena. They represented a small percentage of those present. Nearly every seat remained occupied.

"Early on the morning of the massacre in El Paso, Texas," Calderón went on, "I received a call from the president of the United States. Since then, we have spoken many times on the telephone and in person. He is not like his predecessor. I could tell you what he intends to do, but that isn't necessary. I would rather he tell you himself!"

Doors opened and a stream of armed troops began filing into the arena in pairs. To the crowd's amazement, each pair consisted of a Mexican soldier, and an American soldier. Two hundred troops formed a ring around the platform where President Calderón and others stood.

Next, a Secret Service detail appeared, and walking in the midst of it was President Michael Stonebreaker. He was accompanied by the Joint Chiefs of Staff in full dress uniform.

The surprise of the spectacle sent the crowd rushing to its feet. The deafening roar of cheers, boos, yells, and curses all mingled together rose to fill the arena.

Calderón held up his hand until the cries began to diminish.

"Please," he said, "be seated and show your respect for your president, and for the president of the United States. He has come a long way to talk to you today."

The crowd quieted as the Americans stepped onto the platform. The president of the United States was flanked by the Joint Chiefs, with the Secret Service forming a protective circle around them.

"Ladies and gentlemen," President Calderón said, "it is my pleasure to present to you Michael Stonebreaker, President of the United States."

The crowd was on its feet cheering, clapping, and whistling. Here and there a few boos rang out, but those who were corrupted by the cartels were mostly wise enough to remain silent.

President Stonebreaker came forward and joined President Calderón at the podium. They stood side-by-side as the crowd cheered. Calderón reached out and took Stonebreaker's hand in his and the two men raised their hands high. The crowd cheered even more.

They dropped their hands and Calderón said, "I want to share something with you appropriate for this moment. It is from the Holy Bible, the gospel of John, in the thirteenth chapter, beginning at verse thirty-four. 'A new commandment I give to you, that you love one another, even as I have loved you, that you also love one another.'

"These are the words of Jesus to his disciples the night before He went to the cross. I am sure that some of you are believers and others are not, but the words are true, whether you attend church or not. I would be a hypocrite if I claimed to be a man of faith. I have not been inside a church in many years. I need to go and make confession."

Calderón turned and gestured toward Michael Stonebreaker.

"You see," he continued, "I have been reminded by the man standing next to me that there is something far bigger and more important than the sound of my own voice. Love may be a strange word to hear coming from a man like me. I am, after all, a politician, and I will admit, politicians are most often driven by their own egos and the desire for power. President Stonebreaker has shown me there is a better way to govern. I will be grateful to him for the rest of my life."

The sound of the crowd faded into silence.

"We must come together in our resolve, but this is only the first step," Calderón said. "What is about to happen here in our beloved land is something few could have envisioned. Rather than explain it to you, I have invited our guest to do so. I am in total agreement with him. I believe that many of you will be convinced by what he has to say. Others here will take a wait-and-see position. Still, others will deny the truth he brings here today. Politicians, police officers, and military personnel are charged with protecting the people. At least that is part of our job description. However, we have a problem here in our nation that is not faced by many others. The time for that problem to come to an end is now. Please listen to our guest carefully. Your future, and the future of your family, depends on it."

Calderón stepped back from the podium, leaving the president of the United States standing there alone.

Michael raised his hand in greeting and the crowd cheered. He waved for the crowd to sit down, and when the noise had subsided and all sat silently Michael Stonebreaker began his address to the Mexican people in flawless Spanish.

He had begun learning the language in high school and continued through college. He had begun to practice it again when he started his studies with The Movement. When asked why he had taken up the language again after so many years, Michael's answer was simple. "With an estimated thirty-five million Spanish-speaking people in America, I have no desire to ignore more than ten percent of the population," he'd often say. "I want to be able to speak the language perfectly because I want to be president of all Americans, not just those who speak English."

Large video screens came to life above the crowd. An image of a man on a street appeared.

"This man's name was Ernesto Ruíz," Michael said. "He called himself El Toro. His men called him El Diablo, and for good reason."

The scene shifted to an image of a chamber appeared, and the camera was focused on a coffin-like machine.

"This is El Diablo's Death Machine," Michael said. "It is at torture device designed by someone who had a nightmare for a mind. It is unlike anything anyone has ever built."

The next scene showed the console and a journal lying next to the controls.

"Ernesto Ruíz's hideout was located in the hills near Juarez. The journal you see here contains the names of people tortured to death in this horrible machine. The first name is that of the man who designed and built the machine. El Diablo did not want the man to ever build one for someone else. There are one hundred and twelve names in the journal. Twenty-eight men, seventeen children, and sixty-seven women. Eleven of the children were under the age of ten."

Gasps and cries ensued from everywhere in the arena.

"They could have been your children," Michael said. "The women could have been your sisters, daughters, or nieces. The men could have been your brothers, husbands, or sons."

Cries of outrage mixed with sobs among the crowd.

The scene on the screen changed again.

"Nearly a hundred horrible tortures were built into this machine," Michael said. "It was designed to torment and kill in the most horrific ways possible, possibly even more excruciating than boiling, burning, or beheading people."

The camera showed a hand flipping switches and the machine whirring to life. The crowd watched as the machine rotated at high speed.

The next scene showed what remained of the town of Lago.

"This was where El Diablo's army was located," Michael continued. "A town called Lago, he renamed it Hell. It was burned to the ground. Over four hundred and fifty people died here."

The scene on the screen changed, showing a street in an American suburb at night, illuminated by bright lights. There were bodies lying everywhere.

"These are police videos of the scene in the El Paso suburb where El Diablo and his men murdered American citizens. Innocent people were torn from their beds, driven into the street, and slaughtered."

Michael paused for a long moment, letting the scenes on the screens play out. Then, the screens went dark.

"El Diablo and his men are no more," he said. "As to his fate, I will let you think about that. Some say that when justice is rightly served, the punishment fits the crime. I will only tell you this: his fate did."

When Michael said this a shudder ran through the crowd.

Silence descended on the arena.

The president of the United States looked at the crowd for a moment. Then, he said, "The day of the Mexican cartels is ended. The day of freedom has come! You see before you Mexican and American soldiers standing shoulder-to-shoulder." He paused before going on. "However, the scene before you is not yet complete."

A door opened and the highest ranking Mexican military leaders entered the arena. They strode down the aisle, stepped up to the platform, and spaced themselves evenly between the American Joint Chiefs of Staff.

"At a time known only to your president and myself, American troops will enter Mexico from every corner of the compass," Michael said. "They will be here at the invitation of your president and your government leaders. They will be working side-by-side with your military and police. When I said that the cartels are coming to an end, I meant it. We will be waging war on them until every last one of them has been found, tried, convicted, imprisoned, and/or executed should their personal crimes merit death."

The roar of the crowd was so loud that President Calderón stepped forward and yelled, "Silence! You will hear all that needs to be said!"

When the noise subsided, Michael continued.

"We know that some here are in the employ of the cartels. You may think us fools, but we are anything but foolish. It will be the intention of some of you to grab your cell phones when you leave here and warn your cartel contacts that we are coming. Whether you do so or not, you will be found and arrested as well. The airports and transport systems are closed to you. You will not be traveling anywhere. We are beginning a process today to clear or arrest each of you. When you are cleared you will be free to return home. If you are corrupt, we will determine your degree of guilt, and your punishment will fit the crime.

"Our troops are coming. Nothing will stop them. We will take as long as is necessary to find and destroy the cartels. Your northern border has been closed. Our warships are along your coasts, in the Gulf of Mexico and the Gulf of California. Our special forces are already in place. Our goal is to create a safe nation for all of the Mexican people. We will not be swayed from our intention. However, that is not the only reason we are here. For decades your people have been streaming over our borders in search of a better life and greater opportunity. Many have died in the attempt. Criminals have also come into our nation in search of opportunities to commit more crimes. Drug traffic over our border is horrendous. It is all coming to an end.

"If Mexico could have a healthy, vibrant economy, the need to cross the border into the United States would be limited to tourism and seeing family members in the US. We are here to help you build such an economy. It begins now. Do we want to make you another US state or territory? No! That is the last thing we want. We want Mexico to remain Mexican. We want to be good neighbors and friends. What kind or program will this require? It is one that has been designed to enhance the unique differences in all things Mexican.

"Many years of planning have gone into this program. It will be implemented carefully, with checks and balances along the way, and adjustments where necessary. It will be reviewed and guided by your people, not ours. It will affect every aspect of every occupation in Mexico, and involve resources and their preservation, energy development, farming, fishing, manufacturing, financial institutions, transportation, infrastructure, health services and hospitals, research and development, and education – especially education. Nothing has been left out.

"Some of you will be wondering why we are engaged in such a program. Because it should be obvious to you that this is going to go on for a long time. It will take many years. Why are we making such an effort? The answer is a simple one. We want peace on this continent. We live in North America, my friends. Yes, I name you friends, but if we go on with business as usual, we will be engaged in another war that could end in destroying all of us.

"When we achieve the peace we desire, it will set an example for Central and South America as well. Mexico, Canada, and the United States working together can be that shining city on a hill that the world looks to and finds desirable because of our economies and cooperation with each other. Economic competition doesn't have to sacrifice principles because of misguided or greedy people who believe it to be a zero sum game. Frankly, that's a stupid way to think and work together! On the contrary, everyone can win.

"Finally, I will leave you with this thought. You are police and military officials. Where I live, such people are charged with protecting the public from harm, both internally and externally. I am one of you. I was a military officer before I took this job. I am a combat veteran. I have known both fear and anger in battle. I got through it because of my training, my fellow soldiers, the oath I made to my country, and my God. Whatever you believe today, I ask you to embrace the situation before you. What is going to happen in Mexico will be happening with you, or without you. It would be better if you were a willing partner.

"Finally, I leave you with an old Mexican proverb to consider. Once the dog is dead, the rabies ends. Won't you join us in killing the rabid dog that is the drug cartels? Work with us to accomplish this great task; we will have your backs as you will have ours. God bless you. Thank you."

President Michael Stonebreaker stepped away from the podium and grasped President Nicolas Calderón's hand. Together they stepped between the ranks of the military heads behind them and joined hands with those men in a visual symbol of their solidarity.

Even as the crowd shouted its approval, some were thinking that it was time to find a way to flee the country, or at the very least to hide their ties with a cartel.

CHAPTER 48

The work of the film crew continued under Adriana's direction. Ray Karwel and his assistant had left for Hollywood.

Rick and Adriana had said a painful goodbye, and Rick and his people had flown to their respective homes.

When Rick walked into the living room his father and brothers surrounded and embraced him with heartfelt relief.

The Man Who Loved the Gulf said, "You didn't tell me that you got shot! Are you okay? Had I known you were going to get hurt, I would never have permitted you to go."

"What matters is that he missed," Rick said. "I am just fine, father. It's all right. We did the right thing. The Navy SEALs are fantastic! They saved the day!"

Derek said, "Tell us about it."

Rick spent the next hour recounting the tale.

When he described El Toro and the Death Machine, Duke said, "I wish we could reanimate the S.O.B. and run him through that machine a hundred times. He did that to women and kids? What kind of twisted freak would do such things to another human being? How can anybody hate that much, or be that screwed up?"

"Remember Ollie in Nebraska?" Damien asked. "He had the same kind of personality." He shook his head in disgust. "There are some really whacked people on this planet."

"Don't remind me," Rick said. "I didn't want to throw the switch on Ernesto. Thankfully, Maria stepped up and took care of business."

"Remind me not to get on her bad side whenever I see her again," Duke said.

Everybody laughed.

"She might be giving a SEAL a call," Rick said. "He gave her his number. I think he's in love."

"That would be a real battle of the sexes," The Man Who Loved the Gulf said.

The laughter went on for a long time.

"Let's go to the Gulf Maiden," The Man said. "I told my cousin that I would meet with the president of the United States to discuss doing business in this hemisphere. I need your input. You see and hear more than I do. Bring me up to speed."

"Are you sure this is a good idea, Father?" Duke asked. "We try our best to protect your privacy. Doesn't this open you up to vetting and scrutiny from now on?"

"My cousin set it up. He'll be with me, and Stonebreaker will have the head of the CIA and his brother with him. We'll meet in a totally safe location."

"The CIA? Couldn't that lead to big trouble?" Derek asked.

"What about his brother?" Rick added.

"His brother, Henry, is a Marine, and he is as level-headed as anyone could be," The Man replied. "Stonebreaker trusts him with his life, and he likes having him around. He writes speeches and offers advice. The guy works with his hands on heavy equipment. My cousin filled me in. Henry can be trusted."

"Yes, but the CIA is not something we need in our backyard," Damien said. "What about that?"

"You forget, Damien," The Man added. "My cousin is more secretive than I am. The change in leadership in this country came about because of him. They don't just owe him respect. They owe him more than anyone has ever been owed. It has been said before, but he ought to have a statue of himself on every corner. He literally saved this nation. They respect him so much that they would not do anything to make him upset. He is my only blood relative in this world. When he convinced me to do this, he said that he would have me disguised as him, and we would play out a charade. Henry Stonebreaker has never met him, and the CIA head and the president have only seen him on a couple of occasions.

"I nixed the idea. I want him beside me in that meeting. Maybe I am getting senile, but there are people outside of the four of you who can actually be trusted. We have hundreds of people who work for us who we trust every day. The people who employ my cousin are even more clandestine than I am, or the CIA, for that matter. They know all about me, and I know nothing about them. I probably never will know who or where they are, but my cousin assures me that we have nothing to fear from them. They've come to us twice for help now, and twice we have delivered on what they needed."

"It's your call," Duke said. "We know you're more careful than anyone, but we just don't want you placed in a position that's dangerous."

"I'll be fine," The Man Who Loved the Gulf said.

Rick said, "There one more thing"

"What's that?" his father asked.

"I met a woman," Rick said, deciding bluntness was best.

Derek laughed. "Hey, brother, every woman in America wants to meet you! What's new about that? Is she pretty?"

"The word, Derek, is beautiful," Rick said, with a crooked smile.

Duke laughed. He put his hand on Rick's shoulder. "So, who is this beautiful woman?"

"Adriana Santos," Rick said.

"You've all met her. She was on the Gulf Maiden at the meeting."

Damien said, "No way! She's drop dead spectacular, my brother!"

"Yes, I would agree with that," The Man said.

"I've asked her to marry me," Rick said.

His father and brothers were speechless. "But— " was all his father managed to say.

Rick laughed an easy laugh. "The look on your faces is priceless! We haven't set a date yet, and we're not sure if we can work it out because my place is here, and her work is in Rio," he said.

Duke said, "How—?"

"Well, there's much to work out still," Rick said.

Damien was the first to make a complete sentence.

"You mean the King of Broken Hearts is finally retiring from the field?" he asked. "Is this woman a sorceress? Man, what has happened to you?"

"I am in love, brother," Rick said. "I've never met anyone like Adriana. When I am with her I feel like a schoolboy. She is so intelligent it's hard to keep up with her! She is interested in everything! I talked with her non-stop from Rio to Juarez. We covered so many subjects I couldn't keep track of them. I want to spend the rest of my life with her."

Duke finally managed to say, "Whoa! You love her for her mind? What's got into you, Rick? I never thought you'd give up the ladies. You're the only guy in the world whose little black book comes in a 10-volume set! This is incredible."

Rick said, "Look, I told you what I asked her. She loves me, too. What happened in Nebraska changed me. I don't know how to explain it. When a maniac has you on a torture table it kind of puts things in perspective."

Rick looked at his father. "She is from the old world," he said. She has never been with a man. She is a believer, like your cousin. She is so good that I don't even know how to think about her. I love her with all my heart. I want more out of life, and that isn't said out of disrespect for you or my brothers. I love you and I will be your son and their brother for as long as I live. This is real. It's the most real thing that has ever happened to me. It will take time for me to sort it all out. We are in no hurry. It needs to be right.

"The truth is that if the issues involved are too difficult to resolve, she and I will end our relationship. She said that if God wants two people to be together, and they are willing to follow His leading, that their dream will come true. I'm not a believer, but I am not beyond thinking that there is something more to life than just what I want from day-to-day. I didn't mean to drop this on you this way, but you are my family. If I can't trust my thoughts and feelings with you, who can I trust?"

There was silence in the room for a long moment.

Then, The Man Who Loved the Gulf reached out and placed his

hands on Rick's shoulders and looked at him. There were tears in the older man's eyes.

"You are my son, and these are my sons," he said, gesturing to include all of them. "If God is real—and my cousin is busy convincing me that He is—I am overwhelmed by the gifts that life has given to me these past few years. It appears He may have another gift for me."

Rick said softly, "And what would that be?"

"Grandchildren!" The Man said. "I never thought I might have grandchildren. I'd like that very much."

Nothing more needed to be said.

CHAPTER 49

The invasion was set to begin at 2:00 a.m. on the second day of September. Following the meeting in Mexico City, nearly three hundred police and military personnel were still being questioned as to where their loyalties lay. The others had returned to their cities, towns, and hamlets. All were sworn to secrecy.

President Stonebreaker had placed General Avery Thompson in charge of the Americans assigned to command posts in each Mexican state. Thompson was already positioned at central command in Mexico City where he was busy laying out the invasion plans with the top Mexican military and police officials. In a joint effort, every cartel headquarters would be destroyed, and any of their members who survived the attack would be rounded up and placed in maximum security prisons without possibility of release.

The entire operation was shrouded in secrecy. Everyone involved understood that if they leaked what was about to happen, they would be arrested, stripped of rank or position within the police or military, jailed, and held until they were tried and convicted.

Calderón and Stonebreaker were not fools. They were men who understood human nature, and they had no doubt that the cartels would find out quickly what was going down. That, however, did not matter. What mattered was their mutual resolve to complete the task of eradicating the drug cartels. If it took a year, or five years, it would be done. It was irrevocable. As Michael Stonebreaker had said before the assembly in Mexico City, the day of the cartels was over.

In a joint news conference at noon on September 2nd the two presidents would stand side-by-side and tell their people what was happening. In some areas of Mexico the fighting would be all-out war. In others it would be less violent, but nonetheless every cartel compound would be razed. No matter how many cartel members were located, they would be removed from society, tried swiftly, and executed or imprisoned for life.

The forensic accounting effort would go on until every last person who had helped the cartels was found, arrested, tried, and convicted. If it took a decade, Presidents Calderón and Stonebreaker agreed, that was fine. The job would be done. No criminal was going to escape.

President Stonebreaker and Vice President Dryden met in the Oval Office to discuss the impact of the invasion and subsequent shutdown of the cartels on the United States.

"There are unique issues the US will have to face in the aftermath, obviously," Michael said. "When the flow of drugs across the border from Mexico dries up there will be consequences."

Neither man was comfortable with the thought.

"What madness would addicts inflict on others when their supply is gone?" Eric wondered aloud. "Not to mention the growing prescription drug abuse problem. Opioid addiction is devastating communities across the country."

Michael turned a page in the binder they had been reviewing. It contained the whole of The Movement's plan to revitalize and restore the government, economy, military, and people of the United States.

"The Movement, in its wisdom, has accounted to some degree for that, as well," Michael said. "They have been stockpiling drugs for some time.

"Illicit drugs from Mexico, when the door is closed and locked, will be available to addicts through hospitals and clinics—for a time," Michael said, looking up from the document.

"A media public awareness campaign is set to begin on the day of the invasion," he continued. "Addicts will learn that their illicit drug pipleine is cut off, but there will be a number of legal sources for getting the drugs and treatment they need."

"What about funding?" Eric asked.

"They will have to pay for the drugs they receive to help fund the effort," Michael said. "Mandatory drug treatment that will require them to be drug free in a reasonable amount of time will be covered by insurance, and corporations with a vested interest in retraining these men and women to become productive members of society will help foot the bill.

"Police and health officials will have their work cut out for them, but the reality of the end of the drug war will be presented to addicts everywhere," Michael said.

"At the end of a war the losing army has to stop fighting and go home," Eric said. "However, the craving for drugs is often so terrible that addicts will do anything to get relief. And those addicted to coke, meth, and heroin are in a far worse place than marijuana users."

Michael nodded. "Authorities will no doubt realize quickly how hard times will get for many of these people. Crime rates will likely spike, including violent crime. When someone is out of their mind over drugs, they will rob or even kill others to get what they want.

"Drug dealers in America are about to have their supplies terminated. No one wants to lose their cash cow, but this particular cow is about to be locked in the barn permanently." Michael drummed his fingers on his desk before going on. "A new day is coming to the illegal drug market in this country. And it's going to be difficult for those affected by drugs for some time."

"I'll get right on making the heads up calls to get the ball rolling with our state governors," Eric said. "Police forces all over will need to be prepared for what's coming this side of the border once the cartels are dismantled."

"Good," Michael said. "Unfortunately there's more to be dealt with as we shore up our southern border; there is also the issue of illegal aliens already here in the US."

"There's no question that many companies and farmers depend on workers from below the border. Undocumented workers have less of an impact on their bottom line," Eric said, "until they get caught."

"Agreed," Michael said. "Reality can be stark and unforgiving. Politicians have been screaming at each other for decades over the issue of what to do about these people. The American public has been polarized over the problem as well."

"Few things are simple when they are examined closely," Eric said, rubbing the back of his neck. "Solving the problem is going to be messy, no two ways about it."

"Building the Mexican economy is going to take time," Michael said. "The Movement was well aware that something had to be done when it crafted its plan. The issue had become such a battleground for liberals and conservatives."

He sighed before going on. "The invective was piled higher and deeper every day on talk radio and other media outlets. Everyone had their own ideas about how to stop the screaming."

Eric nodded. "Unfortunately there was absolutely no consensus. Some people wanted to ship all of the illegal aliens back over the border," he said.

"Yes," Michael said, "and others wanted them all rounded up, tried, convicted, and jailed. Many in the previous administration had seen some sort of amnesty or path to citizenship as a source of votes to keep their party permanently in power."

"Even to the extent of the former president doing an end-around Congress by implementing the Deferred Action for Child Arrivals program by executive order," Eric said.

"Thankfully, the former government is gone," Michael said. "Now the people in the shadows must be brought into the light of day. Illegal workers and the employers who depend on them have a symbiotic and, for the most part, beneficial relationship. Our job will be to find and deal with the bad actors and criminals among the ranks of illegal aliens. That leaves a whole lot of people who are simply trying to survive."

"No one disputes that sneaking over the border and into the country illegally is wrong," Eric said. "But up until now the question has been what should be done with these people."

"Yes," Michael agreed. "Thankfully, The Movement has brought us closer to an equitable answer.

"When President Calderón and I make our joint announcement to the nations, we will also be explaining what will be happening to illegal aliens currently in the United States."

Michael thumbed through several pages in the binder.

"It is physically impossible to uproot twelve million or more people from one country and ship them back to another," Michael continued, "so it will not be done. They will not be able to be used for their vote by any political party while in the program. Instead the focus will be on the value of the work they are able to do. It's eminently clear that individual states do not have the money to support them through public assistance programs."

"Entitlements are being examined and revised as rapidly as possible from the top down," Eric said. "From the federal government down to the state level The Movement's program for spotting fraud is getting a workout, but it's proving to be effective."

"Certainly the work each government agency is doing to send duplication, unnecessary regulations, and ill-advised programs and functions the way of the dinosaurs is equally impressive," Michael said.

"And in you, my friend," he continued, "people who had no voice are about to be given one. They will have an advocate. You will be given the power, authority, and funding to finally make the aliens welcomed in America."

"Thank you, sir," Eric said. "I'm honored. I'm also pleased that President Calderón has agreed to partner in the effort. Mexico will be funding the program, even while the training, education, and outreach goes on in the States.

"I'm working to finalize the avenues through which illegal aliens in the program will be given the choice to remain here and begin the path to citizenship through the existing process, or to return to Mexico to practice their newfound skills. I'm proud to be spearheading the effort to create real opportunity for these people to get a leg up that is not on the backs of American taxpayers."

Micheal smiled. "The ages old maxim, 'If you want to eat, you must work' is certainly being implemented from the foundation of the program," he said.

"Yes, sir," Eric said. "There will be no free lunch. Laziness will not be tolerated. If people are able to work, they will have to do so."

"That said, how are things looking on the education and tax fronts?" Michael asked.

"Children will continue to go to American schools at the expense of the Mexican government," Eric said, "and wages earned by illegal aliens are set to be taxed reasonably to offset the cost of services at the state and local levels. There is also a process in the works for ensuring that a fair number of participants return to Mexico permanently or temporarily to share their skills and contribute to the growth of the Mexican economy in exchange for the money it contributes to the program."

Michael nodded his approval. "They will do well with you as their champion on this side of the border," he said, "and with Nicolas Calderón representing them at home."

"Thank you, sir," Eric continued. "The overall objective is simply to train people for higher-level skilled jobs. Better lives depend on a willingness to work hard and succeed. The many changes to Mexico's economy and national well-being will bear fruit for everyone who is willing to strive for the best. Achievement will be rewarded. There's opportunity in the air."

"Indeed," Michael said. "The world is changing. The northern half of the western hemisphere is on its way to becoming a more healthy and productive cooperative entity. Capitalism and free enterprise will reward the dreams of those seeking to create a better world for themselves and their families." Michael smiled broadly. "I'm glad to be on the right side of those efforts."

Eric returned the smile. "I'm glad to be there with you, sir."

CHAPTER 50

Michael Stonebreaker stepped off of the campus of William and Mary in Williamsburg, Virginia, shortly after giving a speech on federal aid. After he left the campus, he promptly got into his motorcade limo and drove off. However, he was not leaving the area.

Henry Stonebreaker was waiting in the parking deck on the William and Mary campus when a limo with tinted windows pulled into the deck and parked in a space.

He walked toward the limo as three men wearing sunglasses got out. The men were dressed casually as tourists, and their sunglasses were not out of place on the warm sunlit day. Two of the men resembled one another enough to have been twins.

Henry had been instructed to dispense with any introductions and to simply escort the men to the meeting. He directed them to a nondescript black Lincoln parked nearby. The men said not a word to him in return. They got into the car and Henry got behind the wheel. He drove them to a point near the colonial area.

Henry and the three men strolled down the path to a church where "Closed" signs had been placed on the entrances. He ushered them into the sanctuary and led them to a doorway at the rear of the church.

Henry opened the door and he and the men entered the room.

Michael Stonebreaker turned to look at the men as they entered the room with his brother, Henry.

"Gentlemen," Michael said," if I may break protocol, I would like to introduce my guests here today. I'll introduce you formally to my brother, Henry Stonebreaker, who brought you here."

Michael shook hands with the mysterious Mr. Smith who had become a regular visitor to his office. Next to him stood a man who so resembled him that he could have passed for his twin, and a younger man who was the most handsome man Michael had ever seen.

The president directed the men's attention to the lovely woman with whom he had been speaking when they entered the room.

"Now, I would like you to meet CIA Director, Helen Abramson. She is here because she is very much concerned with our southern border these days, and she is actively monitoring intelligence from inside the region at this time."

Helen Abramson greeted each of them warmly with a smile.

The Man Who Loved the Gulf nodded his head in greeting. He studied her closely, noting that even as a professional and beautiful woman she exuded an air of potential danger. He would choose his words carefully in this meeting.

"I realize that you cannot identify yourselves," Michael said, "and I would not ask you to do so. Your privacy is paramount."

Michael indicated chairs around a table, and they all took seats. He looked expectantly at the mysterious stranger.

"Mr. President," Smith said, "Thank you for meeting with us."

"On the contrary," Michael said. "I'm the one who is thankful. In a few days the world will change. I need all the input I can get because of what we face. Our relationship with Mexico is about to be altered on every level. Obviously, I have enough on my plate each day, and my knowledge of the region is limited. I grew up in Pennsylvania, and while I can read briefs and reports all day long, it doesn't mean that I know all the things I need to know to make good decisions on the Mexican front."

The Man Who Loved the Gulf had been silently studying President Michael Stonebreaker. He sensed the hidden power in the man. This was no one to trifle with. The keen intelligence in the man's eyes, the way he carried himself, the sound of his voice, his bearing and manner all said that he was a man of both intellect and physical strength. He began to see what his cousin had told him about Michael Stonebreaker was true.

Mr. Smith had begun his introduction of The Man Who Loved the Gulf to President Stonebreaker and the group. "Mr. President, one of the most accomplished men in the world sits next to me. He has built a business empire in Canada, the US, Mexico, Central and South America. He values his privacy beyond everything. After much exhortation, he agreed to come with me to this meeting today. He did so against his better judgment. Also, he probably gave in because, as you can see, we look alike. We are cousins."

Michael laughed and smiled. "I would have never guessed that!" he said. "Would you, Helen?"

A tension had been broken. Light laughter rippled around the room.

"Mr. President," Helen said, "there are so many handsome men in this room that I feel like a schoolgirl who just wandered into a meeting of the varsity club at high school. I wouldn't know where to begin telling you all apart."

Her voice and smile radiated southern charm, but there was a glint of steel in her eyes. Everyone laughed, but The Man Who Loved the Gulf saw the steel. He had a feeling Helen Abramson had the ability to get men to talk about things that would be best left unsaid. He reaffirmed his earlier intent to be careful.

"My cousin is right, Mr. President, Ms. Abramson," The Man said. "Our keen resemblance betrays our kinship. Though I am honored to meet you, my attendance at this meeting proves blood is indeed thicker than water."

The Man flashed a smile as disarming as Helen Abramson's.

"You like having your brother with you," The Man said, "and I like having family with me, too. The man next to me is my son. I brought him along today because I wanted him to meet you for a reason. He and his team are the people who took down El Diablo!"

Michael smiled at Rick and took his hand to shake it again.

"You, sir, have my undying gratitude," Michael said, "and the gratitude of the president of Mexico, as well. No one knows about what you did, and we'll keep it that way, but you saved us a lot of grief!"

Rick saluted the president. "Semper fi, sir!"

"A Marine," Michael said. "I could have guessed!" He saluted Rick in return.

"Mr. President," said Mr. Smith, "my cousin has businesses and connections throughout the western hemisphere. He has learned much about doing business successfully in the region, so much so that I have asked him to share what he is comfortable in sharing with you."

Henry Stonebreaker said, "Is there a market for bulldozers? I've spent a lot of time fixing them. Maybe I could help you fellas?"

Everyone laughed.

"We owe you an incalculable debt, young man," Henry said, saluting Rick.

"Uh-oh, we're in trouble now," The Man Who Loved the Gulf said, "We've got two Marines together. If the stories begin, we'll be here all day."

Any remaining tension dissipated completely, and laughing, the group settled in for their discussion.

The Man Who Loved the Gulf talked about doing business in the southern region.

"Doing business in Mexico is different than doing business in Central and South America," he began.

He talked about heads of state, people of influence, dictators, corruption, the perception of Americans, and fitting into the grand scheme of things.

"Knowing when to hang tough, and when to withdraw is an invaluable skill born of experience in the region," he said.

The Man explained the peculiarities of the various countries, why he employed people who were native to those areas, how he learned to adapt, and mistakes he had made early on.

"Some Americans mistake the sometimes accented speech of people who speak English as a second language for a sign of intellectual inferiority," The Man said. "Having spent many years conversing with Spanish speakers and others in their native languages, I can tell you just how wrong an idea that is."

He shared how he had learned to respect and have genuine affection for people everywhere south of the US border.

An hour passed quickly. By the end of it no one in the room

doubted that The Man Who Loved the Gulf was extraordinary, and he had particularly impressed Helen Abramson.

It quickly became obvious to Helen that The Man was a genius at business. She appreciated that he did not seem to find it necessary to impress anyone with his accomplishments, thought that was exactly the effect. She could certainly see how his dispassionate, rational, and utterly sincere demeanor had contributed to his phenomenal success.

It was also apparent to Helen that The Man was a student of history and a lifelong learner; he seemed to be a living, breathing expert on all things concerning the western hemisphere. dedicated to excellence. and intelligence were evident to all in the room.

Helen Abramson was fascinated by The Man. He exuded an almost seductive energy that dominated the room when he spoke.

Her thoughts fled to her husband, Albert, who had died four years earlier. The trauma of his battle with pancreatic cancer and subsequent death had nearly consumed her. She had thrown herself into work to escape the utter abyss of grief that lay just beneath the surface threatening to overwhelm her. When The Movement had approached her about running the CIA, she had welcomed the challenge, and the distraction.

Two years after Albert's death she had ventured out, enjoying dinners and parties with a few male acquaintances. But she had lost the only love of her life, and there had been no one who had come close to stirring her heart and challenging her mind as Albert had.

Helen returned her attention to The Man. He reminded her of a film star from an earlier age. He was strong, charming, self-assured, and brilliant. She did not know if she would see him again, and that would be a loss. She would like to get to know him better.

Michael was also impressed by The Man. He had gotten used to the fact that he would never know the name of the cousin, The Movement's point man inside the corruption in Washington, and he realized that this man would remain an enigma as well. However, before the meeting broke up he made of point of securing a future meeting.

"I hope you will consider meeting with Director Abramson and me again on options for expanding our business relationship with Mexico and elsewhere below the border in the future," Michael asked The Man as the meeting ended and they stood to say their goodbyes. "In a few days I will be announcing a major change in Mexican-US relations. If you are comfortable, sir, I may call upon you to review the plan we are putting forward. I believe your input would be incredibly valuable to our success."

The Man Who Loved the Gulf smiled warmly and shook the president's hand.

"Mr. President, it would be my pleasure," The Man said. "I will provide whatever help I can. Doing more business is always my goal. I wish you Godspeed in your endeavors, sir. I know I would not want to deal with the challenges you face."

The Man's cousin raised his eyebrows but said nothing. The Man had mentioned God. *Perhaps I am rubbing off on him?* the cousin thought.

The little group commenced shaking hands. When The Man Who Loved the Gulf took Helen's hand in his she looked into his eyes, fully intending to flash an appropriately professional smile. But as she felt the warmth of his hand around hers, she suddenly found herself blushing like a schoolgirl. She quickly regained her composure and delivered her goodbyes.

The Man had seen Helen Abramson blush, and he smiled before graciously taking his leave.

Back in the limo Rick turned to The Man Who Loved the Gulf. "That was quite a meeting today," he said.

The Man nodded his assent.

"In fact," Rick continued, now grinning, "I suspect that I might not be the only one with a woman in my life. What did you think, Father?"

The Man Who Loved the Gulf looked thoughtfully at his son and smiled.

"Yes," he said, "but you must remember that there is a vast difference between the lovely Adriana and this woman, son."

"What is that, sir?" Rick asked.

The Man Who Loved the Gulf looked at Rick with a glint in his eye. He said, "This woman could have me killed if I jilted her."

CHAPTER 51

Whether it was Divine Providence or simply good luck, the cartels were not aware that big trouble was coming when America invaded Mexico.

In the wee hours of the morning of September 2nd, troops quietly descended on their targets from every point on the compass. General Avery Thompson was fond of reminding the troops, "Even thugs have to sleep!"

U.S. military units moved into position alongside their Mexican counterparts. It went without saying that the joint effort would be a demonstration of the US military prowess, but it would also be an opportunity to showcase the impeccable character and intgerity of American servicemen. General Thompson gave strict orders that everyone from the highest ranking officer to the canine MWDs be squared away.

"Let me make it clear," he said, "we are guests of the nation of Mexico, and we are to be the very best of guests at all times." He paused before adding, "But we are armed guests, and it's all right to kill bad guys without hesitation. We won't be asking permission to shoot."

Mexican troops had also gotten the order to serve as gracious hosts through their commanders. The eradication of the cartels was to be a joint operation. Each side needed the other to get the job done.

President Stonebreaker communicated in no uncertain terms that invading Mexico to wipe out the drug cartels was serious business. People were going to die. The United States and Mexico together were declaring war on the drug cartels. They would be neutralized and their members taken, dead or alive. It would take a long time to find and eliminate all them, particularly those cloaked in the various echelons of Mexican society, but that would be done, as well.

The commander-in-chief met questions about a timeline with steely resolve.

"No one is kidding themselves," he said. "The mission will be over when it's over. We will take as much time as necessary, until the last drug lord is dead or."

At noon the presidents of the two nations would stand shoulder-to-shoulder and explain to their people how the world was about to change.

For now, it was time to begin.

In retrospect, General Thompson would later tell President Stonebreaker and President Calderón that he believed it had been through Divine intervention that the cartels remained ignorant of the heavy troop and equipment movement that had taken place during the night.

Showtime was set for 2:00 a.m., and the wake-up call came in the form of ground force artillery strikes from armored vehicles and airstrikes from helicopter gunships, drones, and stealth bombers.

Hell had now left Lago and come for all the rest. El Diablo was joined by hundreds of cartel members in the next world.

To their credit, some cartels fought back, but they were no match for the kind of firepower that was raining down on them. They began to give up. First, one or two surrendered, then a handful, and finally large groups threw down their weapons and put their hands in the air.

Veteran troops from operations conducted in the streets of Iraq and Afghanistan moved into urban areas, chasing down cartel members to the same bloody and fearsome end. They learned quickly that the only difference was that Taliban and Al-Qaeda terrorists believed that they would be rewarded in the next world for conducting jihad. Cartel soldiers suffered no such delusion. They didn't want to die if they could avoid it.

By 10:00 a.m. General Thompson was ready to deliver the first situation report to President Stonebreaker.

"Not one cartel leader had believed that the United States would do such a thing," General Thompson said. "In their wildest drug or alcohol-induced dreams, they never thought it possible that the greatest military force in the world would confront them. It's more than sobering.

"We're bringing them a real come-to-Jesus revelation," he continued. "We're destroying everything they've accomplished by spreading poison from their despotic domains."

"Excellent," Michael said. "What's the casualty report?"

"Some of our soldiers, American and Mexican alike, paid the ultimate price," General Thompson replied, "but the count is lopsided compared to losses among the cartels. We are wiping them out, even while we're doing everything possible to protect our guys. We're working our way through the rural and urban areas, and we've got each other's backs."

"Civilian casualties?" Michael asked.

"Unfortunately, there is collateral damage to report as well," Thompson said. "It's impossible to avoid it in every case, particularly in places where law-abiding Mexican citizens live among cartel members, or in strongholds where they've dug in. We're doing all we can to avoid harming the innocent.

"One of our choppers was blown to bits by a surface-to-air missile over a compound controlled by the Los Zetas cartel. We sent in a stealth bomber and turned the whole compound into a massive black hole in the ground. Nearly one-hundred people on the ground were killed in the process; thankfully most were Zetas."

"I'm pleased that American and Mexican troops are moving hand in glove toward the singular goal of destroying the cartels," Michael said.

"Thank you, sir," Thompson said.

"What about drugs? Weapons?" Michael asked.

General Thompson replied, "We've uncovered stockpiles of both hidden in buildings, barns, warehouses, private homes, basements—everywhere," Thompson said. "Interrogating prisoners is yielding intel on the locations of ever more vast collections of guns, meth, coke, and marijuana. The drugs are being destroyed with flame throwers. We're collecting the guns and other weapons to deliver to Mexican authorities. They may end up with the military or the police, or they may be melted down and made into cars and refrigerators. The money and other valuables are being turned over to the government to pay for a lot of the property damage and related expenses."

He added that since Mexican jails were already overloaded, American combat engineers were overseeing the erection of detention centers in the field to hold prisoners temporarily.

"No doubt all over Mexico people awoke in the early morning hours thinking that, from the sounds they were hearing, the world was coming to an end," General Thompson said.

"In one sense," Michael said, "It is ending. But the demise of the cartels heralds a new future of possibility for Mexico."

Just before noon, news correspondent Kelly McDonnell and a host of reporters from the major TV and cable networks pooled in front of two podiums placed side-by-side at the Mexican-American border between El Paso, Texas and Juarez, Mexico.

The engineers had performed mic checks. Tele-prompters were in position, and cameras were ready to transmit. There would be no alternative programming on this day. Every TV channel in America and Mexico would carry the broadcast. No *Leave it to Beaver* or *Spongebob* reruns were scheduled to be shown. Telemundo would not be broadcasting as usual.

"We're here on the US-Mexican border between El Paso, Texas and Juarez, Mexico to mark a pivotal moment in the history of relations between the United States and Mexico..." McDonnell began her lead-up to the speech.

Due to the world-changing content, a unique format had been developed for the presentation. Viewers may not know this, but Mexican President Nicolas Calderón, and US President Michael Stonebreaker are fluent speakers of both English and Spanish. The two presidents will be alternating paragraphs in Spanish and English during the speech, essentially, addressing both nations simultaneously without an interpreter. The speech will, however, be close-captioned and delivered in ASL for the hearing impaired.

Promptly at noon President Calderón and President Stonebreaker stepped to the microphones.

"My fellow Americans..."

"Mis compatriotas Mexicanos..."

So began the speech that would alter the relationship between the peoples of Mexico and the United States forever.

Speaking clearly and carefully, the two men told their nations together that the day of the cartels was ending. They spoke of the joint war being conducted by Mexican and American troops fighting side-by-side against the bloodthirsty criminals who were being destroyed even as they spoke. They explained that it would go on for as long as it took to rid the nation of criminals.

President Stonebreaker recounted the El Paso massacre carried out by El Diablo and his men in which they'd killed more than one hundred Americans.

President Calderón described how the murderous El Diablo and his army had been wiped out.

Neither man spoke of the Death Machine or the nuclear weapon the despot had obtained.

The Mexican president declared that those hidden in Mexican society who had been supporting the cartels would also be found, and that they would be arrested and prosecuted. If found guilty, they'd be imprisoned for long sentences or executed.

The U.S. commander-in-chief praised the Mexican and American military for their bravery in bringing down the cartels. He explained that the troops were doing everything they could to avoid civilian casualties.

The two heads-of-state spoke alternately in Spanish and English, giving a powerful description of the revolutionary plan to improve the Mexican economy, build and re-build infrastructure, and develop energy resources. It included creating a strong and vibrant business climate to stimulate innovation and research and development. Among its chief goals was providing excellent education for all children and adults.

The speech went on, and all over America and Mexico people gazed in rapt silence at the two men on TV screens or listened on radios or mobile devices as the dawning of a new world was described.

As they neared the conclusion of the speech, President Stonebreaker and President Calderón stood shoulder-to-shoulder in a display of solidarity to their countrymen, assuring the nations of their intent to make the North American continent the strongest economic powerhouse in the world.

At the last moment they were joined by a third man—the prime minister of Canada, signifying that Canada would be a full participant in the effort to make North America a place that would do business with the world for all its citizens.

The three men joined hands and held them high together. In English, Spanish and French, they said, "May God bless our union!"

———

The talking heads took over, stunned by the speech, not knowing how to react, not having anticipated what was going to happen, not having received advanced notice of the contents of the speech. They were amazed. Some praised the speech, and some tried to degrade it, saying such a thing was impossible, doomed to fail, stupid, and irresponsible. Their egos had been bruised mightily. How dare they be left out of the loop! Still others welcomed the new era, saying they hoped the noble goals of the speech would be achieved, and praising the chief executives for their daring vision and commitment to such an incredible dream.

———

As the battles raged on throughout Mexico, those who had secretly served the cartels tried their best to escape the country. They soon discovered that roads and beaches were blocked and monitored. Airports were locked down, and small airfields were under guard. Marinas were locked tight, and every means of escape that authorities could manage to guard held traps waiting to be sprung. Some managed to escape, but hundreds were arrested.

Military aircraft patrolled the skies everywhere over Mexico, offering pilots of small planes taking off from hidden or obscure airfields a choice: land or be blown out of the sky. Coastguard cutters monitored every coastline, drones were in the air, and boats of every size were being confronted, stopped, and searched. The noose was being tightened.

CHAPTER 52

President and Mrs. Stonebreaker stood along with Vice President and Mrs. Dryden on the North Portico as two limos slowed to a stop along the semi-circular driveway.

Captain Everett Williams and his wife Adrienne exited the first car with their son Chuck and daughter Susan.

Captain Williams' commanding officer, Colonel Ron McKenzie, took his wife Carol's arm and escorted her from the second vehicle. Their son, Stephen and twin daughters, Mary and Margaret followed closely behind.

The presidential couples smiled, warmly exchanging greetings and introductions before ushering their very special guests into the White House.

"Welcome to The White House," Michael said, smiling as the group assembled in the East Hall. "We are truly honored to have you here. As our very special guests, the first order of business is a private tour! When one walks through living history, there is no better person to conduct the tour than someone who actually lives in it."

"You are very special guests to us, indeed," Joan said. "After the tour we'll be enjoying a private dinner together in the Old Family Dining Room. The room has been refurbished and reopened to the public, however, on this occasion it's been reserved to host our very special dinner party," Joan said.

Michael and Joan led their guests down the Center Hall Stairs to begin the tour of the public rooms on the Ground Floor, including stops at the Library, with its collection of books about American history and life, and The White House Bowl bowling alley in the Basement.

"One of my favorite rooms in the house is the Vermeil Room," Joan shared as the group entered that room from Center Hall.

"I love looking at the portraits of former first ladies. I often think about how each of them made this place a home for their families, and at the same time made hosted some of the most powerful people in the world here."

She pointed out paintings of iconic first ladies that adorned the walls of the room, as well as the impressive collection of gilded silver on display.

Michael led the group through the Visitor's Foyer to the entrance of the White House Family Theater in the East Wing.

"Wow! Do they show real movies here?" Stephen McKenzie asked.

"Sure!" Michael said. He patted Stephen on the shoulder. "This room had an exciting history before it was turned into a movie theater," he said. "It used to be a coatroom!"

Everyone laughed and tried out the four extra comfy armchairs up front reserved for the president, his family, and special guests.

As they left the movie room and walked along the East Colonnade, Michael pointed to the garden beyond the windows.

"Just outside is the Jacqueline Kennedy Garden," he said. "It's one of the most tranquil places on the grounds."

"It really is delightful," Joan said. "Pink tulips flood the view from here with gorgeous color in the spring. Against the backdrop of the lush green of the boxwoods and lawn, it's truly stunning."

Michael led the group back to Center Hall, up to the First Floor and into Cross Hall. He shared bits of the history of the White House and its many occupants as they walked.

On the State Floor they marveled at the elegant furnishings and exquisite artwork in the Green and Red rooms along Cross Hall. They gawked at the magnificent chandelier and were captivated by the sweeping view of the South Lawn afforded by the Blue Room.

Inside the expansive East Room, Michael gathered everyone together in the center of the room.

"The East Room is the largest of the rooms in the Executive Residence," he said. "This room has witnessed countless historic events. Bill signings, receptions, addresses, weddings, and even concerts by famous musicians all have taken place here over the years."

He looked at the Williams and Mckenzie children with a twinkle in his eye.

"It's also hosted less official events!" he went on. "Amy Carter roller skated here, and so did the Roosevelt children!"

"May *I* rollerskate here, Mr. President?" seven-year-old Susan Williams asked, wide-eyed. "I have my own skates!"

Laughing with delight, Michael bent to look Susan in the eye.

"We will just have to see about that!" he said.

"Michael, darling," Joan said, smiling at her husband and Susan, "we have about an hour before dinner; why don't we treat our guests to cocktails on the Truman Balcony until then?"

"I couldn't think of a nicer way to end our tour," Michael said. "Except maybe rollerskating!"

He winked at Susan before standing up.

He took Joan's hand and the two of them led everyone upstairs to the Yellow Oval Room.

"Please, make yourselves at home," Michael said.

The group settled in with cocktails and hors d'oeuvres and admired the inviting elegance of the room. A soft palette of yellow accented with equally soft celadon on stylish, comfortable sofas gave the room a decidedly cozy feel despite its formal decor.

Michael opened the door and the party moved out onto the balcony to take in the view of the South Lawn and the Washington Monument.

"Mom, Dad," said Mary McKenzie," I think I can see the Capitol Building!"

Michael and Joan and their guests shared observations about the White House and chatted until Michael announced it was time for dinner.

"Ladies and gentlemen," Michael said, "I've been informed that dinner is just about ready to be served." He gestured toward the staircase. "Shall we make our way downstairs?"

Michael led the group to the Old Family Dining Room, stopping on the way through the prestigious State Dining Room.

"I would be sorely remiss if I did not share with you what Joan and I consider one of the most inspiring treasures of this beautiful house," Michael said, approaching the stately fireplace mantel.

"Franklin Roosevelt placed some very special words here," Michael said. As he spoke he reached out to touch the carved surface of the mantel. "They're part of a letter John Adams wrote to his wife upon moving into this house as president."

Michael recited the words inscribed in the fireplace, words he'd memorized upon moving into the White House to serve as president of the United States.

"I pray to Heaven to bestow the best of blessings on this House, and all that shall hereafter inhabit it. May none but honest and wise men ever rule under this roof," he said.

A chorus of "Amen" rose up from among the guests. They lingered a moment before Michael led the way to the Old Family Dining Room.

When they were seated and comfortable, President Stonebreaker stood up to address the group. When everyone else started to stand out of respect, he said,"Please, everyone, I insist you all remain seated."

He looked around the table at his wife and their guests for a moment before settling his gaze on Captain Everett Williams, his wife Adrienne, and their children, Chuck and Susan.

"I am profoundly honored to be in your presence this evening," he said.

He looked in turn at Colonel Ron McKenzie with his wife Carol, their twin daughters Mary and Margaret, and son, Stephen.

"Being the president, it is hard for people to keep things from me," Michael said. "I have found out, for example, that you and your families also share the kind of relationship that Joan and I share with my very best friend Vice President Eric Dryden and his dear wife,Yvette." He smiled warmly at his friends. "That makes me very happy.

"Joan and I have been blessed to have these two extraordinary friends in our lives from the time we were married. We have watched each other's children grow up, shared vacations together, and seen the world evolve and change.

"It gives me great joy that Eric, Yvette, and all of you are here to celebrate the safe return of Adrienne and Chuck to their family.

"Vice President Dryden and I were career army," the president said to Colonel McKenzie and Captain Williams, "just like the two of you, before we were called to our current roles.

"The duties of this office are such that I must often wear what I call my official face, and it hasn't been very often since I took office that I've been able to spend real time with family and friends." He paused for a moment, and there was a glint of tears in his eyes. "I can think of no more real reason to gather than to celebrate the bonds of family and friendship."

Joan reached out and took his right hand in hers.

Michael gave his wife's hand a gentle squeeze.

"The White House is a treasure trove of history and the embodiment of countless public occasions in the life of our great nation," he said. "Many private and equally cherished moments have no doubt been celebrated in the Old Family Dining Room by the families who've lived here and their closest friends, which is why Joan and I chose it as the perfect setting for dinner tonight. In fact, President John Quincy Adams and his wife Louisa Catherine were the first to designate it for meals with their family back in 1825. Tonight, Joan and I are happy to share it with you as part of our American family. It is family that gives this nation its strength, and faith that keeps us going."

Michael waved a hand in the direction of two empty seats at the table.

"You may have noticed that two chairs are empty. Tonight I have the privilege of introducing you to two extraordinary people. Unfortunately, for security reasons I cannot disclose their real identities, but I would not deny you the honor of sharing in the auspicious occasion of their engagement to be married."

The president gave a slight nod of his head to a steward. The man opened the door, and in the next moment it was like a god and goddess had entered the room.

Adrienne was on her feet immediately. There were tears streaming down her face.

Captain Williams stood and put his arm around his wife.

"Adrienne, dear," he said, "are you okay?"

Everyone was talking at once, concerned about her.

Joan pressed a handkerchief into Adrienne's hand, and she quickly used it to dab at her tears.

"Yes, I'm all right," she said. "I'm all right. I'm crying because I'm so happy! Everett, this is the man who saved Chuck and me. He came for us with his men, and he saved us!"

Rick and Adriana stood smiling as everyone in the room gathered around them.

Captain Everett Williams reached out and wrapped Rick in a bear hug. Tears were streaming down his face, but he did not care.

The captain said through his tears, "Thank you for saving my wife and son. Thank you! I'd almost given up hope. I-I didn't know how they would be saved, but somehow you were there."

Captain Williams released Rick from his embrace. He was pleased to see that the tough young Marine was misty-eyed as well.

"Captain Williams," Rick said, "your wife, Adrienne is one of the bravest women I have ever known. She did everything she could to save your son and herself before we arrived on the scene."

Rick placed a hand on Chuck Williams' shoulder. "What your son did was beyond brave!" he said. "The fact that they had gotten away from that hell hole before we found them made all the difference!"

Rick turned to Adrienne. "Do you remember the woman who exchanged places with you?"

"Of course," Adrienne said. "She was so brave!"

"I cannot tell you her name," Rick said, "but it was only fitting that she be with me when we entered that place. She is an outstanding member of our team. The man who kidnapped you and Chuck was, without question, the most monstrous of men. But he made the mistake of attacking the woman who replaced you in that chamber, and it ended very badly for him. In the end justice was delivered."

"You're wife and son are very special people, Captain Williams. I'm happy to have been part of the team that brought them back safe to you," Rick said. "Speaking of special people, let me introduce you to the amazing woman with me here tonight."

Everyone applauded Rick and Adriana, gathering around them

and congratulating them on their engagement.

Finally, Joan said, "We had all better sit down. There is a truly wonderful meal about to be served, and your memorable experience of our nation's capital continues after dinner."

The president added, "Washington is a fantastic town, steeped in the history of our country. Joan and I want to make sure you thoroughly enjoy your time here, so during the next few days I have arranged a private tour of the capital, including a special treat tonight at the Lincoln Theater. I won't say more so as not to spoil the surprise. On that note, let's enjoy this meal together, and then you're off for a night on the town!"

The meal and conversation that followed were wonderful.

Michael closed his eyes at one point and thought of the special room in the garage behind his boyhood home where his father and grandfather had played cards. He heard the sounds of their voices in his memory.

Joan noticed his smile and closed eyes. She leaned toward him and whispered, "What are you thinking about, Mr. President?"

He opened his eyes. "I was thinking about family, sweetheart. We're blessed to live in this nation."

She said, "True, but not everyone would agree with you. Some hate living under the laws of this country, and others are unhappy because of their circumstances. Not everyone has been as blessed as we have been."

Michael grew serious. "Look around this table. See the faces here. They represent the people of this country. Our ancestors came here by many routes and under harsh circumstances. Eric and Yvette's ancestors came here on slave ships in chains, and now he is the vice president of the United States. If he desires it, I believe he will be president. I trust him more than most men. America needs more people like him and the others gathered here with us. Of course, those who genuinely need help should be given it, but those who seek the goodness of this nation and its people must contribute their work if they are able. As stressful as it can be at times, there's also a therapy in work." His mouth softened in a smile. "Even in the work of being president."

"I couldn't agree more," Joan said, leaning in and brushing his knee.

Michael and Joan and their guests continued sharing stories and enjoying the splended meal as the time quickly slipped away. Around eight o'clock the steward came and whispered in the president's ear.

"Pardon the interruption, everyone," he said, drawing their attention to where he stood at the head of the table. "I'm afraid that the limos are waiting to take you to Lincoln Center for the show. We will have to say goodbye, and we need to wish our special guests safe passage as well."

As everyone gathered to leave, Captain Williams and Adrienne made their way to Rick and Adriana.

Adrienne said, "I wish I could know your names."

Rick said, "We wish we could tell you," he said, "but that would be unwise. We may never see each other again, but I want you to remember us always."

Adriana smiled and took the older woman's hand in her own. "And keep us in your prayers," she said. "We need them."

There were hugs and well wishes all around.

Rick turned to find the president standing in front of him.

"Would you ask your father something for me?" Michael asked.

"Yes, sir," Rick said. "What do you need?"

"I need two things, actually," Michael said. "His cousin has carried something to him for his review. I need his input on it as we move forward with Mexico."

Rick nodded.

"Secondly," Michael continued, "I would like you to tell him from me that one day I hope to spend time with him, and that his son is one of the bravest men I have had the pleasure of meeting."

Rick blushed. "Thank you, sir. I work with the best people," he said.

The president took his hand and Rick felt the strength in it.

"As to you, well, I wish you and Adriana a wonderful wedding and a long and happy life together. If the two of you are as deeply in love as you appear to be, I think that my wish will come true!"

Rick smiled and saluted the president. "Thank you, sir."

President Stonebreaker returned the salute.

"We're both faithful to the same things," he said. "You helped rescue two very important people, and saved Mexico and America a world of pain. You have my eternal thanks, young man. The best to you."

Rick leaned close and whispered into Michael's ear.

"My name is Rick, Mr. President, but please don't tell anybody."

Michael Stonebreaker laughed. "I'll take that to the next world," he said. "Be well!"

President Stonebreaker and his wife watched their guests pile into the waiting limos.

Joan leaned into her husband, her arm resting on his shoulder.

"You've done well, Mr. President," she said softly. "You've done well."

EPILOGUE

Eight months had passed since the war in Mexico had begun. Spring held the promise of seeing an end to the open conflicts with the cartels as a result of the combined efforts of the Mexican and American military forces. Nevertheless, it had not been easy. Some of the cartels had fought fiercely and many brave soldiers had died. Thankfully, the end was in sight.

The Man Who Loved the Gulf had made good on his promise to advise President Stonebreaker on the plan to revitalize the Mexican economy. He had spent long hours reading and analyzing it. He'd taken it apart and put it back together over and over again. He'd spent four days with key people in his companies, particularly those who lived and worked in Mexico discussing every aspect of the proposal, sections of which they'd also revised.

When they were finished, The Man contacted his cousin and presented their findings, which were then conveyed to President Stonebreaker.

President Michael Stonebreaker sat in his office with The Movement's mysterious Mr. Smith and Vice President Eric Dryden.

Smith had just delivered feedback from The Man Who Loved the Gulf on the Mexican revitalization program.

"My cousin applauds the plans The Movement proposes for moving US relations with Mexico forward in the wake of the decimation of the drug cartels and the newly secured border," he said.

"Most of the changes he's proposed are extremely insightful," Michael said. "Brilliant, even."

"Thank you, Mr. President," the man from The Movement said. "My cousin is honored to offer any input that could prove useful. I will convey your sentiments."

"Excellent. I will share these recommendations with President Calderón for final review," Michael said. "The beauty of The Movement's plan is its flexibility. Nothing has been carved in stone."

Vice President Eric Dryden had embraced the work of coordinating efforts to halt illegal immigration and build a mutually beneficial workforce development program between the United States and Mexico.

"Indeed," Eric said. "Mexico and its people are in the driver's seat."

President Calderón had expanded his group of trusted advisors beyond his secretary Margarita and her son Rinaldo. After reviewing it himself and upon their recommendation, he had given his official stamp of approval to the revitalization plan delivered to him by US President Michael Stonebreaker.

Now, he stood before Mexico's thirty-one state governors to deliver that plan and begin its execution. They'd agreed to appoint a delegation of representatives from among the people. The delegation would report to the governors and be responsible for evaluating and implementing the program at the community level. Key ground-breaking pilot projects were set to begin in every corner of Mexico.

President Calderón cleared his throat and addressed the group.

"Esteemed governors of the United Mexican States, a dream is being born on our soil. The drug cartels have largely been wiped out, and their remnants are being tracked down and dealt with day by day. A future with real opportunity for all of our people is being shaped here at home..."

Aboard the lovely Gulf Maiden, The Man Who Loved the Gulf watched the waters for signs of life and was rewarded for his patience. The Man had seen the Gulf of Mexico in all of her moods, from quiet lapping waves on a nearly still lake, to the raging waves of storms that smash into the mid-Florida Gulf Coast.

Watching the movement below the surface of the water, he

thought about his cousin. Aside from a few tense days working with the governments of the United States and Mexico on the new plan to improve relations between the two, their lives had returned to a peaceful quiet, which The Man rather enjoyed.

Tomorrow, he thought, *I will sail to the Captiva.*

The Captiva Blue Hole was about thirty-two miles off Boca Grande and one of The Man's favorite places to go diving.

He woke up early the next morning and had his crew set sail.

He was deeply pleased that the beautiful Helen Abramson had agreed to accompany him on a dive.

She followed his lead as they swam together around the perimeter of the hole. He indicated by hand gestures that she should follow him, and he slowly led her deeper into its depths. She impressed him with her skill and ability. Though he was confident she could handle herself in the water, The Man's dive mates swam nearby watching and protecting them.

They were lucky this day. The fish were plentiful, and he enjoyed seeing her excitement over the creatures that swam by them in a variety of colors, shapes, and sizes.

Helen peered into a hole and was startled by an octopus that was more frightened of her than she was of it. It sped away from her on a jet of water.

The Man watched for a few moments more as she swam gracefully among a school of silvery spadefish.

He directed her to a favorite spot of his, a shelf about twenty meters ahead of them. As they approached they saw a goliath grouper that must have weighed at least three-hundred pounds. It lazily turned away from them and swam deeper into the hole.

Far too soon for The Man, one of his men signaled that it was time to return to the surface.

They took their time ascending the line that extended down from the ship above, spending a full minute at each of the knotted stopping points marking thirty foot intervals.

They Gulf Maiden loomed large, cutting a majestic figure above the water. They broke the surface and swam to a platform lowered from the ship.

The Man's dive buddies steadied the platform while he helped Helen get onto it. She removed her respirator.

He grinned as they were drawn up to deck level.

"Did you enjoy seeing Captiva?" The Man asked.

"It was absolutely fantastic," Helen said. "Thank you for bringing me here! This is a wonderful break for me."

"I assure you, the pleasure is mine," The Man said.

He looked at her. She was incredibly lovely, her silky wet hair glistening around her shoulders in the mid-afternoon sunlight. He wanted to kiss her, but remembering she was the director of the CIA, he simply smiled at her.

On deck, they helped remove each other's scuba tanks. The crew gathered up their tanks, masks, and flippers and went to stow the gear.

"Please take your time in your cabin, Helen," The Man said. "Dinner will be at six. I hope you like swordfish and salad. The others will join us then. I'll see you at dinner."

"See you then," she said. She smiled a dazzling smile and turned to walk toward an entrance that led below decks.

His eyes followed her. He thought, *This is crazy. Am I falling for the most dangerous woman in the world?*

He shook his head and made his way to his stateroom.

Everyone began gathering at 5:30 in the lounge to enjoy cocktails and easy conversation before sitting down to dinner.

The brothers Dupree were away on business, but Rick and his beloved Adriana had been pleased to accept The Man's invitation. His cousin had also managed to fly in to join their table.

The Man thought Helen Abramson looked fantastic in a blue skirt and crisp, white blouse. Her hair was tied in a ponytail, and her smile was warm and pleasant. He caught the light scent of her perfume whenever she leaned in to make a point or laugh with delight.

What in heaven's name was he doing inviting the head of the CIA out for a day on his boat, let alone on a dive with him? Was he out of his mind?

Despite the questions, for some reason he felt at peace. *It's time I broaden my world a bit*, he thought.

The Man Who Loved the Gulf looked at his cousin. Somehow, it seemed fitting that his cousin was here, too.

He cleared his throat. "Would you do the honors, Cousin?" The Man asked.

His look-alike smiled, but instead of offering a blessing, he turned to Rick and placed a hand on his shoulder.

"Would you say something, Rick?"

Rick, smiling slightly, took Adriana's hand in his.

"Let's pray," he said, and bowed his head.

The others joined him.

"Dios ha sido bueno…and for that we are thankful" Rick began. "May it please you, Lord, to bless this gathering and this meal, and to enrich our lives with new opportunities to learn of you. Amen."

When Rick ended the prayer, The Man looked up and into the deep pools of Helen Abramson's eyes.

She steadily returned his gaze.

It's going to be a beautiful meal, The Man thought, "*filled with beautiful possibilities, indeed.*"

www.ingramcontent.com/pod-product-compliance
Lightning Source LLC
Chambersburg PA
CBHW030429310726
48979CB00009B/1685/J
9780983842767